LIFE 2.0

CIARA FINEMAN

This book is dedicated to Lily Fuller. Without her, I never would have finished writing Life 2.0. Thank you for being an amazing supporter and listening to me when I need it and when I don't. That small conversation probably didn't mean much to you, but it launched me towards writing my debut novel! Thank you for continuing to be someone who supports me time after time. I love you!

This book is also dedicated to Fawcett, my bearded dragon. This book was released on her birthday, not that she'll count it as a birthday present! She was the first pet I adopted that was purely my responsibility. She loves me more than anyone else, and I love her as much as my heart can handle. She's an amazing creature to spend my evenings with. Yes, I know. I love animals too much. But they make me happy and I wanted to show her some love on her birthday!

CHAPTER ONE

Sparkling in the light, colors dancing over the walls... that's what I want to remember when I see it. Not any of the million things that actually come to mind, just that. Where I close my eyes and I'm back there again. I can almost smell the air and the way her perfume made me feel like I was home, or hear the TV on in the background, a movie still playing that we're no longer paying attention to as our fingers get lost in each other's hair. I can feel the flutter of my heart when she entered a room, the pull of my stomach when I was struck once again with just how beautiful she was, or taste the meals she put so much effort into, but always ended up burnt. When I close my eyes, I can almost see her smile or the way she looked at me... I can almost picture the first time we met instead of what I see now.

Almost.

Just like every time I hold the ring between my fingers, all that comes over me is silence and sadness. The dim lighting of the room doesn't do the ring's beauty justice. Neither do my thoughts, but those are harder to fix. If I could wish them away, I would have a long time ago. I definitely wouldn't be sitting on my couch with a bottle of vodka on the table, a blanket pulled tightly around my shoulders, and my wife's wedding ring in my hand.

I squeeze the ring in my fist for a second before letting it drop so it hangs on the chain around my neck, falling under my shirt. I tried to keep it on my finger, next to my own ring, but my fingers are several sizes too big, and the thought of trusting someone else with it to change the size... well, if they lost it, I think I'd be sick. Plus, this way, it's out of sight, hidden, so I don't feel like people are staring at it those rare times I go out into the world.

When finally I got out of that house and left my old neighborhood, I didn't have to be The Girl From The House On The Corner. With my house being on the news for so long, people tended to remember me. Which is great, because they all remembered me as the girl shown in the background of the reporter's video – or at the very least I'd be seen as the girl who didn't get murdered. How sucky would it be to be remembered as the person who *did* get murdered? Well, not that I would know, I'd be dead, so...

I reach around the blanket pulled tight to my shoulders for my drink sitting on the side table. Raspberry lemonade and vodka, the only thing that solves any of my problems. Not that it'll really *solve* any of them. For that to happen, there'd have to actually be a God, and if I remember anything from that night, it's that there can't possibly be a God. If there is, he can go fuck himself for all I care.

I down the rest of my drink, grabbing the bottle. As I fill the cup halfway and reach for the lemonade, my doorbell rings. I'm almost surprised since the room feels so dark and the streets seem so quiet. If I didn't know better I would say that it's the middle of the night. The clock on the shelf proves that to be wrong — it's mid-afternoon.

Setting my cup down on the table, I go over to the door,

opening it quickly. As the door swings past my face, I have a brief moment where I feel like scolding myself for not checking who it was first. I quickly calm down as I push the door open and see who's standing in front of me, a wiry grin on his lips. "Lincoln?"

"Hey, Maz." He leans forward, peering behind me, trying to see into the apartment. "How's it going?"

I open my mouth to speak but then pause for a second. That's his first question? "How's it *going?* I haven't seen you in..."

"A long time, I know." He takes another step in, looking around the room. "Can I come in? It's kinda cold out here."

I sigh under my breath, backing up and opening the door for Lincoln to come in. "Why are you here?"

He looks back at me, running his hands through his light ginger hair, already starting to work his way around the room. "What, I can't come and say hello to my little sister?"

"Not really, no. You flew here to talk to me, really?"

Lincoln waves my question off. "Oh, no. I'm at a convention about the school building trip I was a part of for a while. I just thought I'd drop by."

Drop by? "I — well," I go to the coffee table, picking up some of the trash lying around. "I haven't had a guest in a long time." I crack a half-hearted smile.

His nose scrunches as he pokes a pile of dirty laundry with his shoe. "Hmm, yeah, I see that. You okay?"

My eyes dart away from him, and I busy myself with dropping everything in the kitchen trash. "I kinda got fired, so I've been in a bit of a shitty mood."

Lincoln's face pulls in worry. He looks like he's going to offer me advice but quickly puts on a smile instead. "Well, maybe that job wasn't good enough anyway. What are you doing now?"

"Uh... nothing. I couldn't get myself to go to my last job.

No reason to think I'd do any better at a new one." I lean my stomach forward against the back of my couch, watching Lincoln wander around the living room.

He picks up an almost empty bottle of vodka, the last bit of liquid sloshing around as he swirls it. "So you don't have a job right now?"

"No, I don't."

He sets the bottle down and turns his million-watt smile on me. "That's perfect, then!"

"Uh, what?"

He comes to the front of the couch, kneeling on it in front of me. "Come back to Florida with me."

I lean closer — I clearly didn't hear him correctly. "Like, for Thanksgiving?"

"No. Well, yes, but then also to stay." He pulls an envelope out of his pocket and holds it in his hands, tapping the edge of it against his fingertips. "All of the other fosters miss you a ton. I just talked to Olivia about how she wishes she had you to talk to about girl stuff."

The corner of my lip tugs up into a half-smile. "I miss everyone too."

"*And*," he hands me the envelope, "You already have a ticket."

I open the envelope and, sure enough, there's a ticket for two days from now. "You bought me a plane ticket?"

He clams up like he wants to answer. "Not me, exactly..."

"Who?"

"Phoenix bought it. But it's just... he's worried about you, Mazey. I mean, the two of you used to be connected at the hip, inseparable. Now... you haven't talked to him in almost a year." Lincoln taps the ticket, "He wants you to be happy, to be with other people – not cramped in your apartment without any social contact for months. You don't have anything or anyone here for you anymore. Besides, he could really use some adult company..."

Phoenix.

Phoenix would be there. I can't figure out if that's a good thing or a bad thing. On the one hand, I can't imagine coming face-to-face with him again – having to actually *talk* to him again. On the other hand... if I could just hug him, I think everything would be alright. It's not exactly like I'm doing anything here. Going to Florida may actually be a good idea. "I... where would I live?"

"I already talked to Mom and she has a spare bed in Vincent's room."

I shake my head, looking down at the ticket in my hands. Suzan. Am I ready to face her after all this time? Am I ready to say everything that's been left unsaid? Can I show up at her house and expect her to welcome me with open arms? "She said yes?"

Lincoln narrows his eyes at me, "Yeah... why wouldn't she?"

She didn't tell him? "Nothing. I just feel so disconnected from everyone."

"I promise you'll feel at home as soon as you walk in the door. You used to come over a million times a year. Summers, birthdays, holidays — what's another extended vacation? Plus, the weather is much better than it is here in Seattle. At least at this time of the year." He nudges me with his finger. "So? Whaddya say?"

I reach up to my neck, where my necklace rests beneath my shirt. Pressing my hand against it, I know my answer. "Yeah. Yes, I think I'd like to get the hell out of Seattle."

Inside the house, I see the hustle and bustle of people playing, cooking, *living*. The scent of chili, a staple in this house, wafts through the air. There are bikes dropped on the lawn and the front door is open, with just the screen door closing it in. I stare down the hallway, noticing the pile of toys on the porch. Every kid here is going to grow up spoiled. I walk towards the driveway, past the cars that have been here since long before I moved in and have been here for the years since I moved out. Looking up at the massive house in front of me, I shut my eyes and let the subtle breeze wash over me. Well, the breeze and the stickiness in the air around me. The leaves rustle on the trees and the faint sound of kids playing outside from the next-door neighbor down the street travels through the thin woods.

I feel the energy that the house has when everyone's just coming home from school, and they're all sitting by the TV for the hour of screen time they are allowed before they have to do their homework. Upstairs, a curtain rustles as a window is opened and the window screen is popped out and pulled into the room. A few seconds later, I see a pair of feet slide through the window. A guy, average height with deep brown hair, drops onto the roof below the window. He reaches back inside to grab something and as a second person slides through I see what's glittering in the first guy's hands: a bong. Behind the first guy is someone I know well, only now he has a bright shade of green streaked through his hair, which I'm sure makes his green eyes pop.

He sweeps a gaze around, and I catch his eye. "Mazey?" He takes a step forward, baffled by my presence. My decision to surprise everyone is proved worth it with the look on his face. Before I can say anything back, he continues, "Holy shit! What are you doing here?"

"Suzan didn't tell you?" I walk closer, so I don't yell across the driveway.

Vincent shakes his head. "No. What? Nothing happened, right?"

"No." I shake my head quickly, giving him a reassuring smile. "I think this might actually be a good thing. I haven't really made up my mind yet."

He throws his hands in the air, "Well, tell me already!" He moves around his friend to the edge of the roof and smiles down at me

"I'm moving in."

"What!" He smiles at me, joy filling his face, making my heart feel warm. "Dude, how is that not a good thing?" Vincent goes to the end of the roof and hangs off the edge, sliding down and onto his feet so gracefully I know he's done it a million times. His friend, seeming as confused as he should, drops the bong back inside the window, laying a jacket over it before following Vincent. In seconds, Vincent runs over, throwing his arms around me and squeezing tight.

I hug him back, head pressed against his chest when it used to be near his neck. As I pull back, I look over him, "God, you're huge! How much have you grown since the last time I saw you?"

Vincent's face drops, "I, uh, stopped growing a little over a year ago."

I offer him up a smile – one that must fall short by the pained expression he gives me. "Yeah, sorry. I wasn't really paying attention the last time I saw you, I guess."

"I'm... I'm sorry, I didn't mean to–"

"You didn't do anything." I squeeze his arm, giving him the best smile I can. "But, uh, introduce me to your friend. Who is this?"

Vincent looks back at the guy behind him, "Oh, this is my friend, Jake. Jake, this is my old foster sister, Mazey."

"Mazey..." He mumbles, trying to place the name. As soon as the piece clicks into place, he looks at Vincent, who gives him a terrifying glare. Instead of saying what he probably wants to, Jake shoots a dazzling smile at me and reaches his hand out for a handshake. His silver eyes seem to sparkle in the light. "Nice to meet you."

I smile back. "Yeah, you too."

Grinning at me like a kid on Christmas morning, Vincent leans back against the beat-up car parked behind him. "I've really missed you."

"I've missed you, too. All of you." I nod towards the door at the noise trailing outside from the commotion going on. I look up at the rooftop where the two guys just climbed out of the window. "When did that start happening? Suzan doesn't know, I'm guessing?"

Vincent laughs, "Ha! No, like I'd ever tell her. Would you?"

"Hell no, especially not anymore." I stop, hoping I didn't say too much.

Vincent glances away, looking like he's not sure of something. After a second of thought, he asks me something he's probably been trying to figure out for a while now. "What happened between you two? I mean, she was with you in Seattle one minute and the next she was back here pretending nothing happened."

Sighing, I lean back against the garage in front of him, trying to give myself time to think of what to say. Suzan never did say anything to the rest of the family, even after all this time. If that was for my sake, Phoenix's, or her own, I'm not sure. At least she kept her mouth shut. At this point, if everyone knows what happened, it would only do more harm than good. Besides, I just came back, I don't want any drama. I've had way more than enough for my entire freaking lifetime. "It wasn't anything, really. I did something stupid, and Suzan was upset about it."

"If you say so," Vincent trails off and turns to his friend, who's already starting to back up to the end of the driveway. He nods to Jake, "Sorry to bail, but with Maz back, we'll probably be hanging out with her tonight."

I chaff, "You don't have to change your plans for me. I'm here, at least for a little while."

"Yeah, well I see him all the time, so..." Vincent teases him.

Jake waves me off. "Don't sweat it; family's important. Enjoy your night, y'all."

Vincent waves as Jake walks away, "See you tomorrow." Once Jake is gone a little ways away, Vincent grabs my two bigger suitcases from the sidewalk where I left them. "Come on! Everyone will freak when they see you."

I grab the remaining bags and follow him to the porch. Through the screen door, I see someone walking down the hall, away from us, with a bag of chips under their arm. Knowing the time, Suzan will likely take that snack away from them the instant she sees it. She's serious about her family dinners. To the right, I hear people in the kitchen, cooking away. They're all laughing and chatting about something. Pushing through the screen door, I almost trip over a pair of shoes, stopping on the welcome mat behind Vincent. The hallway floor is a mess, littered with toys, backpacks, clothes... since when has Suzan let a single item go out of place?

Tucking a stray piece of hair behind my ear, I notice a MacBook half falling out of one of the bags at the base of the stairs. No one bought me a laptop when I lived here. A short, chubby girl walks out of the kitchen, holding plates, cheeks flushed, and hair pulled into a messy bun. Tense shoulders tell me she's on kitchen duty with Suzan. She jumps when she sees us.

"Vin, what the hell are you doing? Weren't you just upstairs?" She looks at him and then over at me, brows furrowed in confusion as she notices the suitcases. I'd be confused as well if I didn't already know exactly what happened. She must be a new foster kid. I haven't exactly been keeping up with everyone over the last year. It wouldn't have been hard for me to miss that they took in someone else; from my best guess, she looks like she's in middle school – twelve or thirteen. thirteen. Suzan always did have a bleeding heart for kids who are getting too old to be adopted by other people. Life must be looking pretty good for Suzan's new foster daughter. She looks at me then turns to Vincent, head cocked. "Who's this? Don't tell me you've already gotten over Lexi."

"Eww, hell no! Still with Lexi." Vincent looks back at me, nose scrunching up.

I raise an eyebrow at him, "Who's Lexi?"

Vincent lets out a nervous chuckle, "Just, uh, nobody."

"Uh-huh, whatever you say." I smile at him mischievously.

Vincent gives the new girl a look that very clearly says "*fuck off*," which tells me this Lexi chick must have a story behind her. "This is Heather, who's supposed to be setting the table."

Heather looks at me, then back at Vincent, then very quickly back at me. "You look familiar."

I nod slowly, "Yeah. I'm in a lot of pictures around the house."

"You were a foster kid?"

"Yeah. I aged out like seven years ago, though. I'm Mazey." I give her a small wave, not able to do much more with the bags in my hands and on my shoulders.

In the living room at the end of the hall, I hear an excited voice, "Is that Mazey?" as footsteps shuffle around, the TV pauses, and people emerge from the room.

She looks at me closely, "Mazey... like, 'the Girl-Whose-Wife-Died,' Mazey?"

I look down at my feet, shaking my head. "God, is that how people introduce me, now?" I look up at Vincent, seeing Olivia, one of the only foster sisters I talk to, come into the hall. She motions to people I can't see, whispers running around the hall, and the rustling of more people becomes louder. Little baby Georgie stumbles out of the room, tripping on his own foot. Well, I guess not *baby* anymore. He's gotten so big. I look at Heather, inwardly grimacing at the way I reacted. She can't help how much it still hurts, no need to take it out on her. "Yes, I'm Mazey. Sorry for snapping."

She looks over at Vincent, then to her other side, where Olivia stands. "Sorry, I didn't mean to—"

"It's fine. I'm just a little too sensitive about it." I drop my bags on the ground under the entry table. Olivia comes over, brushing past the new girl to throw her arms around me, the multiple charm bracelets on her wrist clinking lightly as her hand presses to my neck. I hug her back, noticing Suzan coming out of the kitchen. Her sloppily thrown-up hair showing her neck glistening with sweat. She eyes me, surprised, but also with slightly furrowed eyebrows, that "*oh goodness*" look taking over.

I see most of the kids I expected to see, only missing a few of them. Suzan's constant need to always keep the house full is both annoying and endearing at the same time. At the end of the day, she's only trying to do what's best for these kids. She always tries to help *everyone*. Here she is offering me a room in her already crazy full house. And, seven years after I moved out, after all. While I could go on forever thinking of all the ways she falls short, she's always offering a helping hand.

"Mazey?" She has a shrill pitch to her voice as she comes over to me slowly. "What are you doing here?

I purse my lips. "Staying here? Did Lincoln not actually talk to you?"

"I just assumed you'd say no."

"To coming home?"

She clamps her mouth shut and pats the front of her apron. "Well, it's not like it's *your* home anymore, right? You have one of those in Seattle."

"I wouldn't..." I clear my throat, eyes down at my feet. "Can I stay here?"

She looks at the kids gathered around us. "I'm just not sure if I have enough room for you right now—"

"I have an extra bed in my room." Vincent steps forward, throwing his arm over my shoulders. "I could go for some company."

"I don't have to stay if you don't want me to..."

Waving me off, Suzan puts a tight smile on her lips. "No, don't be silly. You can stay with Vincent."

Vincent beams down at me, already starting to talk about how fun it'll be to stay together, batting at Olivia as she tries to grab onto my arm. Olivia starts talking a mile a minute about how excited she is to see me again.

Suzan clears her throat, starting in a strained voice, "Well, this calls for a special dinner, I think. I'll go make your favorite dessert!" She shoos people back into a kitchen that's bigger than my entire apartment to help with preparing the food. The new girl goes into the dining room to set the table, and the rest of the kids shuffle back to the TV, leaving Vincent, Olivia, Suzan, and me. Suzan quickly turns her attention back to preparing enough food to feed an army. She's always very flustered while cooking. "Dinner will be done soon, Mazey. You better get ready." With that, she turns and walks towards the kitchen to whip together a feast – she's a sucker for letting kids stay to eat. I'm sure there's a friend or two lurking around.

I pick up my bags with Vincent and Olivia's help and head towards the back of the hallway where the stairs are. Through the archway into the living room, I see I was right – in the mass of foster siblings I see three kids I don't recognize. On the walls are tons of pictures of all of Suzan's foster kids, group pictures from different times. The one that stops me is right at the top of the stairs – a picture of Suzan, her husband, and her three biological kids. I reach up, running my finger on Roxanne's image. I barely see her face anymore since I destroyed all the pictures I had of her around the house. Now I only have my memory.

Roxanne, Ashten, and Phoenix. Gosh, they look so much alike no one could miss that they're related. All three of Suzan's kids have her blue eyes and their dad's copper hair. The only anomaly in the picture is Suzan's strawberry blonde hair against all the auburn. Roxanne and Ashten look almost exactly alike, and when they were younger, it was almost impossible to tell the two twins apart.

Even Phoenix... he looks so much like them, it's crazy. His little goofy smile, the wild hair he had when he was a boy – he's adorable. I move my finger to him, a slight smile on my lips. Seeing him in the picture, his vibrant personality showing through in a single photo, just reminds me of why I came back. My heart skips a beat at the thought of seeing him again, after all this time.

"Mazey?" Olivia calls my name from down the hall.

I step away from the picture and continue towards her. "Sorry."

"I'm glad you're here! I have so much to tell you, Maz. You don't even know the half of it." Olivia beams at me, excitement seeping from her skin. As we finally get to Vincent's room, we dump my stuff inside the door. It's completely different from the last time I was here. A new bed, dresser, nightstand that all match. The only thing I recognize is the spare bed in the corner of the room with plain white sheets under a fluffy dark blue duvet. The steady bedposts barely move as Olivia flops down and pats the blanket beside her. I walk over, kicking my shoes off before sitting at the headboard, pressing against Olivia as Vincent joins us on my other side. After a second, Olivia's face gets slightly somber for someone excited to spill gossip. "How have you been?"

My heart skips a beat – that didn't take very long. I honestly expected them to wait a little bit. I look down, twisting my hands in my lap and shaking my head. "Umm, that's not exactly exciting to talk about. I mean, I haven't done anything too noteworthy lately."

Olivia props her head on the palm of her hand, "You know that's not what I meant."

Vincent kicks her from across my leg, "Stop asking. If she doesn't want to talk about it, leave her alone."

Olivia sticks her tongue out at him, then turns to me. "Do you not want to talk about it? I'm not trying to pry. I'm just..."

"We're worried about you." Vincent finishes her sentence and leans his head on my shoulder.

I reach up and pat his cheek, "I know I'm closed off. People keep saying I should see a therapist. I haven't listened yet."

Olivia squeezes my arm as she lays her head on my lap. "Well, we have the whole night to listen, and we want to hear everything."

I look down at Olivia, then over at Vincent. Suzan is the only person I've talked to about this, and that's just because she forced me to. I hated that conversation almost as much as I hated what was going on around me. But they're not bullying me into it, and they're not here to judge me or ridicule me. I don't have to tell them anything. Just some of the things. The things they'd want to hear about.

Clearing my throat, I look at my hands and start talking, "I got a job at a fast-food restaurant in Seattle. I only had it for maybe three months before I was fired. I just wasn't doing very well with the getting up and going to work part. I felt like I didn't... it's hard to describe. At the same time, I felt like I realized how much we need to live life and go out and do what we want, but also that I didn't deserve to feel the freedom of living life when Roxanne..."

"You do," Olivia mumbles against my leg, "You deserve to live life. Just because someone else can't anymore doesn't mean you have to stop."

I continue, "I wish I could've seen him. I wish he didn't get the peacefulness of dying when they found him. He didn't deserve it." Bryan Johnson. The name burns my stomach, even just thinking about it. I feel anger creeping up in my throat, but it quickly turns to tears instead. They well up in my eyes but don't move any farther. "He got what he wanted, he got her. And I... I lost everything." My throat closes and the last few words come out almost like squeaks. The tears finally spillover, rushing down my cheeks. My chest already hurts, and I've barely begun crying. Olivia sits up and faces me, shaking her head. Vincent links his arm through mine. Olivia sniffles beside me.

I've never hated anyone as much as I hate him. If I could wish anyone to Hell, he'd be my first pick, but I can't. I didn't even get to look him in the eye and tell him everything he took from me. I didn't get justice or peace. I didn't get to spit at him, show him my disgust. I don't know if I could have looked at him, though. His name alone fills me with so much vivid anger that I'm sure that if I were there, and saw him in person, I would have exploded with rage.

Olivia looks at me with tears dripping down her cheeks, "You didn't lose everything, Maz. You still have all of us. We love you, too."

I nod, my mouth slipping into a watery smile, "I know, but having her taken like that, especially when she was... when I was going to–" I take a deep breath, trying to calm myself. "What he *did* to her. What she must have been feeling and thinking in her last few hours–"

My throat closes again, and I quickly feel like I can't breathe. I push away from Olivia and Vincent, needing air, practically scrambling to the edge of the bed. It feels like my lungs are screaming, trying to fill again. I try not to think about her like that and the pain she must have felt. Pain not just from dying, but from the torment and torture she felt in her last moments. He made the last hours of her life a living hell, and I wasn't there for her while she was begging for her life, begging for him to stop touching her, and hurting her. She must have been crying, crying for me or for anyone to make him stop. But he didn't stop, not soon enough, and instead of stopping, he killed her.

"Mazey? What's wrong?"

I feel a pair of hands placed on my thigh, but one of them leaves quickly, wiping a tear off my cheek. As I open my eyes I'm face-to-face with Phoenix. My throat opens, managing to croak out, "Nix?"

Putting his hands on either side of my face, he smiles. "Maz... hey, what's wrong?"

I shake my head, "Nothing, just... nothing." I throw my arms around his neck, resting my cheek on his shoulder as I take a deep breath.

Phoenix hugs me back, "Okay, you're okay." He runs his hands down my arms and quiets me with soothing sounds. Behind me, Olivia clears her throat, making Phoenix's chin lift from the top of my head. "Hey, guys, can we get a moment? I'll calm her down."

There's rustling on the bed behind me, so I let go of Phoenix and turn to see Olivia and Vincent sliding off the bed. "No, wait, I'm sorry. You don't have to go. I didn't mean to freak."

Olivia shakes her head, "Nah, we'll let Phoenix talk to you. You guys can catch up."

"Feel better, Maz." Vincent smiles at me, eyes full of worry.

Phoenix watches them leave, and as soon as they're gone, he gets up off his knees and looks down at me. "What happened?"

I wave his concerns off. "I started talking. Once I start talking about it, I always start crying. It's like a rule or something."

"So, I shouldn't ask you if you want to talk about it?" He smirks at his own joke.

I shake my head, but then I think about it for a second. If I was going to open up to anyone, it would be Phoenix. He's the only one who was there for me no matter what, even when I was pushing him away. I would argue that he saved my life last year. My life and... "Actually, I wanted to talk to you about something."

Phoenix takes a seat on the bed beside me, "Yeah?"

I look up at him, trying to muster the courage. As soon as I meet his eyes, I have to look away. There's no way I can have him looking me in the eyes while I talk. It's like he can read my mind anytime we make eye contact. "About... everything? I'm sorry. I shouldn't have pushed you away so much. I never apologized and we never talked about it."

"You don't have to apologize, Mazey. You were going through a lot."

"Yeah, and so was everyone else. She was your sister,

Suzan's daughter too. Not just my wife." I look up at him, shaking my head, "I had no right to treat you like that. I was sad and angry, but I—" I sniffle, wiping snot all over my jacket. "I didn't push you away because I was angry at you. I just — I was angry at myself." I pause, take a deep breath, and try not to burst into tears for the second time today. "If you hadn't come back to check on me... I — I don't even know what would have happened. You helped me get back on track. You helped me when I needed it the most. Every single time—"

"Mazey." Phoenix grabs my hand and looks me straight in the eyes. "Stop apologizing. I didn't do that because I owed you a favor, I did that because I care about you and you needed help." He finally looks away from me, getting up and pacing across the room. "We screwed up. We both know that, but we're making it right in our own heads. I know why you were pissed at me, even if I didn't like it." He leans back against the dresser, arms folded over his chest, biceps pushing against his shirt sleeves.

I nod, unable to find the right words to reply. I just smile at him, and he smiles back, but his ice-blue eyes are full of sorrow. He's the only one who's never looked at me with pity or treated me like a widow instead of plain old Mazey. It feels momentarily like a weight has been lifted off my shoulders. I knew Phoenix wasn't mad at me anymore, he probably never was, but finally having apologized and *knowing* that we're okay is amazing. Phoenix... he's the reason I'm back here. If I came back for him, then I need to take advantage of that.

He clears his throat, "I heard Mom was making a berry pie. Can I assume that's for you?"

"Heh, yeah. She said she was making my favorite." I get off the bed and walk towards the pile of bags I still need to unpack.

Phoenix walks over and joins me, unzipping a second bag while I finish opening the first. "You really should tell her."

"No way!" I shake my head as I grab my bag of shower supplies out of the suitcase and place it on top of the dresser. "After all these years? That's just embarrassing."

Phoenix takes a pile of shirts and drops them in the top drawer of the dresser. "It's not embarrassing. It's the truth. I mean, one time you lie and say berry pie is your favorite, and for what? Years of birthdays and thoughtful desserts made for you and they're all berry pie."

I put the little baggie full of my underwear and bras in a drawer before Phoenix accidentally grabs it. "I just don't want to make Suzan feel bad. Besides, it doesn't happen as much now. When I lived here it definitely wasn't pleasant."

"Now that you're going to live here again you should consider it." Phoenix pauses, a drawer half open, and raises a brow at me. The way he's standing under the light, his normally auburn hair looks more orange than normal. "I mean, you are, right? That's why we're unpacking your bags?"

I evade the question. "You sent Lincoln all the way across the country to ask me something you could've accomplished in a phone call."

Phoenix shrugs. "A phone call didn't seem right. On top of that, he wasn't supposed to tell you I sent him there. He was just supposed to get you back here."

"True." I finish with my first bag and move onto my backpack.

"So," he catches my eye and gives me a look. "Are you?"

"Am I what?" I know full well what he's asking about, but I'm just not sure what the answer to the question is, and my uncertainty will hurt him.

Phoenix rolls his eyes. "Are you staying? In Florida, I mean."

I put my bag down and sigh, "I'm not sure yet."

Phoenix nods, looking down at the bag in front of him and coughing lightly. "Why aren't you sure?"

"I know I don't want to go back to Seattle. There's no reason for me to be there. My apartment is a dump, I got fired from my job, I don't talk to anyone there..." I look up from the hands. "But I'm not sure I want to stay here, either. People here know what happened. It's a pretty small town. I'll be getting shitty looks for the rest of my life."

"What if you had to pick right now?" He finally looks up at me, a blanket I brought squeezed in his hand.

"If I had to pick right now?" I shake my head, a sigh escaping my lips. "I really don't know. That's why I'm here, to figure it all out. I may end up going somewhere new. Somewhere still in Florida, nearby. Maybe a bigger city, not Orlando. Somewhere people don't know who I am, or what happened. Somewhere I can just... be."

Phoenix nods, seeming a little hurt, but not as much as I had thought. He puts the now empty bag on the floor and the blanket on the bed. He steps towards me, dangerously close. He looks down, straight into my eyes, and his face shifts as he grabs my hand. "Please stay," he whispers, leaning closer with each moment that passes, close enough to make my skin tingle.

I open my mouth to speak, to say something, but nothing will come out. When his face is close enough that I want to crawl out of my skin and run away, the door flies open and Dylan, one of the younger foster kids, stands in the doorway. If he wasn't on the other side of the room I would have sworn he shocked us. The jolt of electricity that springs me away from Phoenix sure feels like a taser.

"Mom said to get you 'cause dinner is ready," he announces, then stands there waiting for us.

I nod, walking towards him and taking his hand. "Alright, let's go."

Behind me, Phoenix stays in the room, standing right where I left him. He looks at me as I look at him, both of us debating saying something more. But what *do* I say? He asked me to stay. I have no clue if that's even possible, let alone if I want to. I can't say anything, so I just walk with Dylan to have dinner and forget about everything, even if only for a second.

CHAPTER TWO

"I think when I move out, I'm going to get a dog," Olivia muses as she pins another picture to her bulletin board. She turns to me, eyebrow rising. "What do you think? Should I get a lab or a husky?"

I shake my head at her, flipping a page of the magazine I'm looking at. "I think you should adopt from a shelter. So, probably a pit bull. I also think you have a couple of years to figure it out."

"Well, I graduate in two years. I need to have it figured out before then." She flops onto her bed, chin resting on her palm. "Do you think they don't have huskies or labs at the shelter?"

"I'm sure they do. Other people will adopt the huskies and the labs, though. So you should get the dog that other people won't adopt, instead." I put the magazine down, looking at her. "Do you think you'll be able to afford a dog right out of high school? You're not even really working right now."

She gives me an offended look. "I am too working. I have a job at the boutique down by Publix."

"You work like three hours a week. That isn't giving you much money, and the money you do earn you spend on stupid shit. Like those new shoes you just got today."

She rolls her eyes. "Yeah, those shoes are so worth it. They'll match perfectly with this dress that I got last month that I look really good in."

"What about that hair dye you bought that you never used?" I nod my head towards the plastic shopping bag that's sitting by her nightstand.

"I decided not to bleach my hair. I like my natural hair, the brown makes my eyes look caramel. If it was blonde they'd probably look like poop."

"Poop?" I chuckle. "Your eyes would not look like poop. Nikkie is blonde and he has brown eyes. His eyes don't look like poop."

"Yes," she sits up in her bed, setting a pillow in her lap, "but his eyes are also *really* brown. They look cool and black. Plus, you can't say anything with your gorgeous eyes, I wish I had them."

"They're not even that special."

"*Excuse me?*" Olivia scoffs. "Your eyes are so freaking cool. Hazel looks good with any hair color. You can wear blue *or* green to make them pop."

I bat said eyes and stand up from the chair I'm sitting in. "Thank you, Liv. I'll trade you my eyes for your lips."

"No way, I'm good."

Laughing, I go over to the door. "I'm going to grab food, you want anything?"

"I'll come with you." She gets up from her bed, throwing her hair up into a ponytail.

We go down the stairs and turn into the kitchen where Vincent is chatting with my old foster brother Eric, who's wearing a wife-beater with his frat logo on it and a snapback.

Behind Vincent is a bowl of chips and Eric has at least five chocolate chip cookies in his hand.

I give him a questioning look. "You going to eat all of those?"

"They're for the kids. They're watching *Cars* and I was sent on a snack run. Or, well, a cookie run."

"Don't let Suzan see you giving the kids those cookies. She'll have your head." I open the fridge and grab a cheese stick, quickly pulling the plastic from the sides. I miss these things. I should've kept buying them when Roxanne and I moved out.

Eric nods his head to the front door. "She's out for a while. She said something about errands."

"Well, then you better hope none of them mention it to her on accident." Turning to Vincent, I take a bite out of my cheese. "I thought you said you were hanging out with your girlfriend today?"

He huffs. "We were *supposed* to. She said something came up. Something always comes up."

Olivia snickers. "He's pussy-whipped."

"What?" I look between the two of them. "What the hell does that even mean?"

Eric shakes his head. "He's only with Lexi 'cause she has sex with him."

"His last girlfriend wouldn't give it up so he broke up with her."

My mouth drops open. "Vincent, that's terrible!"

"Look, I'm only seventeen, I'm not looking for a wife. And I got needs. Eric knows what I mean, right, dude?"

Eric puts one of his hands up in surrender, holding the cookies in the other. "I didn't have sex with Valarie for a year. But I'll give it to you, it was a pretty sucky year."

Olivia pushes past Vincent to grab a bowl. "You two are

the reason why I'm waiting until marriage. No one is having sex with me *just 'cause*."

Vincent shakes his head with a sigh. "You're everything that's wrong with the world. Girls don't even tell you they won't have sex until you've already spent a bunch of time trying to get them to go out with you. What a waste."

"You're an ass, you know that, right?" Olivia pushes him again as she grabs a box of Cocoa Puffs from the cabinet behind him.

I look at Vincent. "Yeah, that's a pretty douchebag thing to say."

"Like you don't agree. You and Roxanne started having sex the second you started dating."

I take a second to jump over the fact that we're talking about my dead wife. Then I flick him on the nose. "First off, we didn't. Second, I married her, didn't I?"

Eric chuckles and pushes himself off the counter. "I better go before the kids come looking for me."

Vincent points at Olivia and me. "You guys comin' or what?"

Liv looks over at me and I shrug. "Yeah, we'll all join you. What are we watching next?"

We start heading out. "Buzz Lightyear?" Vincent looks at Eric for confirmation.

"Toy Story." Eric chuckles at him.

"Is that Buzz Lightyear?"

"Yes."

"Then yes."

Vincent throws his arm around my shoulder, walking with me out of the kitchen.

"Mazey, c'mon! You're not even watching the movie." Dylan whines beside me, jabbing into my arm.

I smack at his hand, then take a handful of popcorn from the bowl sitting in my lap and mumble, "I am," before shoving it into my mouth.

Dylan frowns at me, clearly not convinced. He looks back at the screen, then quickly back at me, like he's trying to catch me not watching. "Are you watching?"

"Yes. Belle is getting ready to go to dinner with Beast." I point at the screen, showing him where she's trying on dresses. He seems satisfied with that display of knowledge, not that I'd have to be watching the movie to have convinced him. Belle was my favorite princess when I was little; I watched this movie a million times. I know it like the back of my hand. I mean, I *am* paying attention, I'm just looking away every once in a while. I'm surprised Dylan hasn't fallen asleep yet. The kids had spent the entire morning running around outside, swimming in the pool, and playing with the soccer ball. They've all taken turns sleeping or at the very least, seem pretty drained. Dylan, however, has been very adamant about me seeing every frame of the movie.

Olivia comes in through the archway, arms full of drinks for everyone. She tosses me a can of lemonade and then passes water out to all the younger kids.

Dylan frowns at his bottle. "I asked for a Sprite."

"No sodas before dinner. You know that." She hands Vincent his drink before she settles back onto the couch.

"I wish I was allowed to have sodas." Dylan gives Olivia a look, trying to throw daggers at her with his eyes, then opens his bottle and gulps down half of it.

I laugh as I take the bottle from him when he's done with his sip so I can spin the lid back on. "You can when you're older. It's something to look forward to." Before I can say anything else, the doorbell rings and Dylan jumps up, running off to answer it. Apparently, that's one of his new habits. In the few days I've been here, I've only seen someone else answer the door twice – once time because he was asleep, and the next because he was in the bathroom. I hear him open the door and say something to the person there. "Who is it, bud?"

"Phoenix!" Dylan yells back, way louder than necessary, as he walks around the corner with Phoenix close behind. He jumps back on the couch next to me and wraps himself into the blanket. "I missed the best part!"

I grab the remote out of his hand as he tries to rewind it. "Everyone else has already seen it. You know what happens, anyway."

"Mazey?" Phoenix calls from the doorway, coat and shoes still on.

I take a drink of my lemonade before answering. "Yeah?"

"Can we talk for a second?"

"Uh... yeah." I peel myself out from underneath the fuzzy blanket, throwing my half onto Olivia's lap. As I lift the popcorn bowl from my lap, Dylan's hands go up to grab it, so I give the bowl to him, leaving my nearly full lemonade on the coffee table. My heart flutters as I go over to the doorway, adjusting my shirt as I walk, wanting to look somewhere other than at Phoenix, but not able to. "What's up?"

His eyes are locked on something – my necklace. It's sitting on my shirt, the ring sparkling in the light. He reaches forward and picks it up, holding the ring in his palm. "This is..."

"Roxanne's ring, yeah." As if it's an instinct, I start twisting my own ring around my finger.

Phoenix drops the necklace back onto my shirt. "I've always thought this ring suited her perfectly."

I smile tightly. "I know, you said that the day I showed it to you."

He looks over my head at the room of people behind me. "What are y'all doing?"

"Watching *Beauty and the Beast*." I tuck the ring under my shirt and clear my throat. "You said you wanted to talk?"

He nods. "Yeah. Can we go somewhere, though?"

"Go somewhere?"

"I was thinking of Frank's Bar?" He motions towards the front door.

I start walking and he follows behind me. "Seriously? That's what you're picking?"

"Yeah, why not?"

I stop to put some flip-flops on and let my hair down out of the messy bun it's in, checking it in the mirror as I talk. "Nothing, just hoping you're not doing it as something cheesy."

Phoenix scoffs. "Just 'cause that's where we met doesn't mean I'm going to use it for everything."

"You've done it before. It's not completely unimaginable to me." I open the front door and hold it for him to walk through.

He does, smirking at me. "That was for a reason, though. Besides, I'm pretty sure we swore not to talk about that."

"Whatever. We got over that ages ago."

"Don't speak for the both of us there, Maz." He looks over at me, dragging his eyes from my feet to my nose. "We both know what happened after that."

My mouth falls open as I try to say something, but I can't. I do know what happened after that. He seems to be making sure I remember just as much as he does. Phoenix raises an eyebrow, calling me out on the fact that I'm still just staring at him and have yet to answer. As he stares into my eyes, I quickly become very aware of how close he is, how I can see the lines of darker blue running through his pale blue eyes. The smell of his honey shampoo washes over me, and it's all I can do not to reach up and run my fingers through his hair.

I squirm under his gaze, trying to swallow, but my throat is so dry all I end up doing is coughing. That does give me a great excuse to look away, however, which is exactly what I needed. Without looking at him, I go to the other side of the car and pull on the handle. It's locked. I look back at Phoenix, finger tapping against the handle.

Phoenix shakes his head, a chuckle rumbling in his chest. "You've always been so weird about this."

"Weird? About what?"

"This," he flicks his finger between us.

Oh, geez. "Yeah, for good reasons, too."

"Not anymore."

My mouth falls open in shock. "Even more so now!"

Phoenix comes back over from where he was standing on his side of the car, staring down at me. "Look, I'm sorry for bringing it up. I won't do it again. Can we just get in the car?"

"I'm not going to lie, I don't believe you. You're going to bring it up again the second we sit down." I back away slightly, not able to think clearly when he's this close to me, shaking my head. "Last time you brought me to Frank's—"

"Last time I took you to Frank's was years ago, Maz." He sighs, leaning against the car door. "Look, I'm not trying to do anything other than be friends again, okay? We used to be best friends. Now that you're moving back, I..."

Leaning against the car next to him, I nod. "I know. I miss you, too."

"But...?" He chuckles. He knows exactly what I'm about to say.

"It just feels like I'm betraying Roxanne."

Phoenix turns to me. "You have to stop living your life

like you're living it for her. I know you loved her, and I get where you're coming from..."

His words fade away slowly as my eye catches something behind him. On the other side of the street is... Roxanne? My heart drops. I've talked to Phoenix twice in the five days I've been here, and now I'm seeing my dead wife? She looks too clean and pretty, not how I see her when I close my eyes. She looks... happy? I want her to be happy, but why would she be smiling like that. And waving at me? She's waving at me and walking towards me.

I squeeze my eyes shut, not wanting to look at her anymore, but all that does is make me picture her the way I saw her the night she was killed. Bloody, broken, sprawled on the floor. Lifeless eyes staring at nothing. Blood trailing out of her mouth, and her hands tied above her head. No, I don't want to see her anymore. I open my eyes and she's standing right in front of me. Only, that's not Roxanne, is it? It can't be.

"Mazey?" She has a concerned look on her face, and her hand reaches out to touch me.

I jump back, trying to pull air into my lungs. "Wha... what are you... why–" I can't even finish the sentence before I see it all in front of me, even without my eyes closed. The guilt-tripping look she gave me as I walked out the door that night, the look that ended up being the last look she'd ever give me. And the look in her eyes when I found her... the look of nothing. No emotions or feelings in her eyes like there normally was. I see the blood-stained carpet underneath her, the stab wounds all over her body.

My stomach reels and I drop to my knees, vomiting onto the grass. I feel someone rush to my side and pull my hair from my face. After a few moments, my heart slows down. I wipe my mouth with the back of my hand, leaning backward, and against someone. He whispers – it's Phoenix. Someone walks around in front of me, wearing sandals, and Roxanne would never wear sandals. Plus, she has a freckle on her nose. Roxanne doesn't have that... Ashten does. "Ashten?"

She has a worried look on her face. "Are you okay? What just happened?"

I look back at Phoenix, then up at Ashten. I feel ridiculous that my first thought wasn't of Roxanne's twin but rather of Roxanne herself. I haven't seen Ashten since the funeral. "I, uh, I thought you lived in Texas now?"

"I do. That's where my husband is from." She looks over my shoulder at Phoenix, raising her brows in question. After a second, she tries her best to put on a smile and points to the man walking up to us. "You remember Greg, don't you?"

Heat rushes to my cheeks at the thought of someone I barely know just saw me puke my guts up. I push to my feet with the help of Phoenix and turn to Greg. "Hi, yeah. We've met... I think."

Greg steps forward and holds out his hand. "Yes. Christmas two years ago."

"I'd shake your hand, but I kinda just wiped my mouth with mine, so..."

He chuckles. "Uh, yeah. Well, good to see you again either way."

Phoenix squeezes my shoulder then turns his attention to Ashten. "What are you doing here?"

"We're here for Thanksgiving. Figured it'd be better to get settled in the night before. With the baby coming–"

"You're pregnant?" My eyes drop to her stomach. She doesn't look pregnant. She may not be very far along, and she is wearing a very loose shirt.

Ashten beams, resting her hand on her stomach. "About fifteen weeks."

My eyes well up and I can't help but feel the ache of the *what-ifs*. The *what-could-have-been*s. If we had had more time,

Roxanne could have carried our child. I push away from Phoenix, making everyone stop talking, and walk away from them as fast as I can. I hear someone calling after me, but I don't respond, just shove open the gate to the backyard. Wrapping my arms around my waist, I try to hold back tears.

There's no reason to cry right now. I've been crying practically nonstop since I got here. It feels like the summer Roxanne died all over again when I couldn't even take a breath without being sad that she couldn't anymore. I was getting better. Yeah, I wasn't doing great, but I was better than before. Before I got fired, I was in the highest place I've been since Roxanne died. I thought there might finally be a light at the end of the tunnel, when before it had been completely black. A huge, gaping pit of nothing swallowing me whole. It was like the night I found her, dead and lifeless on the ground, I shattered into a million pieces. Day-by-day, I'm getting some of those pieces back, fitting edges back together where I can, but I'm still broken. One gust of wind can send all those pieces flying back out into the darkness, hiding from me until I can muster up the strength to find them again.

I drop onto a bench swing, pressing my face into my palms. I don't want to fight anymore. I'm tired of trying to find those pieces when I just keep losing them again. I'll finally get one in my hands, and then it falls to the ground and shatters into even smaller pieces. I miss her so much. If she was here... if I was trying to fix myself with her by my side? At least then it would feel like it was worth it. I would have someone not only to help me but to be the *reason* I'm putting the pieces back together to begin with. Who am I fixing myself for now? Who's going to be waiting at the end of that dark tunnel, with light shining from behind, arms open wide to welcome me back?

"Mazey?"

I look up to see Phoenix, hands shoved in his pockets, standing in front of me. I open my mouth, trying to find the words, hoping something will come out, and for once, they do. "I miss her so *much*. More than I think I would ever have the time to express in words."

"I know." Phoenix sits next to me. His weight makes the swing move backward, then forward again. He uses his legs to stop the movement. The light breeze rustles the leaves as splashing and laughter fill the air. The kids are probably in the pool. In the silence that's resting between Phoenix and me, I feel all the things we've left unsaid. I snuggle my knees to my chest, trying to block the slight bite of the wind. It's been so long since my last Florida winter. I almost forgot how nice the air smells.

I smile down at the ground. "It's like... sometimes I can feel this pressure in my chest. I feel like I can't breathe, and the world seems so small, but... that's what it feels like when I try to remember her from before. When I sit there and I think about how nervous she was on our first date, so nervous she accidentally dropped her ice cream on my skirt, and normally I would have been so mad... but that night I just laughed, and when she finally laughed back I was so captured by the sound that I just stopped and the world faded away so it was just me and her, and that laugh–" My voice catches in my throat, and I have to stop.

Phoenix grabs my hand and squeezes it, eyes watering, too.

"I wish that when I close my eyes, and I think of her, that I would think of the years we spent together. That I would think of the hours we spent cuddled up on the couch watching TV. Or the way she always managed to get me to tell her the answer to the math problem she needed help with, even if I didn't want to. The night of our senior prom, when she made me swear I wouldn't look at her dress, claiming it was bad luck. But then on our wedding day barged into my dressing room completely done up, saying she just had to look at me. I wish I could think of happy memories, like when we were looking at houses and she always felt like she had to remind me that we needed lots of bedrooms so we could have a big, happy family like she had growing up. Or the way she proposed to me, starting her speech by telling me she refused to get on one knee because that's how a guy would do it, but then acting surprised that I knew she was proposing before she asked me to marry her."

Taking a shaky breath, I drop my head onto my knees. "I don't think of any of that when I think of Roxanne. I only think of that night. I can't get the image of that guy out of my head. Of how terrified she must have been when she saw him for the first time, and how much pain she felt when he was raping her–" My voice breaks, and I squeeze my eyes shut, that exact image burning itself into my eyelids.

"Mazey..." Phoenix's voice is trembling, and when I look up at him, I see the sorrow I'm feeling reflected in his eyes. He runs his thumb over the back of my hand, then scoots over and pulls me into his arms.

I tuck my head under his chin. "What I said to you that night... the only thing that keeps me sane about it is that she never lived to hear it. If I had gone home and she had been alive, I would have broken her heart that night."

Phoenix pulls me closer – as if it's even possible. "But you didn't, Maz. And if she hadn't died, and you hadn't talked to her, you would have been lying to yourself and to her. Telling her would have been the right thing to do."

"It doesn't feel like it would have been the right thing when the last thing I did to my wife when she was alive was betray her." I look up at Phoenix, my mind wandering to the other parts of that night, the parts that came before the worst thing I could have imagined. There was a time when I took Roxanne for granted, and before I could make that up to her, she died. If I could go back in time... I honestly don't know what I would do, but I do know for sure I would have been by her side in her last moments, even if they were my last moments, too. I would have told her I loved her, that I was sorry for the mistakes that I had made. That I wished I could take them back. But that didn't happen, and I can't go back in time. So, instead, I get to live with the grief and the guilt.

Phoenix wipes a tear away from under my eye, resting his palm against my cheek. "There was a time when this could've been normal. A time where thinking about Roxanne didn't bring you this much pain. I'm worried that you feel this much pain because of me."

"You're not the one who killed her."

Phoenix shakes his head, a tear rolling down his cheek, and just like him, I reach up and wipe it away. "I was the one who kept you away from her when he was there."

"I chose to be there just as much as you did. And," I trail off, my brain stopping me before I finish what I'm about to say. As I look at Phoenix's eyes and see not only pain in them but also love and acceptance, I open my mouth and finish the sentence before I can regret it. "If Roxanne hadn't died that night, it would have been the best decision of my life."

Phoenix gasps in a hushed tone as if he didn't expect me to say it just as much as I didn't expect to be able to. Without him saying anything, I can feel his answer. He leans forward, pressing his forehead to mine, eyes squeezed shut like he's thinking really hard.

I reach between us and brush my thumb against his lip.

This must have halted his train of thought because his eyes snap open, bluer than I've ever seen them. My heart pounds in my chest as I take a wavering breath. I can see his mind is made up. The puzzle pieces snapping into place, and his reasoning and rational thoughts being locked away. I can see the moment he's finally decided he's going to kiss me. And from the look of determination I can see on his face, I assume he's seen the same moment in my eyes. He smiles.

I can't see his mouth, but I can see it around his eyes. I take a deep breath, deciding the same as him. At this moment, I can't think of a single reason not to fall right into his arms.

"Phoenix? Mazey?" Suzan snaps, standing a little ways away. She doesn't waste much time closing the distance between us. I practically fall off of Phoenix's lap with her last steps, my heartbeat already picking up pace with the clipped tone in her voice. *Shit.* "What the *hell* do you think you're doing?"

Feeling like I'm still the broken teenager she brought in, an excuse is already at the tip of my tongue. Luckily for me, Phoenix is quicker on his feet and he answers first.

"Mom, calm down–"

"Calm down?" She scoffs, eyes blazing. "I cannot believe the two of you! You've barely been back five days, Mazey, and you're coming into my house and disrespecting me like this? When Lincoln called and said you were coming back, I knew it was a mistake. I shouldn't have let you back into my home."

I get off the bench, arms crossed over my chest. I feel like I'm being scolded, which I am – that's exactly what she's doing. Doesn't mean I want to feel like I am, though. "Suzan, please just– Suzan?"

She turns and marches off, only looking back to give us a disgusted look.

"Suzan, come back, are you seriously leaving?" My mouth falls open. "She's storming away like a child. God, I could swear the last time she did this to me I was in high school." I huff, wiping under my eyes to hopefully get rid of any smudged makeup.

Phoenix sighs from his place on the bench. "How are you even surprised? She did the same thing when she found out about us the first time."

I turn to Phoenix, a question already on the tip of my tongue. "The first time?"

"Yeah, back after Roxanne died. Did she not tell you she knew?"

"Oh, no, she let me know she knew." I snort, a groan working its way up my throat. I didn't know she talked to Phoenix about it, though. "I guess I should go after her?"

Phoenix nods. "Yeah, we should go." He gets up off the bench, but I shake my head.

"Us going together will only make it worse. I'll go alone."

"Okay, but I'll be here if you need anything." He squeezes my hand, a reassuring smile offering me some comfort.

I smile back. "Yeah. Thanks." I start down the little dirt path through the trees, leaving the bench that I used to call my safe haven. Well, I guess it still is since I found my way back here. I push aside small branches poking out from the huge trees, hearing less of the sounds of nature and more of the kids in the backyard. I guess they finished movie day. As I break through to the clearing, I spot Olivia, who's laying poolside in a bikini, sipping on the straw coming out of the canned drink in her hand. Knowing her, it's probably her fourth Fanta of the day. The only good things her parents left her with are her beautiful looks and her killer metabolism. Trying to sidestep the splashing from the kids in the pool, and ignoring the shouts asking me to join them, I finally make it to the back door.

I head to the kitchen first, where I expected Suzan to be making dinner. Instead, I just find Ashten pouring herself a glass of OJ.

She looks up as I enter, a motherly smile pulling on her lips. "Hey."

"Hey," I clear my throat, "have you seen Suzan?"

"No, actually, I think she just left. Didn't say where she was going, though." Ashten returns the pitcher to the fridge, then leans back against the counter as she takes a sip of her drink. "Is everything okay? I told her what happened, and she went around trying to find you."

I shrug. "You know Suzan. She's just pissed like usual."

"Oh, well, sorry. When she asked, I didn't even think that you might not want me to tell her."

"No," I walk over to the island, "you're fine, it was something else." I wave her off.

Ashten nods, taking another sip of her juice. "Well, I'm sorry, anyway. For freaking you out. I should have told you I was coming... I just didn't think about it. Again. Me and my not thinking." She chuckles kind of nervously into her drink as she finishes it.

"It was stupid that I freaked out like that. It was just that I was thinking about Roxanne, and then you came out of the car, and–"

"Well, I do look almost exactly like her. People actually call me Roxanne now that she's dead than they did before, which never really made sense to me." She rinses out her glass and then puts it in the dishwasher. "I guess she was just on their minds more." She shrugs.

"I kind of forgot the small things, ya know? Like the freckle – that's how I always used to tell you two apart when I first met you. After all this time without seeing Roxanne... small details just kind of get lost."

Ashten nods thoughtfully. "I never really thought about that."

"I never really thought about it either, until now." I smile at her. "Sorry I flipped out."

"Sorry I flipped you out."

"Truce," I hold out my hand like we used to when we were kids.

She looks at my outstretched arm, and instead of grabbing it, she wrings her hands together. "So... where were you and Phoenix going? Do you need to leave still?"

I drop my arm and lean on the other side of the island from her. "He just wanted to talk about... stuff."

Ashten scoffs, shoulders tensing as she gives me a look that says *do-you-think-I'm-stupid*? "Stuff? Really?"

"What?"

Ashten stands up straighter, pressing the palms of her hands against the countertop. "Look, Mazey. Roxanne and I were close."

"Yeah, I know. I was her wife. I heard you talking all the time."

She nods slowly like she's hoping I get her point. "Close enough that she told me everything."

"Yeah, I got that? I'm not sure what you mean."

"I know about you and Phoenix." She blurts out, lips pressed together. "She told me about how he followed you around, tried to get you to leave her. I know that you loved him. Do you still? Love him, I mean."

I'm shocked by her tone – like she's trying to catch me in a lie. "Yeah, of course. He's my best friend... at least, he was."

"You know what I mean, Mazey. Look, if you and Phoenix are friends, that's fine. But you were married to his *sister*. Don't think for a second that it's not shitty to do this to Roxanne, even if she's dead."

"Ashten–"

Behind me, someone walks in before I can finish my sentence. I turn around to see Dylan standing in the hallway. "What's for dinner?"

I look back at Ashten. She shrugs. "I'm not sure. I don't think Suzan is cooking tonight."

"She always cooks." Dylan whines, coming farther into the kitchen. As he stops, his eyes light up. "Does that mean we can eat whatever we want?"

Ashten clears her throat. "Uh, no, bud. That just means Mazey and I are in charge."

Dylan looks at me and turns on his 'charm.' "Can we *please* go out to eat? I haven't had pizza in *forever*."

"Forever? Man, that's a really long time." I look back at Ashten and she shrugs again, eyes on her fingernails. "Okay, why don't you go tell everyone to get ready. You have ten minutes, or we're not going."

His eyes widen. "Ten minutes? I gotta run!" He rushes out of the room. "Guys! Get ready," he screams as he goes down the hallway.

Behind me, Ashten sighs. "I'm going to go grab Greg. He's taking care of Georgie."

"Okay." She heads out of the room. I head upstairs and grab a jacket. As I'm coming back down, Phoenix is standing in the hall.

He raises a brow at me. "I heard we're getting pizza 'cause Mazey said so?"

I nod. "Yeah. Suzan left. I figured why not."

"You okay?"

I give him a tight smile. "Yeah, I'm fine. Help me find the car keys. We're going to that place in the strip mall."

"Getting that many kids in and out of a restaurant will be hard." He holds out his hand to help me down the last step.

I only think about it for a second before grabbing it. I put on my jacket as I smile at him. "Good thing you'll be there to help us."

"Good thing, indeed."

I sit on the couch in the living room with Nikkie and Eric, who have decided that instead of finishing their finals that are due in a few weeks, they're going to play video games. Dropping F-bombs like they're sailors and chugging beers like the frat boys they are, they focus with the kind of attention they only have for shooter games. Beside me, Nikkie chucks his controller at Eric, jaw twitching. "You have to be cheating."

"You're sitting right here, you'd see me cheat, dude." Eric picks up the controller and tosses it back at Nikkie.

Nikkie catches it. "Nah, you have to be. You're doing something to the game before I come in. I lose every time."

Eric rolls his eyes, taking a swig of his beer. "You're just a sore loser."

In the hallway, a swarm of kids, both fosters and their friends, march from the kitchen to the backyard with Phoenix following behind them. I wave at him, feeling my heart skip a beat as he smiles back.

Nikkie leans back on the couch. "Phoenix has been here so much recently."

"Isn't he always here?" I look out the window, eyes trained on Phoenix as he helps Georgie open a bottle of water.

Eric shakes his head. "Not anymore. He stopped coming a while ago."

"Around the time that Roxanne died." Nikkie turns to Eric. "When was the last time he'd been over?"

"Uh…" He snaps his fingers, pointing the same finger at Nikkie, hair flopping in his face as he turns. "That play the kids did for their elementary school. Back in May, I think."

Nikkie shakes his head. "No, it was Heather. He came to her welcome dinner in August."

I tuck my legs under me, leaning my arm against the back of the couch. "He really doesn't come over anymore?"

They both shake their heads, turning the game back on. I know Phoenix isn't exactly close to anyone here. It's kind of hard to be when everyone is so far from your age. Other than Lincoln, who's a year older than him, the closest people were Roxanne and Ashten, his biological siblings, who are five years younger than him. I know for a fact that he, Roxanne, and Ashten had never been close. The opposite, in fact. Phoenix didn't like them when I got here, and his opinion of Roxanne definitely hasn't grown since then. I've always felt bad for driving them even farther apart. Despite that, Phoenix used to be here all the time. He helped with the kids and took them to their after school activities. He came for dinner, and for every game and recital... what happened to make him change that?

I take a pause from guessing when Suzan walks past the living room archway and towards the back door. I haven't seen her since yesterday when she took off. She got back while we were at dinner last night and hasn't come out of her room since. I get off the couch, stepping over Eric, and rush to get to her. She's in the laundry room, clothes from the laundry basket being dropped into the washer.

"Suzan?" I step into the room.

She sighs, setting the basket down on the top of the dryer and closing the washer's lid. "What, Mazey?"

I roll my eyes behind her back. "Look, I wanted to apologize. I didn't mean to disrespect you, or anyone else. I promise Phoenix and I won't do anything else like that here."

She turns around to face me. "You won't do it here, but you'll do it somewhere else?"

"I don't know..."

Her face goes red and her eyes get some of that fire behind them that she passed down to all of her kids. "After what you did to Roxanne, you're going to do it again?"

"It's a lot more complicated than—"

"Mazey, stop manipulating my children. Just stop. If you can't keep your hands off my son, then you should go back to Seattle."

Manipulate her children? "I'm not manipulating anyone."

"First, you mess with Roxanne, and now you're dragging Phoenix along? You're playing with his heart. If *you* hadn't convinced him that night to—"

"I didn't convince him of anything. God, I just... I came here to apologize. To tell you that I wanted to make up. I was hoping that we could go back to how it used to be before Roxanne died. But I can see you're not interested."

Suzan tilts her nose up at me. "The fact that you're asking me to go back to how things were before my *child* was murdered shows how little you ever really cared about Roxanne."

"I *loved* Roxanne—"

"Hey," Nikkie comes through the curtain in the doorway. "Am I interrupting?"

I back away from Suzan and shake my head. "No, not at all. What's up?"

"Eric and I were going to grab a beer. Want to come?"

"Don't we have beers here?"

"Yeah, well, we want to go to a bar. You in or not?"

I look back at Suzan, but her attention is already back on the laundry, her shoulder stuff as she drops in the detergent. I turn back to Nikkie, smiling tightly. "Sure, why not. Let's go grab a beer."

CHAPTER THREE

I stand in the hallway outside of the kitchen, foot tapping and mind whirling. Inside, I hear Ashten and Suzan; they've been cooking since before I woke up, the smells of a home-cooked meal filling the entire house. Suzan loves Thanksgiving, and the food is the most important part. I just want to go in and talk to her, but I just... don't want to have to talk to her *and* Ashten together. I'm close to just saying screw it and going in there before Asthen leaves, but it's not like I have anything else to do, so standing creepily in the hallway is as good an idea as any.

I jump as the back door is thrown open, a group of kids rushing in, dirt trailing in from their shoes. Suzan isn't going to like that. Eric follows in behind them, a phone pressed between his shoulder and his ear, talking in a soft voice. Just as I'm about to walk away and forget it, Ashten pushes past me, going out the front door with her car keys hanging off her finger. Taking the opportunity before I miss it, I go into the kitchen.

The room is a mess, not unusual for Suzan when she cooks even a regular meal. She has the tendency to use every pot, pan, or bowl that's available. She's leaning over the oven, a meat thermometer in her hand, steam rising all around her. I wait until she's closed the oven before I speak. "Suzan, can we talk?"

She looks up from the counter, wiping her hands off on the apron around her waist, an impatient sigh already through her lips. "Mazey, I don't have time to talk right now."

"I think it's important that we figure this out before lunch. I'd have a hard time celebrating Thanksgiving knowing you're still mad at me." I walk farther into the kitchen, hands fiddling in front of me. I stop them, clenching my fists instead. I make sure to look Suzan in the eyes. "How can I fix this? I don't want you to be mad again."

"Again?" She scoffs as she grabs a bowl of sweet potatoes and starts washing them. "I never stopped."

I nod, my resolve faltering a little bit. After all this time, she still feels the same as she did right after her daughter died? "Okay... then how do I fix *this*." I motion between us, taking the final steps to the island, standing on the opposite side of it from her. "I miss talking to you, even if it was just on the holidays."

Suzan shakes her head, setting the last potato back into the bowl and draining the sink of the sitting water. She grabs the peelers on the counter and starts peeling before she answers my question. "I don't think you can. When I look at you," Her eyes flicker up to me, then quickly back down to her hands. "When I look at you, all I can think about is Roxanne."

"We can get past that, right? Eventually the pain of remembering her won't be as bad." I look at her, trying to get her to look back up to me, but she won't. I press my hands against the counter, leaning on them. "You promised to take care of me, Suzan. You took me in when I was still a kid, and you promised you'd take care of me."

"That was a long time ago, and you know I do that for everyone."

"Bullshit," I snap, finally getting her to look up at me. "When you promised everyone else, you actually kept that promise."

"How can I love you or care for you when I can't even look at you? You killed Roxanne." She holds my eyes for a second longer before going back to peeling her potatoes with harsh strokes.

"I didn't kill Roxanne, please stop saying that. I feel bad enough as it is—"

"And you should. She was my *baby*."

I push off of the counter, arms going wide at my sides. "We're all supposed to be your *babies*. I needed you. After Roxanne died, I needed you, and you chose someone dead over someone alive."

"I chose my daughter over you; don't make it into something it's not." She drops the potato she's holding and gets another one.

"I'm not making it into anything!" I practically scream. She chose her *daughter* over *me*? I've always known that's how she felt, but to hear her say it... "Why the hell did you even foster me if you weren't going to be able to love me?"

Suzan shakes her head, peeling more than just the skin off of the potatoes. Huge chunks fall into the bowl. "I intended to, you just didn't turn out to be who I thought you were."

"No, you brought me in because you were sad, right? What, you were crying over Robert and you just decided to bring me in, mess with my life?"

She looks up at me, a vein throbbing in her forehead, her grip on the potatoes turning her knuckles white. "Don't you dare bring my husband into this."

"You're bringing my wife into it, right? And you know what, this is what makes it all so much worse. You know what it's like to have the person you love ripped away from you, and yet you're making sure I feel worse." I jab my finger at her, feeling my other fingernails pressing into my palm.

"What happened with me and Robert isn't anything like what happened with you and Roxanne, let's get that straight."

I keep my eyes locked with hers, our glares matching in intensity. Leaning against the counter with one hand, pushing my finger at her with the other, I make sure she hears every word I say. "Next time you're feeling sad that Robert died, or better yet, that you couldn't have your own children, leave us foster kids the hell out of it. You should've listened to the universe when it was telling you not to have kids. It was trying to protect people from having such a shitty mother."

"Mazey, what the hell?" Ashten comes into the kitchen with a huge box of cooking supplies in her hands. "What's going on?"

I look back at Suzan, shoulders tense. "Nothing, I was just going to leave." I let my glare sit on Suzan for a second longer before turning to push past Ashten, storming out of the kitchen.

Out of all the things I've been worried about recently, this might just be the most ridiculous yet. I've been looking at myself in the mirror for the past half hour, trying to make sure I look okay. I feel like I have to impress someone, that I'm interviewing to be reinvited into the family. As if when people look at me they still see me as the broken girl at Roxanne's funeral: shuffling and crying, a complete mess. Definitely not what I want people to think of when they think of Mazey Sutton. When I decided to go ahead and come here right away, I was thinking it'd be nice to actually spend the holidays with them. Start coming back into society. Spend this *jolly* time with my family instead of alone.

More recently, I've decided that it's not just *anyone* I want to be here with. It's a specific someone. I fiddle with the neckline of my dress again, wishing there had been a turtle neck I could have borrowed from Olivia's closet. Not that I could even wear it, it's too hot in Florida for any winter clothes. At least the necklace would have been covered up.

Like many times before, I think about all the people who've told me I should've taken the necklace off by now. Sometimes I think they might be right, but I quickly push that thought away. I haven't taken it off since I put it on all that time ago. The ring sparkles as it sits on my chest. It'll be the first thing people notice when they look at me, even if they never knew who Roxanne was. Today everyone will notice the seat beside me, where Roxanne should be sitting. It'll be pretty hard not to notice that. A dress couldn't fix that no matter how much or how little it had to it. This ring still won't help much, either.

But this is the only thing that Olivia had that worked. Most of her dresses are tight-fitting on her already, and with my wide hips and disproportionate chest, they were even worse. At least the bottom half of this one is loose. It's a step up from the other dresses. Though, I can't complain much since I was the idiot who traveled home a week before Thanksgiving without anything to wear *to* Thanksgiving. I mostly brought sweatpants and baggy tees. The nicest clothes I brought with me are ripped jeans. Olivia and Vincent kept telling me it was fine, that I don't have to dress up, but I don't want to get any more attention than I need to. Pity looks already feel like a punch to the gut. Judgmental looks, somehow still full of pity, won't hurt any less.

The doorbell rings downstairs for what feels like the millionth time today. Having a massive family sometimes works against me, especially when they witnessed first hand how bad I took Roxanne's death. How many of them were bridesmaids at our wedding and how many of them have moved on with their lives while I'm still stuck in the past. Huge families also don't help with things like having enough seats for holiday dinners together; every year, the family that started off small grows a little more. Sometimes I feel like it's growing without me.

I look at the clock in front of me, sighing when I see the time. I'll have to head down soon. I have a max of fifteen minutes until someone comes up to get me, and that's already pushing it. Deciding I'd much rather go down on my own than be ambushed by who knows who, I fluff my hair out again. I *should* go by myself, but I think if I do, I might hurl. Once a week is good enough for me. It's just... for some reason today feels different. With Suzan mad at me, and it being my first holiday back, I feel like today matters more than the others. Which is ridiculous, today will be the same as any other day. And my nerves aren't going to change anytime soon; I'm going to feel just as freaked out in fifteen minutes as I do right now.

A knock on the door makes me jump. I look at myself in the mirror once more, trying to yank my dress up enough to hide the necklace, but quickly decide against that when the skirt rises above my butt. This dress is just not practical. I curse myself again, like I have a dozen times today, for not having thought to get something in advance. Taking a deep breath, I open the door to find Ashten standing in the hall. The ring catches her eye but she quickly looks back up at me. I knew it'd be the first thing anyone noticed.

"Mom wants everyone downstairs to say grace before Sam

starts cutting the turkey." She steps aside to give me room to move into the hall.

Closing the door behind me, I avert my eyes from Ashten, not liking how uncomfortable I feel around someone I'm supposed to be close to. "Sam's here? He never comes anymore." My oldest foster brother moved out before I even got here. He's thirty-three now with a white-collar job, two kids, and a trophy wife. He barely even made it to Roxanne's funeral.

Ashten shrugs. "I guess so. The rest of his family's here too."

Well, there are some people who might not think about Roxanne when they look at me. We start walking towards the stairs. "Is everyone here?"

"Phoenix is running late, but everyone else is downstairs." Ashten and I go down the stairs, slowly going into the smells of the food, the sounds of people talking and laughing. Eventually, I see the faces of my family. The people standing there come over smiling, hugging me, and saying hello, or telling me they like my dress. As I reach Sam he smiles at me, moving to the side and revealing his wife, Tracy, bouncing a little swaddle back and forth.

She looks down at the baby in her arms, the newest addition to our family, Evelyn. She sees me looking down at Evelyn with the hint of a smile. "Do you want to hold her?"

Dylan pops around her legs, looking at the baby with awe. "I want to hold her!"

Sam chuckles. "You just did. You'll get another chance in a bit, okay? Ready?"

I nod, taking Evelyn carefully from Tracy's arms as Sam circles behind me and leans over my shoulder, smiling down at his daughter. I put my finger in her hand and let her grip onto it. "She's so beautiful."

The doorbell rings, and Dylan instantly forgets about the

baby, running off. "I'll get it!"

I gently rock back and forth, smiling down at the small creature in my arms, a sense of calm falling over me. "God, she's so small."

Sam nods, pinching his daughter's cheeks making her coo. "She's way too small, isn't she?"

"Way too small..." I look up, eyes locking onto Phoenix, standing at the end of the hallway, gaze stuck on the baby in my arms. As he works his way up to my eyes, his face tightens, filled with some kind of deep emotion.

Sam puts a hand on my shoulder, squeezing. "You would have been an amazing mother."

My face drops for an instant, quickly trying to hide it. Evidently, it's visible to others because Tracy grimaces, and Sam steps back slightly, looking dismayed. "I..."

"Dude, why the hell would you say that?" Phoenix comes storming in, looking kind of like he wants to shove Sam, catching my eye instead, seeming to ask me if I'm okay.

I nod but hand the baby back to Tracy. "It's, uh, it's okay."

"Mazey, I'm sorry. I didn't mean it like—"

"I said it's okay." I give him a tight-lipped smile and move towards the kitchen where almost everyone else has migrated.

Phoenix steps in close behind me, resting his hand on the base of my spine, letting me know he's here.

At the island, Suzan takes off her oven mitts and pushes a strand of hair out of her face. "Thank you everyone for coming today. It makes me so happy to see all of you gathered here to celebrate this day of thanks. I know we have a wide range of beliefs here as always, but you know my rule. If you're not going to pray, at least be silent and respectful. Now, let's pray."

Several people make their way to the island, where they hold hands. Suzan leads the prayer – like she always does.

She's too much of a control freak to let anyone else do it; it has to be perfect. The rest of us stand there in silence. Phoenix takes this time to move his hand on my back, tracing a finger in circles. I look over my shoulder to make sure there's no one behind us, and thank God there isn't. What the hell is he doing anyway? Yes, we almost kissed the other day, but are we really ready to do this? I got lost in the moment and forgot about the world around me. But there *is* a world around me. One that I have to pay attention to and be aware of. I can't just go kissing Phoenix and standing here while he runs his fingers all over my back.

Not only did Suzan *just* freak out, I just freaked out too. I'm not over Roxanne, nowhere close, and while Phoenix might be able to help me get there, do I really want to? I scoot away from Phoenix, looking over my shoulder and giving him a look. He smirks at me but quickly bows his head. When Suzan finishes the prayer, everyone breaks into motion, grabbing plates, spooning food, and pouring drinks. Sam grabs a knife and starts cutting up the turkey.

Phoenix leans down, putting his lips close to my ear and whispering. "Save me a seat and I'll make our plates."

I nod, heading over into the dining room where the adults are supposed to be sitting. I take a seat at the middle of the table. As I sit down, Tracy drops down next to me, a fussy Evelyn in her arms. Evelyn drops the toy she was holding, so I reach down and grab it for her.

Tracy takes it from me and starts shaking it over Evelyn's head again. "Thanks." She looks at the table where I didn't put a plate. "Are you not eating?"

"Oh, Nix is grabbing it for me." I point towards the bustling kitchen. Suzan runs around, busy helping the kids make their plates as they trickle off to the back porch where the kids' table was set up for today.

Olivia, plate piled with almost all carbs, comes into the

dining room. "I wish I was an adult. God, I'm going to be stuck out there with almost all babies. The only other kid my age is Vincent, and his girlfriend is here. He won't even be batting an eye at me. Especially considering what she wore. Her boobs are practically hanging out."

I look down at her dress, a dress tight enough that she may not even be able to breathe right now, and then back up to her. "Liv, I don't think you can say anything in regards to scandalous dresses."

"Scandalous? Who are you, Mom?" She rolls her eyes. "Did I mention that I'm in charge of watching Georgie? That kid is a pain in my ass. He's going to want to try to feed himself, and of course, he's going to fail. A Lot. *Then* I'm going to have to clean him up."

Sam enters, holding a plate in each hand. "Whining much?"

"Sucking much?" Olivia asks in return, sticking out her tongue and leaving the room.

Sam sets a plate in front of Tracy and then a plate in front of the chair next to her. He kisses his daughter on the forehead as he sits down. "Brit is excited to be able to eat on her own this year."

"On her own?" I ask, surprised that his three-year-old is left to her own devices. That'll end up being a mess for sure.

Tracy chuckles. "Yes, actually. She was so excited to be with the older kids that she's been practicing at home."

"Yeah, our daughter has been practicing eating." Sam shakes his head like he can't believe it. "We've got a strange one, that's for sure."

Tracy narrows her eyes at him. "Don't call our daughter strange!"

Sam looks at me around Tracy, eyes laughing. "She's pretty weird."

"Samuel!"

Sam opens his mouth to respond but doesn't get the chance as a loud, bouncing ball of energy bursts into the room. I turn my head around, watching as Lincoln drops his overflowing plate onto the table with a loud thud. Flopping into the seat beside the one I'm saving for Phoenix, he smiles his typical toothy smile at me. Not wasting any time, he stabs a chunk of mac & cheese, eyes darting to the others sitting behind me. "Mazey! Haven't seen you in a fuckin' 'coon's age." He takes a bite of his food, swallowing quickly before continuing. "You look amazing!"

I ignore the obvious lie, debating if he maybe doesn't want people to know he's the one who brought me back, looking back at Sam, who just shakes his head, unable to hide the smile on his lips. Lincoln is the loudest kid in the family, which is impressive since he's thirty-one now and not even a kid anymore. He's always been that way. I hardly even notice his loudness since he's such an amazing person. Loyal as can be, always putting other people first, and the first to try to make you feel better when you're down. He even quit business school to go to Africa and help build a town for a year. That turned out great for him because he found his fiancé while there. The two of them live off her trust fund, going to whatever place needs their help. It's one of the things I've always admired most about him.

"Uh, thanks?" On instinct, my hand goes for my necklace, and I roll it between my fingers.

Lincoln reaches forward and grabs it out of my hand. Another part of his overwhelming personality: not very good with boundaries. "God, I remember when she showed us this ring for the first time. Didn't think there'd ever been a ring better suited for her. You did a good job."

I take the ring from his hands. "Thanks. I tried pretty hard on that one."

Lincoln points to the tablespace in front of me. "You not

eating?"

"I am, Phoenix is getting it for me."

"Ah," Lincoln smirks and gives me a look, "he is, is he?"

I roll my eyes at him. "Yes, he is."

Lincoln's eyes glimmer, like he knows something I don't, but doesn't say anything else. Instead, he shoves another bite of food into his mouth, silencing himself for a moment. I look down at the table, really hoping my cheeks don't turn the shade of a tomato. Around me, people buzz around, quickly moving from one spot to another, slowly filling the room with people.

As the last couple of seats fill up, and the room gets to an almost unbearable volume, Suzan sits at the end of the table. She smiles at Phoenix, who comes in behind her, the same smile dropping as her eyes land on me. I try to ignore the tinge of pain I feel, focusing on Phoenix as he comes over, balancing two plates of food on one arm and two cups in his other hand. I take the cups from him before he drops something and set them down. He places my food in front of me. "Are you bugging her, Linc?"

Lincoln offers a cheesy grin. "Only a little bit, right, Mazey?"

"A little bit seems like a stretch." I grab a fork, digging into the mashed potatoes Ashten was working away in the kitchen to make earlier. "These are great, Ash."

She smiles tightly at me. "Thanks." The sarcastic tone drips from her words.

Lincoln looks between the two of us, a mix of worry and intrigue on his face. "Yeah, Ash, they're really good. I thought you sucked at cooking."

Ashten brightens up slightly. "I'm trying to pick up new things each year, so when I have to start making the whole spread myself, I'll know how to do it all." She turns to her husband, resting her hand on his arm. "Thank God I started ages ago, or I wouldn't have nearly enough of it done by the time the baby comes."

"Yeah, I never did." I try to joke, smiling at Ashten. When she frowns at me, I just take a bite of my potatoes, keeping my eyes on her. Of course, she'd be the one to remember why I never did try. Someone else chimes in, reminding the whole table.

"Roxanne was trying to learn. She almost got the turkey down." Suzan looks pointedly at me as if trying to blame me for leaving the cooking to Roxanne.

I nod. "She loved to cook. I hate it." I feel my back straightening as I look back up at Ashten, then over at Suzan. I'm not in the mood for both of them to gang up on me. Lincoln looks between all of us, eyes wide, the excitement levels almost matching a high school gossip who just heard the juiciest drama of the year. When I catch his eye, he snickers.

Sam turns the conversation over quickly to Nikkie and Eric. "So, how has college been treating you?"

Nikkie groans and dramatically acts like he's dying. Lincoln barks out a laugh. "Finals are coming up, and I swear they're going to kill me."

Ashten finally peels her eyes from mine and looks at Nikkie. "I'm sure you'll do fine."

"Speak for yourself," Eric chimes in, "I'm acing the party scene."

Everyone laughs. Lincoln points at Eric's girlfriend, an impish grin working his lips. "You want me to fight him? I'll fight him."

"Woah, there," Phoenix elbows him, quickly pulling on Lincoln's reins. I'm not even sure why Phoenix tries; Lincoln'll just do something even crazier to get Phoenix to react more. And yet, Phoenix hasn't caught onto the routine after all these years. "I'm sure she can take care of herself."

"I can't complain, he treats me right." Eric's girlfriend grins at him with so much emotion I suddenly feel like I'm intruding.

Nikkie looks away from her, boredom on his face like he's heard this a few hundred times, rolling his eyes. "Get a room."

Sam turns to me, his somber expression making me nervous. "How have you been?"

I give him a tight smile. "I've been... fine, I guess."

Phoenix reaches over and grabs my hand. "You're getting better."

I nod. "Definitely better. I finally found an apartment."

"I thought there was a foreclosure on your house a while ago?" Sam questions, leaning around Tracy to see me. Across the table, Ashten pokes at her food, not eating much and frowning at the plate.

"Uh, yeah, back in November last year, so a year ago now." I want to sink into my chair, fade away. Bringing up everything that happened is only going to put me in a shitty mood.

Sam doesn't let up, though, and cocks his head at me with a confused look. "So, where have you been living this whole time?"

"I, well..." I clear my throat, settling my gaze on the food in front of me. "My storage unit."

"You lived in your storage unit?" Phoenix turns to me, eyes wide. "You were homeless? Wha... how did I not know?"

"I didn't know either," Sam says, looking around the table at everyone else. "What happened?"

I shrug. "The house got foreclosed on. I, I just, I didn't have the money to afford a mortgage. Roxanne barely did either. But it's not that big of a deal, I swear." I rush out the last part, trying to get it out before Phoenix can respond.

"Not that big of a deal? You were homeless."

I look up at him, begging him with my eyes to just drop it for now. "I was fine, I promise."

"Okay..." Lincoln trails off awkwardly, only taking a second to smile at the whole table. "So, who all is staying tonight?"

To his credit, Sam only takes a second to leap to the new conversation and raises his hand. "Tracy and I were talking, and we thought it could be fun to do game night! We haven't seen each other in ages. Might as well take advantage, right?"

Nikkie nods. "Sounds like a fine idea to me. All of us hanging out together? Be just like old times."

"Old times," Lincoln pipes up, "you're what, twenty?"

"Twenty-one—"

"Don't age me, Nik, I'm barely past thirty."

"Neither am I," Sam chimes in, "but when was the last time we all sat down and played board games?"

"Phoenix and I played video games just last week." He nudges Phoenix with his arm.

Ashten huffs, glaring pointedly at Phoenix. "Yeah, from different apartments. That hardly counts."

Lincoln sits back in his seat, conceding. "Fair play. I like the idea anyway."

I groan quietly, not liking the idea of having to spend any more time with everyone confined to one small space. Phoenix, hearing me, moves his hand to my leg, squeezing it. I smile up at him softly, silently thanking him for being there. At the end of the room, something makes a loud, smacking noise. I look up to see Suzan with her hands flat on the table, eyes glaring directly at me.

"Mazey Kim Sutton!" Everyone hushes immediately, eyes all pointed at Suzan. "How *dare* you continue to behave like this."

Phoenix looks from me to Suzan, worry suddenly in his eyes. "Mom—"

"Don't defend her, Phoenix." She doesn't take her eyes off me as she talks. "After how you treated my daughter, after the *disgrace* you felt before, you're going to continue this?"

I swallow a lump in my throat. "Suzan, please don't. We can talk outside–"

"Because you're ashamed? You don't want anyone to know?"

"Yes. Please–"

"You don't deserve favors. Not if you didn't learn from your mistakes the first time." She stands up from the table, palms still stiffly planted. "You had sex with your wife's brother, and now you want to do it again? Wipe that pitiful look off your face."

Lincoln places a hand in front of Suzan, almost as if trying to keep her from jumping at me. "Look, Mom, we know Phoenix was Mazey's first. Roxanne wasn't exactly quiet about it when she found out. You don't have to bring it up again–"

"Lincoln, shut your mouth right now." She turns her attention to me, tears seeming to come to her eyes. "You cheated on my baby. You couldn't even be bothered to be there for her when she was killed. You couldn't keep it in your pants long enough to see her life through!"

I flinch as if I've been slapped, feeling everyone's eyes shift from Suzan to me. "I– I, I didn't–"

Phoenix stands up to match his mother, jaw clenched. "Stop. You're only embarrassing yourself. What happened that night–"

"What happened that night never should have happened!" Suzan snaps.

I jump out of my seat, and if I was closer, I might have slapped her. It'd serve her right. "You have no idea what happened that night!" I scream back, leaning in front of Phoenix and over the table to get closer. "You haven't had to live with that guilt for the last year and a half. And you know what? You also weren't the one who had to find her wife dead on the floor. You didn't have to wash her blood out of the carpet or feel unsafe in your own home because you were scared the man who killed your wife might come back for you. You didn't have to see her every time you went into the bedroom or cringe every time you saw something that *might* be blood. You weren't the one who got locked up when the police found her because you were a suspect. You didn't have to be in the room when they described in explicit detail *how* he raped her, and how long she was in pain."

The people around me gasp, and I can feel Phoenix's hand on my wrist. A sign of support.

"Yes, I fucked up, Suzan. I cheated on Roxanne, and I have to live with that. Forever. And when you found out only *two months* after Roxanne died, I let you make me feel worse about myself because I was so low I didn't think I deserved to stand up for myself. But you swore to me you wouldn't tell them. You agreed that telling people wouldn't do any good. You swore." My throat closes up, and I hurry and finish before the tears come. "I loved her. Don't try to take that away from me." A tear slips down my cheek, but I quickly wipe it away.

Beside me, Sam looks baffled. "You... that's why you were a suspect?"

I look over at him, sniffling. "What?"

"I never understood why they thought you might have killed Roxanne, but now it makes more sense..."

"That's what you're going to say? Really?" Ashten snaps at him, shaking her head.

At the end of the table, Eric finally speaks up. "Are we just breezing past the part where Lincoln said Phoenix slept with Mazey when she was sixteen? Dude, that's like, illegal."

His girlfriend smacks his arm. "Eric, hush."

Phoenix flops his mouth open and closed like a fish. "That's not exactly what happened..."

I take a deep breath. "Thank you for dinner, *Suzan*, but I don't have an appetite anymore." I push the chair out of my way, moving to leave, but Phoenix grabs my arm.

He looks at Suzan. "Congrats on being a bitch, Mom. We'll let the rest of you enjoy Thanksgiving. Maz and I apparently have some packing to do." He pulls on my arm, taking me out of the room and up the stairs.

I follow until we're in Vincent's room. Well, now I don't know where I'm staying. I mentally start to do the math in my head, and very quickly decide I can't afford a place to live here. All of my furniture is in Seattle; I'd have to sleep on the streets again. I didn't fly across the country to sleep on the streets. As I think of spending yet another cold winter without a home, my blood boils again. Suzan isn't even thinking twice about throwing me out. At least this time it'd be better... a winter in Florida would be better than a winter in Seattle.

I already feel myself mentally preparing. I'm starting to build the walls again, blocking out the pain I was feeling before. I had gotten to a point where the thought of talking to people seemed terrifying. If I started talking to people, I'd have the chance to get hurt again. Maybe I had the right idea all along. Maybe being alone is the best way to live. At least then I wouldn't be feeling so confused. I'd be sure of what I was doing – nothing. And then I could just exist, no worries about what happens next.

Phoenix is grabbing my clothes out of the drawers and throwing them back into my bags. "Let's get out of here before she decides she wants to have the last word."

"Nix, I don't have anywhere to go. I just screwed up my only place to live." I watch as he goes back and forth to grab all my stuff, too shocked to even help.

Phoenix pauses long enough to grab my hands, look into my eyes, and smile. "You can stay with me. I don't want you to go back to Washington."

"I don't want to go back either, but..."

"Look, right now, you don't have many choices. You can stay with me until you figure it out. Hopefully, you decide that you want to stay. I want you to stay." He squeezes my hands, then let's go and starts packing again.

"Phoenix, wait. Just pause for a second."

He stops as he drops a pile of shirts in the bag. "Yeah?"

"Thank you."

"For what?"

"For standing up for me with Suzan. And for being here for me."

He smiles at me. "Anytime, Maz."

I nod, grabbing the clothes he's been throwing in the bag and folding them. Thankfully, we finish packing everything with no knocks on the door or anymore yelling. The one thing I still can't get over is that everyone knows. Everyone knows what happened that night, and I'm scared this means I came back here for nothing. That the only thing I'll accomplish while I'm here in Florida is messing things up more. It's like I can't move a finger without breaking everything.

The hatred in Suzan's eyes could only be matched by the disgust on Ashten's face. The way she curled back away from me, jaw twitching, fist clenched. If she wasn't upset with me for betraying Roxanne before, she definitely is now. Even with Phoenix's hand in mine as we walk down the hall, I can't help but feel the weight of the mistake we made the night Roxanne died. There hasn't been a day that's gone by since then I haven't thought about it. That I haven't thought about her.

Phoenix looks back over his shoulder at me as we go down the stairs. The family pictures hanging on the walls that wrap around us seem to be laughing at my pain. Years of happy memories for the family I'll never be a part of. As we reach the bottom of the stairs, my lungs tighten, my breath halting. I can't decide if I want to get as far away from the pictures as possible or if I want to stay on the steps, so I don't have to see Suzan again.

The closer we get, the louder the roar of the dining room gets. I start to hear bits of the conversation as Phoenix and I step off the last step and into the hallway.

"–because she screwed up doesn't mean you needed to embarrass her like that, Mom." Lincoln's voice cuts through the crowd's volume, not surprisingly.

"She *never* should have done that to our sister. Roxanne deserved better than this." Ashten cuts in, voice thick with emotion but still sharp as a knife.

"Mazey is our sister too–"

"Like hell she is!" Ashten cuts Olivia off, sounding about a second away from snapping. "If she cared about Roxanne, or any of us for that matter, she never would have done something so terrible."

"What does this have to do with any of us?" Olivia barks back.

I hover against the wall just outside of the dining room, trying to take a second to recoup before having to walk past them and out the front door. Phoenix stands behind me, veins bulging as he clenches his jaw. I squeeze his hand, just wanting him to give me another second.

"What kind of people would we be if we just let her do this to Roxanne?" Ashten sneers, and I see her pace to the archway of the room, back facing us.

"What kind of people would we be if we made Mazey feel worse after everything she's been through?" Olivia jumps on her question immediately, not showing any hesitation.

Ashten's mouth drops open for a second as she looks lost

for words. After a moment, she folds her arms over her chest, back straightening. "Mazey hasn't gone through anything worse than Roxanne did. If *this* is what she was doing while Roxanne was being tormented, then she deserves everything coming to her."

Phoenix pushes past me, moving into the doorway, shoulders squared. I follow behind him, looking at the crowd of people in front of me.

Olivia looks at me, the fire dropping from her face. "Mazey..."

Phoenix nods to Lincoln, "Can I talk to you for a second?"

Lincoln immediately gets up, coming over to Phoenix. As we go towards the front door, Olivia calls out after me. "Mazey, wait!"

I look back, shaking my head at her. She drops her eyes, shoulders slumping. I push out the front door and head to the car. Phoenix pulls Lincoln to a halt, talking in a hushed voice. I can't make out what they're saying; all I know is that Lincoln does not like whatever Phoenix told him. After a *very* long pause, the two of them come over to where I'm standing by the car.

"What's going on?" I look at Lincoln, then Phoenix. "What was that?"

Phoenix shrugs. "It was nothing. I just have to get some things ready for you to stay with me, that's all."

"Yeah, we're just going to go do something for a little while." Lincoln smiles at me, grabbing my bags and throwing them in Phoenix's trunk.

I look at Phoenix again. "What? Why?"

Phoenix slams the trunk closed. "Nothing, it's fine. Have fun with Linc."

Lincoln grabs my arm, leading me away as Phoenix hops into his car. "What do you want to do?"

What the hell just happened?

CHAPTER FOUR

Phoenix places a bowl of mac & cheese in front of me, smiling proudly. "Bon Appétit."

"Wow. Instant mac & cheese, I feel so special." I joke, grabbing my fork and taking a bite – it's still really good.

Phoenix sticks his tongue out at me like he's five. "It's what I had time for."

"Well, it's pretty good. So I'll take it." After wandering around the town square and drinking a few too many beers with Lincoln, I'm exhausted. Well, that and my fun scene with Suzan. Oh, and my brain is running a mile a minute, thinking about Phoenix. It took him *hours* to have me come to his place. And when I got here, I was even more confused. He'd moved out of the loft bachelor pad and into a three-bedroom apartment instead. This place is *nice*. I knew he'd gotten a promotion a while ago, at the beginning of the year Roxanne died, but I guess I never really paid attention to how much money he has now. Also, his creepy third room.

He claims it's where he stores the things he doesn't need. I'm not sure how he can have enough crap to fill an entire room, but maybe he's become a hoarder in the last year and a half. Maybe he has a freaky magical rose in the center of the room with petals slowly falling off like *Beauty and the Beast*, and if I touch the wrong thing, his life will be over. Or maybe I'm just being a freak, and I should appreciate that Phoenix is letting me stay in his house and *not* delve into his weird third room.

I watch Phoenix as he spoons some of the pasta into his mouth, not sitting, and instead wandering over to the entertainment center, running his finger over his stack of movies. He stands there silently, picking up a DVD, looking at it for a moment, then putting it back, and repeating the motions with another title. He's silent... a little too silent for someone who's just browsing movies and nothing more. I take the cue and remain quiet, simply watching him and eating the food he made. By the time he finally comes back over, I've almost finished my pasta. "What's up? You look serious."

Phoenix nods, sliding onto the stool next to me. "After Mom bitched at you, there was something you mentioned that took me by surprise. When she found out we had sex the night Roxanne was killed she said something to you. Why didn't you tell me?"

I grimace, not particularly wanting to relive such a shitty time in my life. "Look, I normally would have. But it was last September, right before everything else happened. We haven't exactly been talking since then."

"Yeah, I guess." He slumps forward, leaning his elbows on the counter and dropping his face in his hands. "Well, we're talking now, right? So what did she say to you?"

I honestly don't want to talk about it at all, but what happened between Suzan and I involved Phoenix, too, even if it was indirectly. He deserves to know. "Huh, well, I think the better question is what *didn't* she say to me." I shake my head, looking down at where my feet rest on the crossbar of my stool. If I look at them, I don't have to look at him. "She, uh... she basically just to make it clear to me that I wasn't worthy of Roxanne. That, um, just... just random things."

Phoenix leans forward, putting his hand on my leg, thumb running back and forth. "I had no clue she treated you so poorly. I knew she was mad, but I didn't know she actually talked to you about it, said nasty things. I want to know, Maz. If my mom said those things today, over a year later with our family there, then I can't imagine what she said to you in private. And I swear to you, babe, that I'm on your side."

I look up at him, taking a long, deep breath, eyes locking onto his. "I don't want to screw up how you see your mother."

"She was supposed to be your mom too. She fucked that up big time, with both of us, the moment she opened her mouth tonight."

"Look, Phoenix, Suzan hasn't been my mom... ever. I mean, you don't tell your kid that the best choice she ever made was refusing to adopt me. That me not having the family name was a blessing."

Phoenix squeezes my knee. "She said that to you?"

"Among other things." I look at him, trying to decide how much to say. Yes, he asked me to tell him, but it's possible he doesn't want to see his mom in this light. That his curiosity is getting the best of him and he doesn't really want to know. Though judging by how long he thought about it before saying anything, I'd say he already considered these things on his own. I don't exactly have the right to decide for him. "If you really want to know, I'll tell you what happened one hundred percent. But, Nix, do you really want to hear the things your mom said to me at one of the worst moments in her life?"

"That time was awful for all of us. It doesn't give her a reason to shit on you."

I put my hand on his. "No, it doesn't, and it definitely does not excuse what she did today. Maybe you shouldn't have to hear the words she said just because I had to. Either way, you know me. My memory is awful. Who knows how much of it I even know, right?"

Phoenix rolls his eyes at me. "Yeah, right." His face turns somber as he shakes his head. "You remember every single thing she said. Her words stuck. Because what she said is still stuck with you. I want to know who my mother really is."

"Nix, look, she said some incredibly mean things to me. Terrible things, okay? She told me that I was a disgrace, that she never should have brought me in so Roxanne wouldn't have met me, that..." I feel my heart squeeze at the memory of Suzan and me, standing in the empty hall of a police station, her voice filled with so much anger that she spit as she talked, and her face turned red. The feeling of that weight finally dropping on top of me, the weight that hasn't let up, reminding me that if I had been there... this might not have happened. "She told me she wished it'd been me. That if I needed someone to screw me so bad that I should have let him rape me instead of Roxanne."

Phoenix's hand tightens, becoming an iron grip on my palm. His fist is tight enough to be painful. The kind of pain I can see in him is a pain I know well, the pain of seeing a loved one suffering. Hearing what Roxanne went through was almost worse than hearing she was dead. I never want to hear something so terrible again in my life. I don't want Phoenix to be thinking about this kind of stuff too. Water spills over onto his cheeks, and he grabs me, yanking me to his chest. His fingers grip into my back like he's afraid of letting go.

I wrap my arms around him as well, running them up and down his back, trying to soothe him with shushes. "Phoenix, don't cry. She may not have even meant it. It wasn't all that bad."

"It's not that." He pulls away, moving his hands to my cheeks, planting his eyes directly in front of mine. "If it *had* been you, if that monster had touched you and forced himself on you... I don't know what I would do. How can someone who was supposed to care for you say something so terrible to you? Why didn't you tell me, let me comfort you?" His voice cracks as his throat closes up.

I put my hand over his. "I didn't think I deserved to talk to you. When Suzan was telling me I was the reason Roxanne died, I believed her. I thought that me choosing to see you... my *love* for you was what killed her. I couldn't let myself think about you anymore, let alone talk to you."

Phoenix sniffles, wiping the collecting water from under his eyes. "That's... that's why you didn't talk to me this whole last year? Or tell me you were homeless?"

"Yeah," I pull out of Phoenix's hands, turning away from him. This whole day has been nothing but a constant reminder of things that I want to forget.

Phoenix quickly moves in front of me again, pressing his finger under my chin and looking at me. "My mom is the reason you suffered through Roxanne's death alone?"

"I was the one you decided not to talk to you–"

"But she was the one who put the thoughts into your head. This whole time I thought it was because you regretted everything that happened. That you didn't love me and didn't know how to tell me."

I grab his hands, shaking my head. "No, Nix. I loved you, and that was the reason I couldn't face you. I... I loved you more than I loved Roxanne, and I didn't know how to admit that to myself when I was so heartbroken over her. How do you admit that you didn't love your dead wife as much as someone else?"

Phoenix takes a deep breath, another tear slipping down his cheek. He tucks a strand of hair behind my ear before pulling me into my arms. "I'm so sorry you were alone, Mazey. I just," he stops, his throat catching.

I hear him start to cry harder, feel the wetness of his tears drip onto me. "I'm here now, right? I'm not alone now."

He nods, burying his face in the crook of my neck. "I'm not going to let you be alone again."

The fourth movie of the evening flickers on the screen. It's a movie about... I honestly don't know what. We have a handful of minutes left and I haven't figured out the plot. I can barely remember the main character's name. I know that people are running around, seeming to be making a lot of heartfelt speeches. Maybe they're dying. Maybe they're all going to die, at least then I'd understand something. Though Phoenix seems to be enjoying the movie, and for that, I'm thankful. He's laughing at practically everything – things that are definitely not funny. He hasn't looked over to check on me for the last hour. Progress.

Phoenix chuckles again, his stomach shaking against my legs, which are across his lap. I shift, the blanket falling off my leg. Phoenix, whose hand has been resting on my thigh *over* the blanket, barely notices, and when he slaps his hand against my leg with another fit of laughter, the blanket falls off altogether. His laugh dies out quickly as his hand rests against my skin, but he doesn't look at me or say anything. He leaves his hand there, and I don't complain.

As the movie finishes and the credits roll, I feel his hand start to shift, moving slightly higher. In a purely instinctive move, I leap from the coach. "That was a great movie."

"You were hardly paying attention to it."

I click my tongue, not exactly sure what to say to that. "Still thought it was a banger."

"A banger?" He chuckles, sitting forward and resting his elbows on his knees.

"Yeah, that's what I said..." I trail off, looking away from him, trying to find something else to focus on instead of what might have happened had I stayed on that couch. I clear my throat and busy myself with picking up the leftovers from the take-out Phoenix insisted we order halfway through the second movie. "It's late. What is it, 4 a.m.? Maybe we should, um, sleep?"

Phoenix gives me a weird look. "Yeah, sure." He wanders off into the bedroom, not saying much else.

I sigh, aggravated with myself for leaping away like his hand was on fire. What am I, a virgin? I need to calm down. Who knows if that was even intentional? Maybe his hand just moved, like normal hands do. Maybe he wasn't doing anything sexual at all, and I made it weird. Shit.

I hurry over to the bedroom, wanting to make sure I didn't actually make it weird. As I turn the corner, I almost walk right into the poor man – the poor *shirtless* man. I halt, eyes dropping down his chest to the waistband of his jeans. My breath hitches in my chest, and I'm suddenly very aware of Phoenix's eyes on me. But I can't get my eyes off the v of his hips where his jeans hang low. If they would just go a little lower...

"Mazey?" Phoenix raises an eyebrow at me. "Did you need something?"

I start to shake my head slowly but then realize that I *did* need something. That's the whole reason I came in here. "Uh, yeah. Yes. I was just... what are you doing?"

Phoenix has his hands around the waistband of his jeans and pulls them down, grabbing them and dropping them in a hamper. He turns around, seemingly unaware of the fact that he's standing there in his boxers, looking hot as hell. He raises an eyebrow again. "What?"

"You're stripping."

He nods to the bed. "I'm getting ready for bed. Didn't you say you wanted to sleep?"

"Uh, no. Well, yes, I did, but not like this, no."

"What's wrong?"

I huff. "Phoenix, I'm not sleeping in the same bed as you when you're practically buck-ass naked."

Phoenix chuckles. "Mazey, what? You've slept in the same bed as me before, and in much less than this."

"Yeah, after we screwed. Have we screwed recently?"

He tries to hold back a grin and fails miserably. "Not that I'm aware of, no."

I give him a face that says *seeeee*. "So we're not sleeping in the same bed like that."

"I'mma get hot. You know I heat up like a damn furnace at night."

I sigh, rolling my eyes. "Fine, I'll sleep on the couch. Just get me a blanket and a pillow."

Phoenix sighs right back. "No, I'm not letting my *guest* sleep on the couch. I'll sleep out there, you sleep in here."

"Yeah?"

"Yeah," He nods, grabbing a pillow off the bed and hugs it to his chest. "In that case, I'm taking a shower before sleeping. I'll take it out there, so I don't wake you. Do you need anything from the bathroom?"

"No, I'm good. I can use this one."

"Okay." He leaves the room, taking his pillow with him.

I go to my suitcase in the corner, rummaging through it until I find my toiletry bag. I'm about to go into the master bathroom to brush my teeth when I huff. I should go back to Phoenix and offer to take the couch again. I feel bad for kicking him out of his own room, but I *did* offer. Plus, with the kind of exhaustion I feel right now, I really don't want to have a night full of fitful sleep, tossing and turning. I could just suck it up and sleep in the bed *with* Phoenix. I'm a grown-ass woman; I can keep my hands to myself, I'm not an animal. I'll just offer to sleep in the same bed—

Holy crap.

I stop in my tracks, eyes widening as I see Phoenix standing in the bathroom, bare ass out. My eyes don't know where to look, at his muscular, broad back, or his incredible ass... or nothing, Mazey. Don't stare at Phoenix. What the hell is my problem?

Jumping back, I try as quietly as possible to get back to the room. I close the door, lowering myself onto the bed and taking a shaky breath as images fly through my mind, clouding my judgment. Trying to think of something else, I squeeze my eyes closed. Something that's not hot, and sexy... and dripping wet. Shit. No, I'm not thinking of Phoenix. God, wouldn't this be easier if I didn't know what he looked like naked. As it is, the parts of him I did see are more than enough to remind my brain exactly how the rest looks.

I need to stop this before I do something stupid, but my body has no intention of listening to logic. My stomach tightens as memories of him inside me rush through my veins. He can feed the cute, romantic side of me one second and the raw, hot side of me the next.

My eyes snap open as I stare at the ceiling. I can't act on anything. I can't just storm into the bathroom where Phoenix is showering and tell him I can't stop thinking about him because I saw him naked. That's just... exactly what I want to do. Hell, I think I'd jump his bones if he offered. I need to slow down. Right now, when my whole life is taking a turn for the worse, can I risk screwing things up with Phoenix? He clearly feels the same way, or he wouldn't have insisted on sleeping on the couch.

Okay, *insisting* is a little bit of a strong word considering he offered once and I said yes. Having him sleep next to me in the bed? The small bit of self-control I have now would have taken a dive out the window. The other day he was going to kiss me. If Suzan hadn't shown up, who knows how far that might have gone. So it's not completely out of the question; he may actually want me to make a move. Between the two of us, I am more broken. Maybe he doesn't want to push me too far. Should I be taking that chance when it could end terribly?

I push myself up, so I'm sitting and take a deep breath, then another. I just need to go to sleep – It's already late. Sleeping will just reset it all. I can sleep it off, and tomorrow will be a new day. I may only be worked up from how much has happened today. If I just let my mind have some peace and quiet, I can start with a clean slate tomorrow. I can gauge Phoenix better, see what he's thinking.

Or just leave the man alone. God, I sound like a sex-crazed fool.

Get ready for bed – I just need to get ready for bed. I change into PJs, finally able to take off this terrible dress. Roxanne's ring glitters on my chest – a reminder of yet another reason why I should slow my roll. Roxanne spent her life worried I'd run to Phoenix, and I spent the whole time pretending I didn't care about him. That we were just friends. I'm closer to him than that, but tonight I will only be closer to him *mentally*. There will be no touching Phoenix. Or thinking about touching Phoenix. And there I go again, thinking about touching him. Nope, nope, nope.

I leave the room, going to the kitchen to grab a glass of water. As I do, I can hear the shower running in the guest bath that Phoenix is using. It would be so easy to just go over there and... "Nope," I mutter to myself, pouring the water into a cup, downing the whole thing, and filling it up again. I need to calm down, I sound like a hormone-crazed teenager.

I put the pitcher back into the fridge, leaning against the island as I sip my water again. The sounds of the shower never moving far from my mind. The image of Phoenix standing in that shower, naked and soaking wet, is practically an invitation to my fluttering heart. My stomach clenches into such a tight knot I'm not even sure I could detangle it. Maybe I shouldn't. Maybe I should just see what would happen if I go in there and kiss him.

I find myself standing at the door, staring at the handle, debating with myself. Should I go in or stay out? After another couple of deep breaths, I turn the handle down, stepping into the bathroom. As the door opens, I send a prayer to anyone who will listen that this doesn't completely backfire and embarrass me. I let go of the door, and it drifts closed, with just a crack in the opening. I stare at the shower curtain. I can hear Phoenix behind it. I count to three and then open it.

Phoenix looks up at me, confusion written all over his face. Before I can even register that, my eyes shift lower, admiring every perfect inch of him, including the several a little farther south... and also gripped in his hand. He seems too shocked to move, staring at me as water drips down his nose, coats his eyelashes, and trickles down his lips. He tilts his head, seeming to ask a question, almost like a dog curious at the next move.

What is my next move? I didn't exactly plan this far. I didn't plan this at all. All I know is that now that I'm here, I don't think I could walk away even if I wanted to. My eyes tilt down to where he already stands erect and only one thought remains in my mind. "Were you thinking of me?" I nod down to his waist, not only very curious about the answer but also pleased at the look it puts on his face.

"Of you... your body." He takes his turn, eating me up

with his eyes, shifting his attention to the end of the t-shirt I wear as it brushes against the top of my thighs.

I try to calm my nerves as I muster up the courage to say something back. "Do you want some more inspiration?" Not brave enough to let him say no, I reach my hands down to the hem of the oversized shirt, pulling it over my head and dropping it on the floor at my feet, keeping my eyes closed for a second before opening them to see Phoenix's reaction. His eyes are on my now bare chest, mouth parted.

He looks back up. "Mazey... what are you... are you sure?"

No. I'm most definitely not. Especially if he's going to be asking questions while I'm half-naked. Not like I'm going to tell him that. So instead, I say something else. "Well, you were thinking of me anyway, right?"

He doesn't nod, eyes shifting away instead.

I step forward, putting a finger under his chin to guide his line of sight back at my eyes. "It's not a bad thing. I just figured the real deal is better than your imagination." I take my finger back, quickly turning around before my nerves show all over my face and make this much less sexy than I'm hoping for. Still facing the door, I take a deep breath, then grab the waistband of my shorts and push them off my hips, stepping out of them. Then I do the same with my underwear, leaving them in a pile on the ground as I face Phoenix again. The look on his face totally knocks my confidence. "Am I... is this too far?"

Phoenix shakes his head. "No, no. I just wasn't... expecting this."

My heart drops. Shit, I messed it up. I made it worse again. My hands wander in front of my chest as I sigh. "Oh, I'm sorry. I didn't mean to screw things up. I can, uh, I can leave—"

"Mazey. Stop." Phoenix holds a hand out to me and I take it. "C'mere." I do, stepping into the shower. Phoenix closes the curtain and kisses my forehead. "What do you want?"

Before I can think of an appropriate response, my mouth thinks of one for me. "I want to watch."

"Oh?" Phoenix stops, surprise etched onto his face.

Shocked by my own words, I start to figure out how much backpedaling I need to do. But my brain isn't telling me to run; it's telling me to stay. To stay and watch. So I take a step back and sit on the shelf at the end of the shower, my ass barely even able to fit on it. I stay looking up at Phoenix, trying to look as sexy as possible.

Phoenix chuckles nervously. "You want to watch me jerk off?"

I nod. "Touch yourself for me."

He stares at me, and I can see in his eyes the thoughts throwing themselves around in his head. As he thinks about it, I watch his shocked look shifting to intrigue, then curiosity, and then into a smirk and a devious look. He reaches down and grabs himself in his hands.

My stomach does approximately a million somersaults as my brain tries to play catch up to what exactly is happening. I asked Phoenix to masturbate in front of me... and he's doing it. Holy fuck, that's hot. My mouth slides open, and I can't quite find the will to close it back up. I watch his hand as he slides it up and down, feeling every nerve in my body light on fire, screaming at me to do something, anything. So I do. My legs spread open, a perfect space for someone to place themselves. Instead of *someone,* I reach between my thighs, easing my fingers into myself.

Phoenix groans, squeezing his eyes closed. "Shit, you can't do that."

In an instant, I decide between agreeing or taking the bold route. *Bold.* It has to be bold. "What, this?" I watch as Phoenix opens his eyes, wanting to see what I'm doing. His eyes snap straight to where my finger rubs in circles over the bundle of nerves between my legs. I open my legs wider, leaning back against the wall, moaning along with my touch.

Phoenix mumbles something incoherent under his breath, bracing himself against the wall. He drags his eyes from between my thighs, up my body, to my eyes. "You can't be doing that and expect me to just stand here."

I stop. I have two options: say fuck it and jump the dude, or keep things less... intense and do something else. Well, intense isn't the right word, because holy hell is this intense, but going from zero to one hundred isn't really the *best* idea right now. I go with the second option, smiling at him with what I hope to be a seductive smile. "Oh, do you want me to do this instead?" I lower myself onto the ground, kneeling in front of him, the cold tile biting at my knees.

Phoenix practically licks his lips as he looks down at me. "Shit."

I place my finger on his thigh, trailing it up slowly, not breaking eye contact. "Is that better?"

"Mazey..." He moans, fingers clenching the wall as best they can.

As I take in the pure lust and desire pulling on his face, I feel every last drop of doubt fly away. My confidence takes its place, letting me know it's most definitely ready to take charge. I stop the movement of my hand. "Look at me."

He does, peeling his eyes open, looking down his body to where my mouth hovers.

I smile, continuing my path towards his hips, where my target is. I place my mouth right by his tip, letting my breath fan over him, his dick twitching in front of me. "Keep looking at me, or I'll stop."

"I'm not sure I'll need you to go much longer," he grunts, but he keeps his eyes open. "God, you're going to make me cum as fast as a damn virgin."

I finally reach what my finger has been trailing towards, and I run it down his length. Phoenix closes his eyes again, and I halt. "What, you don't want me to finish?"

"Keep going," He grabs my head, bracing himself on me as he opens his eyes back up.

"Good, this is the fun part." I grab his penis, not hesitating any longer before wrapping my mouth around him. His dick jumps in between my lips, and I take that as an invitation to move my mouth up and down his shaft. His hand grips my hair. I keep my eyes on him, looking straight at him through my lashes as I suck and stroke him with all the enthusiasm I've built up since the last time we were together. His breath hitches in his chest, and he makes a noise that sends sparks all over my body.

His stomach clenches. "Mazey, I'm going to—"

I give him a few more strokes before popping my lips off of him, sitting back on my heels. Not a moment later, he cums on my face. Phoenix moans, body clenching as he orgasms. As he finishes, I wipe the back of my hand across my face. "I think you got it in my nose."

For a second, he just stares at me, but he suddenly bursts out laughing, sliding against the shower wall until he's sitting on the floor. "You just sucked me off and *that's* what you're going to say?"

I chuckle too. "Well, you did."

Phoenix uses his thumb to wipe his jizz off my face. "God, I missed you."

"'Cause I'm great at blow jobs?"

"Yes," Phoenix smiles, shoulders slumped with relaxation. "I also miss you being you."

I nod, leaning forward and dropping my head on his shoulder, letting the water soak my hair and stream down my face. "Yeah, me too."

"You know I was trying to get you to make a move earlier. right?"

I look up at him, eyes narrowed. "No, when?"

He shakes his head in dismay. "Me stripping in front of you didn't give you a hint?"

"You said you were just getting ready for bed. That you slept in your boxers."

"If I was really just getting ready for bed, I would have left the room, Maz." He chuckles at me, flicking the tip of my nose with his finger before leaning closer and putting his lips against my ear. "And I sleep naked."

CHAPTER FIVE

"Oh my God," I sit up so fast my head spins, hair flying into my face. My mind is racing: Suzan and the Thanksgiving lunch, Lincoln and I's stroll, telling Phoenix about Suzan... and Phoenix and me having sex in the shower. I know that last night, being wrapped in his arms, with his lips pressed against my neck, my cheeks, my lips... it felt safe. I felt good, like I was in the right palace, but all I remember after that are my dreams. My dreams where Roxanne was telling me how much I've hurt her, how much I've put her through. It was like she was coming back from the grave to punish me for being with Phoenix again.

I try to open my eyes, but there's so much light streaming into the room, I feel like I'm going to go blind. I can see every single thing in the room, including the naked man beside me. My heart skips a beat before my mind processes how much back peddling I'm going to have to do. "Holy crap." I jump out of bed, almost tripping on the blanket.

Not surprisingly with all the noise I'm making, Phoenix wakes up, eyes peeling open slowly. "Mazey? What're you doing?"

I just sit there, trying to find the words to say. When my brain finally catches up, it decides to go a less graceful route. "We boned."

"Well, I wouldn't say—"

"Oh my God, we did not bone." I gasp as I play catch-up. If the floor opened up and swallowed me whole, I wouldn't complain. At least then I wouldn't have to see the look on his face as he starts to process that I'm not exactly radiating happiness.

He sits up, rubbing his face. "Maz, don't flip, okay? It doesn't have to be a big deal—"

"You don't have pants on."

"Stop cutting me off."

I look down at myself – this is his shirt, which I definitely could have passed on. Maybe I could have worn my own shirt, or maybe some PJs, but no, I didn't, 'cause we had sex. "I don't have pants!" Why couldn't I have kept my horny self from boning him?

"Not boning, Mazey. Boning implies... well, there wasn't any boning, so don't flip." Phoenix reaches forward but quickly stops as the blanket starts to fall off his lap.

I groan, practically stomping my foot like I'm some kind of toddler. "Your dick was in my mouth. Oh my goodness... your penis was in my face!"

Phoenix's eyebrows shoot up as he presses his lips together to try to stop from laughing. "Yes, I know. I was there, I remember."

I throw a pillow at him and he catches it before it smacks his face. Big mistake, because the movement makes the blanket lower on his hips, very close to exposing the exact thing that gave me this problem, to begin with. "Would you put some freaking clothes on?"

"Mazey, babe, don't freak out—"

"Babe?" My heart is fluttering at the sound of him calling

me babe, but my brain tells me that I need to run away – fast. "No, *no*. No 'babe-ing.' I can't, nope. I'm leaving now. I'm.... I'm," I pivot on the balls of my feet and rush out of the room before Phoenix has a chance to speak. I drop myself into the armchair in the living room, mouth gaping and mind spinning. After all this time... I spent almost a year so angry at myself for cheating on Roxanne that I didn't even talk to Phoenix. I cut him out of my life as best as I could. The only reason he came back...

I was so angry at myself. I screwed up, and I never had a chance to fix it, to apologize. Then I come back here, and within the first week, I'm jumping Phoenix? God, it's like when I'm around him, my brain decides to take a vacation and it's my hormones making all the decisions. The first day I met him, when I caught his eyes and he caught mine, everything in me told me to go up to him and talk to him, and I did. Ever since then, my whole body feels like it's screaming when he's around, and it hasn't stopped. If anything, it may be worse now than it was back then, and that's saying something.

Why did I think staying with him would be a good idea? While I don't exactly have anywhere else to go, this wasn't really a good choice either. I could have slept in a box last night and that probably would have been better for us and my heart. I don't know if I can go down this road again. Every time I give in and choose Phoenix, all hell breaks loose. It's like the world keeps trying to tell me to stay away and my heart is too stubborn to listen. What if this just ends in as much pain as it has in the past? What if this screws up our friendship permanently?

He's all I have left. If I lose him, if I mess this up for good, I'll just fall back into the pit I've been trying so hard to get out of. Without the job, the apartment, the thought that *eventually,* I'll get better, what's left? These last few months,

I've been holding on to the fact that I have someone who's waiting for me at the end of the line. That someday, down the line, I could be happy again with Phoenix.

Hasn't that been the plan all along? Even when it was wrong for me to think that I always did. It was the plan the night Roxanne died, and her death didn't change the goal, just how long it'd take to get there. In the back of my mind I've always known that I was going to end up with Phoenix, didn't I? The last thing I did to Roxanne before she died was cheat on her, but can I cheat on her memory too?

"Mazey?" Phoenix squats in front of me and grabs my hands. "Hey, are you okay?"

I take a deep breath, shaking my head. "I don't know. I feel like Roxanne's jumping out of her grave and giving me a piece of her mind. Telling me that I cheated on her once, and now I'm doing it again."

Phoenix sighs, moving to sit on the coffee table in front of me but still holding onto my hands. "Maz... I know you're grieving, and I *know* that you loved Roxanne, and losing her has been the toughest thing you've had to go through, but you've got to stop acting like you owe her anything."

"What?" I'm taken aback by what he's saying. He's usually so... supportive? The first one to offer a shoulder to cry on and the last one to judge or criticize.

"Look, people don't like to speak ill of the dead, so for the past year and a half, no one has said a bad thing about her. But before she died... you told me so many different times the things she's done to you, how she treated you. Everyone seems to keep forgetting that Roxanne cheated on you a ton when you first started dating."

I pull my hands out of his, wrapping my arms around myself. "We were sixteen. We had just started dating–"

"Stop making excuses for her! You were so hurt when you found out, devastated. And yet, when she found out we had sex, she acted like you were so much worse than her. She was the whole reason you took on extra classes to graduate early – you didn't get a real senior year. When y'all were picking colleges, you went to her dream school – she didn't even consider going to yours. She manipulated you for years, made you feel like you needed her to live, and if you don't figure your shit out, she may have ended up being right."

Phoenix leans forward, his hand gripping my knee. "You loved her so much, so there must have been *something* in her worth loving, but you don't owe her anything. You didn't then, and you definitely don't now. I mean, damn, Maz, the whole reason the two of you started dating turned out to be a lie!"

"Please stop," I mutter, looking away from him. "I get it; you two weren't exactly close–"

"She spent the last half of her life stealing the love of *my* life away from me."

"Let me talk–"

"I spent the whole time seeing it all, what she was doing to you... how she always turned it on you–"

"Stop! Stop cutting me off, stop telling me Roxanne was a shitty person, just stop, Phoenix. I loved her."

Phoenix pauses, taking a deep breath before continuing. "I know you loved her, it's just hard to think about her differently just because she's gone. She was the same person, even if she is dead."

I look away from him, running my tongue over my teeth, trying not to cry.

Phoenix stands up and throws his arm up in exasperation. "She's been gone for a year and a half and she still has you under her thumb. When are you going to remember how you felt about her *before* she died? What's important is what she did to you and how she made you feel when she was alive, not what she's doing to you and how she's making you feel when she's dead. That's bullshit, and you have to know it."

"Where is all of this coming from, Phoenix?" I wipe my nose on the back of my hand, nose stuffed from the tears – tears that are starting to pool up in my eyes and close up my throat. Why can't I do anything without crying like a baby?

Phoenix drops onto his knees in front of me, taking a long, deep breath. "I just want you to remember how you used to feel. Not just about Roxanne, but about me and you. I don't want to ruin the way you remember her or how you think about her. I loved her too; she was my sister, but the moment she walked into your life, she started using you, and she didn't stop."

"Ha, seems like a pretty generalized statement. What, she used me for eight whole years?"

"Yeah, she did. Who wanted you to major in biology because it was more 'secure?' Who decided that y'all wouldn't adopt kids but *needed* them to be your own? Who decided to have such a huge wedding you had to take out loans? And who chose to move to Seattle, or to GCU for that matter? It was all Roxanne. And I'm not the one coming up with these examples. It was all you who said this first. You complained about these things for years."

"So, what's your point?" I get up, moving away from Phoenix while he just stands there watching me. "I mean, thanks for the reminder. I wish I hadn't taken her for granted, but I'd much rather *not* argue with you about it."

Phoenix scoffs. "I don't want to argue either, that's not my point." He strides over to me, reaches up, and presses his palm against my cheek. "My point is that you deserve to be happy. You deserve to do whatever you want, with me or someone else. Roxanne is constantly holding you back."

I roll my eyes. "Constantly? I've been here a week."

"I'm not just talking about now. I'm talking about ever."

He smiles down at me, pushing a strand of hair behind my ear. "The night that I went to Seattle to find you... that night was the freest I'd seen you in years. Maybe I'm a little biased, but I really want you to go back to that moment. Just... just remember why you met me in the first place."

My mind goes back to that night. June 15th. The best and worst night of my life. The day that started with petty arguments and ended in bed with Phoenix.

"That night isn't exactly something I try to remember, Phoenix."

"Mazey, look, I'm not saying to sit here and relive every little detail. I'm saying when you answered my phone call, when you chose to meet up with me instead of staying with Roxanne, why did you do it? What made you pick that?" Phoenix's eyes are hopeful, like he needs me to answer this right. Like saying something the wrong way could crush his heart.

I shrug. "When I answered the phone, I was honestly just trying to get away from Roxanne."

"Why?"

I chuckle lightly. "Phoenix, you know all of this. Why are we doing this?"

He groans, spinning away from me. "Because that night you picked me, Mazey. You laid in my arms and told me that you loved me. That you made a mistake when you said yes to marrying Roxanne." He looks at me with such an intense look I may have caught on fire for a second. "You picked *me*. And now you're acting like it never happened."

I swallow hard and search my mind for what to say. How do I respond to something like that? Yes, I did pick him. After yet another headache-inducing fight with Roxanne, I caved. I chose Phoenix's ability to make me laugh, care for me, and charm me over Roxanne's sarcastic tones, passive-aggressive remarks, and controlling personality. But I also chose Phoenix's sharp tongue, impulsive behavior, and all-or-nothing attitude over Roxanne's delicate touch, cheery morning hellos, and dedication to me. The decision wasn't black and white. The way I *feel* about the decision isn't black or white.

I want to blame him, claim he lured me in and tricked me into cheating on my wife. But that's not true, and it's not fair to Phoenix that I keep putting my decisions on him. When I knocked on his hotel room door that night, I knew *something* was going to happen, just not *what*. I can't claim I was lost in the moment, that his excited eyes or his boyish grin were the only things that swayed my decision because, from the second that I answered his call, I knew that I could be cheating on Roxanne in some way. The only question was whether it was going to be physical or just emotional.

I've always known I cared for Phoenix. I always knew he was in love with me, and I let his little flirting go. I pretended I didn't notice the lingering touches or the lustful eyes. That when he held me close, I didn't feel at home in his arms, like I could lay soaking in his perfect honey scent, wrapped in his steady arms forever. I had years to decide if I wanted to be with Phoenix, and I ended up choosing him. Why should that decision be any different now that Roxanne is dead?

The night Roxanne died wasn't *just* the night Roxanne died. It was the day I decided to leave her. It was when I knew that I couldn't just keep hiding in the shadows of what I truly wanted. That taking the leap wouldn't always be a bad thing, especially if there was something there to catch me. I was ready to tell Roxanne everything. Just because she left me instead of me leaving her doesn't mean I have to go back to what I was thinking and feeling before I found out what I really wanted.

So I need to take the leap. I need to trust that Phoenix

feels the same way I do. That he's here for me. I can do that, right? "I picked you."

"What?"

I nod slowly, looking up at him so he knows what I'm saying is exactly what I'm feeling. "Nine years ago, when I met you, I picked you. I picked you from the start. And then I wanted to pick you again that next summer, and again my last year in college, and again the night you came to Seattle. I've known you're who I wanted to pick, but I never took the leap. I kept picking Roxanne."

"Yeah, I was there for the rejections."

I chuckle. "What I'm saying is I can't make the wrong choice anymore. Not just because I *can't* anymore, but also because that night I figured out exactly what I wanted and I was going to fight for it. I'm going to fight for it again. I pick you."

"You pick me?" His lips slowly pull into a smile as the relief flows through him.

"I pick you." I grab his face, reaching as far up as I can on my toes to kiss him.

He pulls me to him, arms wrapping around my waist. He laughs against my lips. "Not fifteen minutes ago, you jumped out of my bed, and now here you are jumping me again."

"Shush," My hands run through his hair as his hands run down my sides, making my skin light on fire. This... this is something Phoenix and I haven't done. The few times we've been together we didn't do much of anything besides have sex of some kind. I think we both always felt like we'd be torn away from each other too soon and were picking our moments. Just kissing was never part of the equation. This makes my stomach dance, but I don't want to just jump into things like we have before. I want this to be real.

I pull away from him, already breathing heavily. Phoenix

rests his forehead against mine, not seeming to want to let go. "What's wrong?"

"Nothing, I just want to take things slow." I kiss him, a quick peck this time.

He smirks, pulling me against him hard. "I think part of me has other intentions."

I gasp as I feel him pressed against my stomach, telling me just what kind of other intentions he could have. I run my thumb across his lip and shake my head. "Slow, Phoenix. Or, my version of slow." I capture his lips with mine, letting him know slow means a little more than nothing. He doesn't hesitate to meet me right back, practically eating me up. We move backward, feet getting tangled together as we try to walk as one person instead of two. I trip on his foot, falling back and bringing him with me, but he catches us, bracing himself against his bedroom door.

He presses me against it with his own body, fumbling for the doorknob that's somewhere beside me. We quickly tumble into the room, finally getting to the bed where he lays me down, looking at me from above. I squirm, the desire and intensity of his look making me want to hide my face. Phoenix lowers himself on me before I can, grabbing my hands with his and raising them above my head. He straddles me, knees pressed firmly against my thighs.

My heart thumps against my chest almost as much as I'm throbbing somewhere else a little lower. This is something the old Mazey would have swooned over. Even just seeing Phoenix the first time I met him had my mind skipping beats. The first time he touched me soaked my panties faster than jumping into a pool, but there wasn't nearly as much heat and tension as there is now. It was more awkward bumping around, whereas this... this could get me off for a lifetime.

Phoenix pulls back, panting above me, his chest rising and falling rapidly. "Mazey, we should stop."

"Stop?" I mumble, still trying to collect the pieces of my scattered brain.

"If we don't stop now, I'm not going to want to at all." He kisses the tip of my nose, smiling down at me with a frisky smile. "If you want to take it slow, then I want to too."

I sit up, still half underneath him. "Okay. Okay..." I squeeze my eyes closed. Yes, it's okay. We need to stop. I want to do this the right way, start over from the beginning. I want to make sure we don't mess anything up. To do that, we need to not be boning, right?

Phoenix rolls off of me, staring at the ceiling. "We're doing this slow..."

"The right way. If we had met that night and you asked me out, what would we have done?"

Phoenix looks over at me with an amused look. "Maz, hon, the first day we met we had sex three times."

"Eh, not sex. Definitely oral."

Phoenix rolls his eyes. "Fine, we had sex once. Either way, if that's what you call slow then I'm all in. Let's do it."

I push him back as he leans towards me, resting my palm on his shirt. "Good point. But I want to do this for real. Like going out on a date, eating dinner and seeing a movie, and you bring me flowers, and I pucker my lips at the end of the night to let you know it's okay to kiss me. But just a peck."

"So you want cheesy?"

I nod. "Yes. I want cheesy."

Phoenix jumps off the bed and leaves the room.

"Where are you going?" I call after him, debating if I should get up and follow him.

Before I make up my mind, he comes back into the room with a potted plant in his hands. He holds it out. "Will you go out with me?"

"What's the plant for?"

He shrugs. "It's the closest thing I have to flowers."

"Oh my God."

He puts the plant down on his nightstand. "You didn't like that one? How about um..." he clears his throat, "are you from Tennessee, 'cause you're the only ten I see."

I chuckle at the way he says it, pulling out a finger gun and everything. "You did not. That's like the oldest line in the book."

"Fine, fine, what about this one? Do you have a map because I'm lost in your eyes."

I throw myself back onto the bed. "You're going to kill me. These are awful."

Phoenix comes over, crawling on top of me again, pressing himself against my body. "Are you from a farm, 'cause you sure do know how to raise some good cock."

"No!" I giggle. "There are 206 bones in my body, want to make it 207?"

"Yes ma'am, I do." He kisses my forehead and then quickly climbs off me. "*But* you'll have to keep your fine ass waiting, 'cause we're going on a date tonight. And it's bad form to bang your date *before* the date happens."

"Oh, is it?" I sit up onto my elbows, watching as he backs out of the room, that lively smile still there.

"Mm-hmm. Though I can't promise I won't be so irresistible tonight that you won't want to jump me right then and there." He flashes a devilish smile at me before leaving the room.

I lay back down, staring at the fan above my head. I sigh. "Fuck me."

Phoenix pops his head back in, "Will do!", and then disappears again.

Oh boy, am I in for a ride.

CHAPTER SIX

Looking at myself in the mirror, I take a deep breath. Having just taken a shower, my hair wrapped in a towel, and my face super red from washing it, I'm looking a little questionable. Earlier this morning, Phoenix "accidentally" spilled a whole glass of water all over his shirt and proceeded to finish cooking our breakfast shirtless. If he's playing games, then so am I, in the form of a skimpy towel that may make me feel a tad uncomfortable. If I wasn't seriously trying to mess with Phoenix, I don't think I'd have even thought of wearing this towel. Come to think of it, why does he even own a child-sized towel?

I shake my hair out of the wrap, hanging it up on the rack. I move the towel to supply ample cleavage, then open the door and look down the hall. I hear him talking around the corner. Just as I walk into the main area, Phoenix calls out my name.

"Mazey, there are some people here to see you." He spins around as he says this, noticing me standing at the end of the hall. "Holy shit."

I look behind him and see a group of my foster siblings all averting their eyes, so they're looking anywhere but at me. "Shoot, uh, sorry! I'll just..." I jump out of sight, mentally face-palming at what just happened. I hear Phoenix excuse himself, and he walks in the room as I do, closing the door behind us. "That was so embarrassing!"

"I know!" He teases, eyeing the towel. "What the hell are you wearing, a hand towel?"

I smack his arm. "No! Or, I mean, maybe, I dunno, but that's not the point." I throw myself on the bed, "Here I am, trying to be *sexy* and *cute*, and what do I get? All my siblings seeing me half-naked."

"Mazey?" Phoenix grabs my arms and pulls me into a sitting position. "You did one thing right."

I roll my eyes. "What is that exactly?"

"This is sexy for sure. Hot, even. If you were trying to get back at me for earlier, this was well played." He smiles at me, kissing my cheek. "I'll be sure to return the favor, but for now, get dressed and come out. They came to talk to you."

I groan and get up off the bed. "What if I don't wanna?"

Phoenix kisses my forehead. "Mazey, babe, don't whine. That's unladylike." He teases with a playful look in his eyes.

"Eww, how old are you?" I grab a shirt and some sweats out of my bag.

Phoenix chuckles. "Shut up. They wanna talk to you. Plus, you may want to clear the air about all... that." He motions to my towel.

I sigh. "Yeah, whatever. I'll be out in a second."

He blows me a kiss as he leaves the room, closing the door behind him.

I quickly get changed and put my hair up into a bun with a scrunchie. I take a second to try to forget how embarrassing that was, but it doesn't seem like the memory is planning on leaving any time soon, so I open the door and walk out into the living room where people are sitting on couches and on the floor too. Phoenix is sitting in the armchair with Georgie in his lap. I eye all of them – Olivia, Vincent, Nikkie, and Eric all look up as I enter the room. "Um, hi."

"Hey, Maz," Vincent smiles at me, patting the spot next to him on the couch.

I look at where Nikkie and Eric are sitting on the floor. "What's going on? It's serious enough that you saved me a seat?"

Olivia shakes her head. "No. It's not serious. I mean, not really. Right?"

Nikkie shakes his head. "We're just here to tell you that we don't agree with Mom or Ashten."

I sit between Olivia and Vincent, giving them both confused looks, not liking how serious they're acting. "You drove all the way over here to tell me that?"

"To tell you and Phoenix that." Olivia smiles at me, pushing a piece of her curled hair out of her face, bracelets jingling on her wrist.

I look over at Phoenix, who shrugs. "Okay. I mean, thanks. But I'm kind of confused."

"We didn't want you to think we felt the same way as Mom or that you don't deserve to be in the family. You do; you're our sister." Nikkie reaches forward and pats my knee, looking a little uncomfortable as he does. He clears his throat, puffing his chest slightly. Never hurts to prove how macho he is, I guess.

I chuckle at the gesture. "Thank you. I appreciate it. At this point, I'm honestly just trying to erase that whole day from my mind." I sink back into the couch, hands placed one on top of the other over my stomach.

"I hope not all of it," Phoenix gives me a devious smile.

I narrow my eyes at him. "Hush."

Olivia gasps, eyes going wide. I see her romance obsession peeking through, ready to discuss all things cute and cheesy. "Oh my gosh, are you guys together now?"

My cheeks flush as everyone's eyes shift between Phoenix and me, wondering what exactly Phoenix doesn't want me to forget. If he were sitting next to me, I definitely would've socked him. "I, uh–"

"No. We're not *together*." Phoenix jumps in, saving me from any more stuttering. "I was talking about the conversation we had. I just want to make sure she remembers."

People shift their attention to me as if waiting for me to confirm. I nod. "Yeah, we just talked about what happened. How I felt about it."

Olivia's gaze lingers on me like she's trying to find the secret we're not telling her. I look away from her quickly.

"So, how do you feel?" Vincent questions, eyes softening as he looks at me.

I sigh, leaning backward on the couch. "Crappy. Weird. Upset. I didn't want anyone else to find out about all that... and I definitely didn't want to have a screaming match with Suzan about it." There's a moment of uncomfortable silence as we sit there, not sure what to say about everything that happened yesterday.

"I'm sorry," Olivia grabs my hand, squeezing it. "I wish we didn't have to find out that way."

"Though we did know about you and Phoenix from before. I mean, Lincoln wasn't kidding. Roxanne definitely made some noise about it." Nikkie chuckles, his reaction now much different than his reaction when he originally found out.

I feel myself cringe. The humiliation I felt that day is only rivaled by yesterday. I can still remember Suzan's shocked face as Roxanne declared that Phoenix and I had sex. The way I wanted to curl up and disappear when everyone looked at me. I was honestly kind of hoping most of my siblings didn't remember. Vincent was only what, eight, Olivia only six. They wouldn't have even known what was happening.

Eric huffs. "I didn't know about it. Like, what the hell, man? I got totally bullied for sleeping with that chick, and that's only three years' difference. Y'all were what, six, seven years apart?"

"Five – don't get ahead of yourself." Phoenix snorts, pointing at me with his free hand. "*Plus* this one didn't tell me she was underage. She said she was nineteen."

Olivia gasps. "You *lied*?"

Vincent chuckles, just sitting back to enjoy the show.

"I mean, I, well... yeah, I did, but that was ages ago."

Eric butts back in. "Okay, but still. Why is it okay if he screwed her underage, but not if I did it."

"Eric, dude, she didn't lie. You knew she was seventeen, and you still slept with her. That's illegal." Olivia gives him a look that definitely calls him out, and it seems he can tell because he sits back, pouting.

Nikkie looks at Phoenix, then at me, then back at Phoenix. "Is that... is that why it was so weird the day y'all met?"

"What do you mean?" I ask as I lean forward to see him. Olivia raises her eyebrows, waiting to hear about mine and Phoenix's uncomfortable second meeting. Vincent twists one of the thick rings on his finger, eyes darting between everyone as they talk. This is all new information for them. I doubt they remember a single thing from the day I met them.

Nikkie points at Phoenix. "That night, when you first came to live with us. Phoenix came in and you both acted *so* strangely. I didn't know why; I just assumed you were weird."

"Me?" I laugh, shaking my head. "I mean, I guess that'd be why. He definitely wasn't very amused when he found out."

Olivia giggles. "Ohh, drama?"

Phoenix rolls her eyes. "No, not *drama*. I wasn't even mad that long. We became friends so fast it was basically forgotten in a day."

Georgie finally wakes up, looking around at everyone and finally landing on Vincent. He points. "Your hair is green?"

"Yes." Vincent leans forward, grabbing Georgie from Phoenix and trying to throw him up in the air and failing. "Good job!"

Olivia groans. "You guys baby the crap out of this poor kid. He's going to grow up being coddled."

"I was coddled and I'm just fine." Eric shrugs. Georgie catches his eye and Eric waves at him.

Nikkie snorts. "Yeah, sure you're fine. I mean, you're practically failing out of college, and *under*age is your favorite age, but you're just fine."

"Oh, shove it, jackass." Eric jabs his middle finger up at Nikkie and then sticks his tongue out.

"Language, dickhead. You know we're not supposed to say that kind of stuff in front of the kids." Vincent sticks his tongue out at Eric to join the battle.

I get up and take Georgie out of Vincent's hands, putting him on the ground. "How about we all just stop talking before you guys ruin Georgie forever?"

"Actually," Olivia gets up, grabbing her jacket off the back of the couch, "we're just going to leave instead. Mom was making dinner when we left, and since we told her we were going to the store to grab some stuff, we'd probably better do that before she realizes it doesn't take an hour to go to grab groceries."

Nikkie gets up as well and pulls me into a hug. "We said what we came here to say, though."

Eric hugs me next. "Don't go tricking any more guys."

I roll my eyes and step back out of his arms. "Not only

can I not, since I'm twenty-six, I also don't plan on picking up strangers anytime soon. Once was enough for me."

Nikkie, holding Georgie's hand with one of his own now, points at me with the other. "Make sure you're here, yeah? If you're staying, make sure you keep in touch and talk to us."

I nod, a warm feeling of hope taking root in my chest. "Of course."

Vincent offers his hand for a high five and attempts the handshake I see guys doing. It's a fumbling mess with my lack of effort. "God, you suck at that."

"Wha– I didn't even know you were going to do that! Some warning would be nice."

He shakes his head at me, going to Phoenix, who pulls off a perfect handshake.

I ignore them and hug Olivia instead. "Thank you for coming over."

"We love you, and we're here for you." She smiles at me as she waves goodbye and the whole group of them leaves the apartment, and Phoenix closes the door after them.

Phoenix locks the door then turns to me, a smile tugging one side of his mouth. "So…"

"What?" I take my hair down and shake it out, not wanting it to get musty. I turn around to grab a blanket that someone must have dropped on the floor. As I spin around to put it back on the couch, I run into Phoenix. "Holy crap, what are you doing?"

He shrugs. "I was just wondering if you may want to put that towel back *on* so I can take it *off*."

I laugh, dropping the blanket onto the sofa and walking towards the bedroom. "Nope. You're picking me up for our date soon, so *I* am going to go get ready." I turn back to smile at him while standing in the doorway. "Maybe you can take my dress off of me?"

As I close the door, I hear Phoenix groan. "Oh lord, please."

As I slide my ring onto my finger, I feel my heart pounding in my chest. I've felt this nervous shake for the thirty minutes since Phoenix left. Before he left, everything felt normal. It was just me and him, like old times, talking and hanging out. I hardly even remembered we were going on a date tonight, even as I was getting ready for it. When he left, though, it all started to feel so real. Like I was going on a date with a stranger, someone I didn't know at all, instead of someone I've known for almost half my life. It was like once he walked out the door, my brain remembered that when he came back, I'd be going on a date. With him.

The only real dates I've ever been on were with Roxanne. On our first 'date,' I didn't even know I was going on a date, it just happened. Well, for me, it did. She told me later she actually had the whole thing planned out. That time I didn't have anything to worry about. I didn't worry about it before, or try to figure out what to wear, or watch the clock tick down, waiting for the moment it started, because I didn't know it was going to happen. It felt less... intense? I knew Roxanne for only a little while before we started dating.

I've known Phoenix for a lifetime, which honestly makes this whole thing that extra bit nerve-racking. He's held my hair back while I puked more times than I can count, so how much modesty do I really have left? I've never shaved anything for him, yet today I shaved so many inches of skin I should get a trophy. And what is it with this sweaty palms thing? If he tries to hold my hand, he's going to slide right off. Not the reason I want him to be talking about how wet I am.

For at least the twentieth time in as many minutes, I want to check to see if Phoenix has come back and is just waiting in the living room, hoping I'll pop out, but I don't. Why he left, I'm not really sure. At the moment, my mind will only spare a few seconds to think about it before I'm back to my worrying and stupid sweaty palms. I look at myself in the mirror over Phoenix's dresser, trying to find anything I can change. My eyes land on the ring that's lying in between my breasts, as if trying to hide. It's like it can sense that I'm still not completely sure if I'm keeping it on or not.

It's a ridiculous idea – I haven't taken it off yet, so why start now? But that's an even more ridiculous question – if I haven't yet, I will eventually. I don't think I'm ready to let go, even if I'm starting to move on. Sure, I can acknowledge how much I want to be with Phoenix and the love that I feel for him, but I can also acknowledge the love I feel for Roxanne. Does it bug Phoenix? When he's looking at me tonight, happy and excited for our date, will his night fall short when he can't stop looking at my dead wife's ring? Or will he accept that I still need that piece of her with me?

I'm being stupid. It's Phoenix, of course he'll support me. He's supported me through every single tough decision and hurdle in my life. He's not leaving me in the dust now. There's no way. Right? I twirl the ring in between my fingers, watching the light bounce off of it and rest on the walls and the dresser in front of me. The colored gems have always thrown people for a loop. They seem to question if it was the wrong choice. Roxanne used to get so many comments about it, questions about if she thought the ring was really right for her. I had no doubt when I picked it out for her. It wasn't *normal* or conventional, but it was perfect. If Roxanne was a ring, she'd definitely be this one.

It always made me smile when I'd hold her hand and feel it, or if it'd catch my eye. As I catch sight of my own wedding ring on my finger, sparkling in a more subtle way than hers does, I almost want to tear it off and get rid of it for good. I haven't been able to take it off and keep it off. In the months after Roxanne died, I couldn't take it off at all. I felt like if I didn't keep an eye on it, then it'd disappear forever. A little like Roxanne. The next step isn't just leaving Roxanne's ring behind, but mine as well.

Move on. Then let go.

I take a deep breath, dropping Roxanne's ring back onto my chest. "Move on, then let go."

A knock on the door jerks me out of my thoughts, and I quickly look at the clock. It's ten past eight. Phoenix is late, and I still have no clue where he went. If he bails on this date and I did all of this getting ready for nothing, I think I'll combust. Another knock comes, so I leave the bedroom, rushing to the door. As I whip it open, expecting a neighbor, or a package I'd need to sign for, I find a pleasant surprise.

Phoenix holds out a bouquet of flowers, taking my hand and kissing the back of it before handing the roses to me. "M'lady."

"My goodness. You're going the whole nine yards." I giggle as I hold the flowers to my nose and smell them.

"You said you wanted to do the real deal, so I'm doing the real deal." Phoenix grins at me like a kid on Christmas.

I grab an empty juice pitcher knowing full well that Phoenix doesn't have any vases, and fill it with water, resting the bouquet in it. "If this is what a first date with Phoenix Hickerman feels like, then I better watch out."

"This is what a first date for Mazey Sutton feels like. No one else is special enough to deserve this." He kisses my cheek, the butterflies already finding their way into my stomach.

As I grab my purse and my phone off the table, I give myself a second for a pep talk. This is fine, it's Phoenix; nothing's going to go wrong while Phoenix is here. "The VIP treatment. You're off to a great start."

After Phoenix locks the door, he grabs my hand and leads me down the hall to the elevator. As I follow behind him I can smell some kind of cologne he doesn't usually wear, one that smells like the Earth. For some reason, knowing he put effort into smelling nice for our date helps calm my nerves, but only a little bit. He pushes the button, making sure to lean as close to me as he can as he does so, and gives me a smug grin. "You look nice."

"Nice?" I scoff, walking into the elevator as the doors slide open. I turn back around, leaning against the cool walls, keeping my eyes on Phoenix as he pushes the button for the first floor. "That's all I get?"

Phoenix raises an eyebrow. "What? Are you saying you don't look nice?"

I shake my head. "No, I just... I dunno."

"Well, you do look nice, and hot, sexy, smoking... is that what you were looking for?" He drops his eyes to my chest, then back up to my eyes. "I noticed the dress. So we're playing it like that?"

I shrug and look away, trying to pretend I don't know what he's talking about, but feeling a little smile on my lips. "Playing it like what? I'm not playing anything."

Phoenix chuckles. "Yeah, right. And what is that?" He leans in really close to me, nuzzling his nose into the crock of my neck. "Are you wearing a new perfume?"

I focus my eyes on the wall across from me, trying not to melt into a puddle. "It's a sample I got from Olivia. Garden Breeze."

"Hmm," He leans back slightly, flicking his eyes up to mine and looking at me through his eyelashes. The elevator opens and he heads out into the walkway. "Wearing the same dress you wore the night we met is no coincidence."

The sudden jump from sensual to joking almost gives me whiplash and it takes me a moment to collect myself and respond. "Oh, is it the same dress? Hmm, didn't notice."

"Well, you missed the mark. This isn't my favorite thing for you to wear." He clicks his car key as we get into the parking lot, unlocking the doors.

I make my way to the passenger side door, silently fawning over the fact that Phoenix is following me over, probably to open my door for me. As we near the door, I look over my shoulder at him. "It isn't?"

"Nope," He leans past me, putting his hand on the door handle, but pressing his lips to my ear. "My favorite thing for you to wear is nothing."

I gasp, smacking his chest. "Phoenix!"

His devilish grin tells me he doesn't regret that in the least. He pulls the door open and steps back to give me room to get in. "A seat for the guest of honor."

My eyes roll. "You aren't coming back from that one so easily." I slide into the seat, trying to hide a smile as Phoenix shuts my door and heads around to the driver's side of the car.

He hops in, turning his key in the ignition and shaking out his arms towards me. He looks me in the eye, a playful look dancing in his, and grabs the sleeve of his button-down shirt. "Maybe this will help?"

"What?" I chuckle, confusion running through my brain.

Phoenix starts to roll up his sleeves, a sly smile pointed at me. "Oh, nothing, just getting a little bit of fresh air."

"Nix…" I eye him as he takes the sleeve on his other arm and rolls it up. My stomach clenches, and I curse him for that. The man knows me too well. Of course, he remembers I told him this. I mean, hearing someone's fetish is forearms is strange enough that he probably kept that tucked in the back of his mind for later use. And now he's pulling it out, practically throwing his arms in my face. "It's not hot if your arms are too close to me. I can't even see them."

Phoenix whistles, well, tries to whistle, which he can't do. "So you think I'm hot too?"

I roll my eyes. "Not fair, you're using this against me."

"Have you seen the way you look in that dress? *Mmm.* This is a fraction of what you're doing to me. I'm just making it a fair fight."

I lean towards him. "It's not a fight if we're both going to win." I tap my finger against his nose before leaning back in my seat.

"So I'm winning tonight?" He clicks his seatbelt into place as I click mine.

I shrug and smile at him, already answering the question before I open my mouth. "Why don't you impress me and we'll see?"

"Oh, yes, ma'am."

Phoenix whips out of the parking lot, changing the channel on the radio as he turns onto the road. The song plays softly as Phoenix sings along to it. I find myself getting lost in his voice, feeling the calm it always brings me, both when he's speaking and otherwise. The sound of *Phoenix* just feels right, like I'm meant to be listening to every word he says or song he sings. Not only that I should be listening, but that he's saying the things he's saying, or singing the verses he's singing because he *knows* I'm there listening – like it's all for me.

"So, where are you taking me, anyway?"

Phoenix looks over at me for a second, a mischievous grin on his face. With his eyes back on the road, he says. "I wouldn't tell you the first fifty times you asked me. What makes you think I'll start now?"

"'Cause now we're *on* the date. We're driving there right now, so it's no harm in telling me."

Phoenix chuckles. "Why do you want to know? You love surprises."

I shrug. "I don't know, I guess..."

"You're nervous, aren't you?" He reaches over and pokes me in the stomach.

I smack his hand away. "Um, no! I'm just not wanting – yeah, okay. I'm nervous."

Phoenix grins. "Aww, you're nervous?"

"Yes, jerkwad. Now don't make it a big deal."

"That's a good thing!" He grabs my hand and squeezes it. "I'm nervous too."

I feel my heart flutter in my chest. That is so freaking cute. "Oh, thank God."

He brings my hand up to his lips, kissing it. "We can be nervous together."

My whole entire stomach does a flip. Or probably several flips. I can't believe we're actually doing this. Going out there and going on a date like a dream come true. Phoenix is holding my hand, saying he's *nervous*, buying me flowers, and taking me to fancy restaurants? I think I might pass out here and now. I think my brain is lagging or something because I can't seem to process that I'm driving on my way to a date with Phoenix, who's nervous, and he's holding my hand and–

Calm down, Mazey. Geez, you're a mess right now. If this were literally anyone else, you'd be keeping your cool. Just because this is super-duper awesome doesn't mean I can lose it. Not that anything he's doing is going to help me *keep* it. I mean, first, he goes and does something sweet like get me a huge bouquet, then he opens my door and *rolls up his sleeves*. Damn him for knowing so much about me. He knows I have a thing for arms and he ran with it.

Not that I can say anything, I *do* look good in this dress

right now. Why own it if I'm not going to use it? It's not exactly like he's complaining. Granted, I'm not complaining about the sleeves either. I'm just saying, not fair. I look down at my hand, where it's sitting on Phoenix's thigh, tangled in his fingers. It'd be so easy to just reach up and – nope. I'm not throwing myself into that again. I told Phoenix slow, and he's giving it to me. I can't just go grabbing his dick and call that slow.

Or can I?

No, I can't. God, there I go, losing my cool again. I look out the window, trying to focus on something else, anything else. Not how warm his leg is beneath the underside of my hand, not the mere *inches* between my hand and something else more exciting. Nope, not thinking about that. Or my stupid abdomen, that's totally in twenty different kinds of knots right now. If my legs had minds of their own, they'd be spreading wide right now, but I'm not thinking about that. I can think about the cute dog on the sidewalk that's pulling at its leash so hard that its owner is tripping over their feet. Or the ice cream shop that's still packed with people in November.

Or I can think about Phoenix, dripping wet in the shower, hand clenched in my hair, eyes caught in mine...

"Mazey?"

I jerk my head in Phoenix's direction, where he looks at me, amusement dripping from his smile. "Yeah, uh, yes?"

Phoenix chuckles, turning his car off and undoing his seatbelt. "We're here. I figured with how intensely you were staring out the window you'd notice that we stopped moving."

"Oh, uh, yes. Yeah, no, I noticed." I nod, taking my hand from his before my brain can go on any more joy rides.

Phoenix shakes his head. "Uh-huh." He opens his door but stops and looks back at me, brow raised. "Are you just going to sit here, or do you need help with that?" He doesn't wait for a response, just reaches over for my seat belt, clicking it open.

I giggle before I get out of the car and take a deep breath. Now that I'm not physically touching him, I'll be fine. I'm good – no more journeys in my head. I'll be staying right here.

Phoenix comes over to my side of the car, grabbing my hand and smiling down at me before grabbing a piece of my hair and twirling it in between his fingers. "Like I said, you love surprises. So *hopefully*, you love this one."

"What did you do?" I question as Phoenix leads me around the restaurant we parked at. "Where are we going? You're not kidnapping me, right?"

Phoenix laughs. "No. I don't plan on kidnapping you any time soon."

If I weren't so confused, I'd be rolling my eyes at the 'any time soon' part, but I still have no clue where we're going. All that's in front of us is a hedge. We stop for a moment, and I see Phoenix's shoulders rise and fall with a deep breath before he motions me forward, and I turn, walking under a hedge arch. Beyond the hedge is a small little courtyard with flowers and bushes, and small trees with fairy lights hanging from their branches. In the center is a fountain, trickling so quietly I can barely hear it. Beside that is a table, decked out in a fancy table cloth, candles, and another flower bouquet in the center. I step forward, noticing something under my shoe – flower petals. The man put a path of flower petals to the table.

I feel my mind trying to put all the pieces into place, to process the scene in front of me. After a couple of seconds, I manage to mumble: "Holy shit."

Phoenix steps beside me, offering me his elbow. "Shall we?"

Heart swelling with love, I beam up at him, a super cheesy grin on my face.

He nudges me with his elbow. "I told you, only the best."

I grab onto it. "This is one hundred percent the best. Thank you."

He kisses my forehead. "Any time, Maz."

CHAPTER SEVEN

I narrow my eyes at the stove, trying to figure out why exactly it's not working. I've turned the knob, then turned it off, then on, then off, and I have no clue why it's not working. I mean, I'd never claim to be *good* in the kitchen, but usually, I'm at least competent. All I want are some damn scrambled eggs. Is that too much to ask? I try to turn the knob on again, and nothing happens... again. I groan, grabbing my phone off the counter to try to find the recipe for mug eggs I saw the other day. Thank God this is something I can do. I set my phone down and get the mug and the eggs. As I crack the egg in, *of course* little chunks of the shell fall in with it.

I grab a spoon to fish them out as best as possible, then add the rest of the seasonings it calls for. I pop it in the microwave, put on the time, and glare at the stove. All I want are eggs, and I can't even manage that. At least Phoenix can cook, but his cooking skills aren't useful to me when he's not here. He was gone when I woke up a little bit ago and hasn't come back since. He could make me eggs, and they'd be good eggs too, but instead, I'm going to get this mess.

I pull the mug out after it's done cooking and poke it with

my fork. Before I can think too hard about what they're going to taste like, I scoop some into my mouth. *And* they're disgusting. Great. I drop the mug and fork onto the counter, spitting the atrocity out of my mouth. Maybe I'll go somewhere? Except that Phoenix probably took the car wherever he went.

Just as I'm starting to debate throwing the mug of my eggs across the room, the door opens. Phoenix walks in and smiles at me. "Hey, you're up!"

My eyes drop directly to the bag of food he's holding. "You brought me food?"

He grins like he's proud of himself. "Yes, I did."

As I walk around the counter to grab it from him, someone else walks through the door. "Lincoln?"

"Hey," he waves as he kicks his shoes off beside the door. When he looks up at me, he points at my legs. "Mazey, hon, your ass is out."

I pull my t-shirt down, trying to make it longer than it is. "Uh, yeah. I didn't realize someone was coming over."

"Sorry, I didn't think you'd be walking around in your underwear." Phoenix's smile says that he doesn't mind it, but I do. Poor Lincoln is looking everywhere but me. "We had breakfast. Hence the food. Figured I'd bring you something back."

"Thank you, I appreciate it." I eye my egg mug. "I was pretty hungry."

Phoenix grabs the mug off the counter, laughing as he examines my horrible creation. "What is this?"

"It's supposed to be eggs in a mug. It tastes like ass." I grumble, taking it from Phoenix and putting it in the sink. "I'm gonna go put pants on." I go into the room, grabbing a pair of Phoenix's sweats to throw on. I tug on the strings to tighten it as best as I can, the ends of the legs already rolled up from when I wore them last night. When I go back out into the living room, Phoenix and Lincoln are sitting on the sofa, a plate of fries in Lincoln's hand. I go in, dropping into the armchair next to Lincoln, grabbing my food off the table where they had laid it out. "Pancakes!"

"Ha!" Lincoln shouts, mouth full of fries. "I was right, pancakes."

I look between them. "What?"

Phoenix sighs. "When we were ordering the food for you, we disagreed about what to get you. I said a breakfast burrito–"

"–and I said pancakes." Lincoln snaps playfully and points at the plate in my hand, where I've already ripped a piece of the top pancake off and stuffed it in my mouth.

I nod. "Yeah, sorry, pancakes over a burrito any day."

Phoenix rolls his eyes at Lincoln as he leans forward to search through the bag on the coffee table. After a second, he groans. "I forgot my leftovers in the car." He gets up, keys getting pulled from his pocket. "I'll be back."

He leaves the room on the journey for his food, leaving me and Lincoln in silence. After just a moment, Lincoln puts his fries beside him and sets his eyes on me. "I have to talk to you."

"Ah, crud." I huff, dropping my pancakes down on the table beside me. "What? What do you wanna talk about this time?"

Lincoln gets a playful look in his eyes. "I thought you enjoyed our impromptu conversations as much as me?"

I narrow my eyes at him. "Get to the point, Lincoln."

He takes my grumpiness in stride as he smiles at me. "Phoenix."

"Uh-huh?"

"You two are together now? Having sex and the works?"

"Lincoln!" I jump out of the chair, arms thrown up beside me. "What the hell kind of question is that?"

He scoffs. "A pretty relevant one, I'd say." He holds his hands out in front of him. "Not really the point, I concede. The point is that Phoenix needs this."

"I'm not in the mood for one of your stupid talks right now. Can we just—"

"Mazey, sit down. Listen to me." He snaps, a serious tone under his words.

I look at him, startled, lowering myself into the chair. "Geez, fine. Talk then."

Lincoln sighs. "We both care about Phoenix, right? That's something we can agree on?" He doesn't wait for me to answer before continuing. "So we both want him to be happy, to get what he wants. What he wants is you."

"We're dating, Linc. He has me."

"No, not just a little bit. Not just maybe. He has to have all of you. You have to be ready to commit to him. Now I *know* that you've already given up and lost so much in your life, so it's not exactly fair to ask you to give up anymore, but... you need to be ready to. For Phoenix, please, Mazey, I'm asking you to just keep an open mind. I'm asking you to be okay with meeting him halfway and being willing to stay with him, no matter what." His eyes are so serious it scares me a little. He's never this serious. "Can you do that?"

I pause for a second as I think of the best response. "Lincoln... you're kind of freaking me out."

"I'm sorry, Maz, I don't mean to. I just need Phoenix to finally get the girl. He's been following you around for so long, pinning after you, I'm just ready to see him with you." He puts the light-hearted smile back on as he nudges my knee. "I mean, that's not too hard for you to do since, like you said, you're already dating!"

I open my mouth to say something, question his weird behavior, but the door opens as Phoenix comes back into the apartment. Phoenix kicks the door shut with his foot. "It's hot as balls out right now. It's November, it should be cold. I hate this weather."

"Wow, so eloquently put." Lincoln laughs, pushing himself off the couch. "And with that, I'm going to leave. I have to relieve... I've got to get home," He looks away, grabbing his wallet and keys off the coffee table.

Ignoring how weird that was, I get up and hug him. "Bye,"

"See you next Friday?" Phoenix asks as they walk to the front door.

Lincoln smacks his hand in a very manly handshake. "Yep. See you then. Bye, Maz." He waves to me, then ducks out the door.

"Is Lincoln okay?" I grab the trash off the coffee table and dump it in the garbage.

Phoenix follows with more trash in his hands. "Why wouldn't he be?"

"He got all... weird." I shove the trash down, so it fits. "He flat out asked me if we were having sex."

"And what did you say?"

I scoff. "I didn't answer. Not that I need to, we haven't."

"Yes, we did. We definitely screwed"

I roll my eyes. "Hardly. Screwing requires things to go in holes."

That makes Phoenix's mouth pull into a smile, a very playful one. "If I recall correctly, things did go in holes. Just different holes."

I smack his chest. "Don't be crude."

"Crude? What are you, my mother? When have you ever been afraid of a little crudeness."

"When the crudeness is about your thing in my holes." I feel my cheeks flush slightly like they used to when I was a freaking pre-teen. What is happening to me? "Just stop talking about it."

Phoenix runs his thumb over my presumably pink cheeks, chuckling. "Mazey Sutton, are you blushing?"

"I said, stop talking about it, jerk."

He pulls me closer to him, hands wrapped around my waist. "Fine, I won't talk then." He leans down and presses his lips to mine.

My stupid cheeks flame ten times hotter, acting like I've never kissed anyone before. Not only have I kissed *someone*, but I've also kissed this specific someone. This is different than the times we've kissed before. When we'd kiss, it was always leading somewhere. Not even in a way where it *eventually* leads somewhere, we both knew going into it that we were having sex. This is much less... I don't know. It's not less hot; the warmth in my veins, and the flush of my cheeks can tell me that. Not less passionate, my stupid fluttering heart and my ridiculously weak knees agree. It's more... innocent?

He's kissing me, and I'm kissing him, but it's not going anywhere. We're staying right here, in his kitchen, kissing. His hands aren't traveling around my body, trying to find my breasts, they're staying in innocent areas – *I've-just-started-dating-this-person* areas. When I'd normally start whipping my shirt off, and Phoenix would start undoing his pants, he pulls back instead.

I look up at him, chest rising and falling rapidly as I try to catch my breath. I nod slowly. "Yeah, I'll take that over you poking fun at me."

"Good, because I plan on doing it again soon." He lets go of me, eyes running all over me.

I rest against the counter, my whole body on hyper-alert for what he's going to do next. "I hope not too soon, 'cause I think my brain just short-circuited."

"Oh, really?" He smiles at me in the cockiest way possible. "My kiss short-circuited your brain?"

I roll my eyes, turning away from him, so I don't have to

look at his stupidly entrancing eyes. "Don't even start. I didn't say that to boost your ego."

"Consider it boosted." He rubs his hands together and slides onto one of the high chairs at the island. "I won't say anything more, but you should definitely prepare to have it happen again."

"Oh, God, just forget I ever said anything." I clean my disastrous attempt at eggs in a mug as I look up at Phoenix.

He's looking right back at me, a much more thoughtful look on his face. "I know you just got here, so I don't mean to push you, but... what do you think you're going to do for money? I've got enough saved up to keep you alive." He leans forward, fingers tapping against the countertop. "You can stay here for... well, I just... figured I'd ask."

I set the mug on the drying rack and reach forward to grab his hands, "I'm not going to live off of your money. I honestly hadn't thought about it. I've been so wrapped up in if I'd even stay or not that I didn't think about after that." I lean against the counter. "I have no clue where I'd even start. The last job I had was at a fast-food restaurant, and before that, I hadn't worked for a couple of years. I have a stupid biology degree, but it's been almost four years since I graduated and I've never had a job related to biology. The closest I've ever gotten was my job at that seafood shop in college where the owner promoted me to assistant manager because I was her only employee and she liked me. I don't know where I'd start now."

"Well, you had *something* you wanted to do before you got shoved into that biology degree."

I nod slowly. "Yeah, I wanted to have a café. I thought it'd be something cute and small. We'd serve ice cream type drinks in the summer, and there could be someone more competent than me making pastries, and I'd make salads. Lincoln always pointed out it could be an internet café too –

charge people by the hour to let them sit in the comfy chairs and use the Wi-Fi. I don't know if I really agree with that one."

"So why don't you do that?"

"Uh, what?"

He shrugs. "Why not do it? That's what you want to do, right?"

"I mean, yeah. That was when I was younger, but–"

"Well, if it still is, then you should do it." Phoenix gets up and grabs a piece of paper and a pen from a drawer, slapping it down in front of me. "Write it all down, figure it out. Do you still want a cute, quiet café?"

I look down at the piece of paper, then back up at him, trying to play catch up. Is it? It feels like so long ago that I was even fighting for it. When I think of a perfect life, it always involves a little café. "I think so, yeah."

"Then try it out." Phoenix puts his hand on my cheek. "You should have your dream job, not just some job that will make you money."

I shake my head. "I need money. My savings are only a purchase away from being zero. I lived off what Roxanne and I built up for almost a year... I need to make money, not play around with something that may never happen."

Phoenix pokes the paper with his finger and gets his serious face on. "Do what is going to make you happy, Maz. Ignore the lies Roxanne pushed on you all those years and focus on what makes *you* happy. As far as I can tell, all the things that made you go for the safe route are gone." He takes the same finger and uses it to push my chin up, so I'm looking into his eyes. "I got you, okay? I'm here to pay for whatever shit you need until you're on your feet. If this café is what will make that cute as shit smile stay on your face, then I think you should go after it."

"Really? It'd take so much work, and who knows how long

it'd take until I'd be able to pay bills or for food? I'd have to find someone willing to work at a business that's just getting started, and what do I know about running a business? And when this was my dream – *nine* years ago, by the way – I had the intention of making some of the food. I screwed up an egg mug today, Phoenix." I feel my voice start to go whiney, and before Phoenix can slap it out of me, I take a deep breath and stare at the paper like it holds all the answers. "It *could* be cute... and the pastry chef and I would become besties. Lincoln could help me figure out how to charge for Wi-Fi like the American capitalist I am. It'd be so freaking adorable!"

Phoenix smiles down at me, excitement levels almost matching mine, which is saying something. "That, right there. Mazey, babe, you should be looking like that every second of every day. If this is what's going to do that, then get on it. Go! *You* are going to sit right here," He scoots me around the counter, pulling out the chair so I can jump on, "and write down everything you want in your café." He plants the paper and pen in front of me. "*I* am going to go run some errands."

"Phoenix! I asked you if you had stuff you had to do. You said no."

He shrugs, already starting to walk. "Welp, oh well. I'll be back before dinner. See you when you have your plan!"

I roll my eyes at his back, watching him go to the front door, shoving keys in his pocket, and winking at me as he closes the door. My smile only gets bigger, which I wouldn't have guessed was even possible. My cheeks are starting to hurt – I can't remember the last time I was smiling this much. I've been here for like a week and my brain has gone through such a roller coaster of feelings. While being here hasn't improved my relationship with Suzan, I'll be damned if bringing me to Florida wasn't the perfect idea. I've been hiding away from everything... every*one* and now that I'm here, I find myself wishing I'd gotten here sooner. Can it be all good if I have barely thought of someone who used to be my everything? Roxanne's memory is with me, and if I'm getting lost in all that's been happening, I'm not remembering her as much.

Who's talking to her every night and mourning her loss? Every second I'm here falling for Phoenix is another second I'm acting like I didn't make the biggest mistake of my life by leaving Roxanne that night. The night she died, I chose Phoenix over her. This last year and a half, I've been choosing her over everyone. Even that can't be enough to make up for how she left this world. Some things can't ever be made up. Will I ever feel like I've repaid her, or will I be pinned down by the debt I owe her for every single living moment I have left without her?

The first time, all those years ago, when I had the chance to choose between Roxanne and Phoenix, and all I had were mere weeks to pick through and pine over my decision, I chose Roxanne. When I made my first decision, did I make the *right* decision, or were the terrible decisions I've made since then because I know deep down that the first choice was the wrong choice?

CHAPTER EIGHT

I sigh as my phone goes to voicemail, again. Every single day since we had our date, Phoenix runs off from breakfast to dinner, always with a different excuse and never answering his phone. Today he said Lincoln needed help hanging a TV. Yesterday it was that he needed a quiet place to work, that I was a distraction. I can't help the nagging feeling that he's hiding away, that I'm the thing he's hiding from.

While Phoenix is gone and Olivia, Vincent, Nikkie, and Eric are all in school, I don't really have much to do. I busy myself with working on the café plans and when I can't possibly use any more brain power, I sit and watch reruns of shows. I'm going to finish an entire series if he keeps this up. Not that I can really be all that upset with him. If he didn't have a job where he worked from home, he'd be gone most of this time anyway. Plus, I just appeared into his life, out of nowhere. Can I really be mad if he has plans other than me?

Even with that, though, as I lay on the couch, staring at the ceiling, while an action sequence takes place on the TV, all I can think about is how much this feels like my life with Roxanne. After college, when she asked me to stop working and be a housewife, I would sit there, doing nothing, all day. It felt miserable, like I had no purpose outside of Roxanne and what she was doing. I'd sit there, between when she left for work and got back from work, and felt like I'd accomplished nothing.

All of this thinking is making me go crazy. Yesterday, while Phoenix was gone, I got so bored I was tempted to go into that third room and organize it for him. The thing that stopped me wasn't how much I hate organizing, it was that Phoenix asked me not to go in there, and I was still really tempted. I pull my phone out from underneath my back, looking at the time. It's a quarter to six, Phoenix should be getting back some time in the next two hours. I'm starving, so hopefully he brings home dinner.

I groan, pushing myself off the couch and wandering into Phoenix's room. My suitcases are still sitting on the floor. I haven't decided if I want to stay here. On the one hand, I hate feeling like I'm in Phoenix's way. I doubt he anticipated me living with him when he flew me down from Seattle. On the other hand, I don't really have anywhere else to go. So, unpacking it is, I guess. I can always pack back up, which I've learned from running out of Suzan's house like my ass was on fire.

I pull one of the cases closer to me, grabbing out a few of my favorite shirts, going into Phoenix's walk-in closet. He's an absolute mess in here, with boxes taking up most of the space behind the shirts and pants hanging up. I have to shove a few out of my way to grab the empty hangers in the corner. As I move a box that's sitting with its lids flipped out, it tips over, spilling everything in it onto the floor. "Shit," I mumble, dropping my shirt onto the wire shelf, bending down to pick it all up.

As I look down at what exactly it was that spilled, I actually feel a question working its way out of my mouth. Phoenix has a box full of kids' books. I pick each one up, looking at the age printed on the front. All are too young for Georgie. Why on earth does Phoenix have a box of kids' books sitting in his closet? As I'm putting the books back in the books, my brain still trying to answer that question, I hear the front door shut and Phoenix calling out my name.

"In here," I shout back as I pick up the books in my hand and stand.

Phoenix comes into the room, "Where are—" He stops when he sees me standing in the closet. He looks to the books in my hands, then back up to me. He doesn't say anything for the full minute I wait.

I drop the books back into the box and close the flaps. I push it back where it was, not failing to notice how Phoenix flinches as I do. "Why are you acting weird? Did something happen at Lincoln's?"

He finally drags his eyes away from the box on the floor and up to my eyes. "Uh, no. No, nothing happened."

"Okay..." I grab the shirts back off the shelf and start to hang them up. "Then why are you acting weird?"

He comes into the closet, grabbing me by the shoulders and guiding me out. "I'm not, just really hungry. I didn't get a chance to eat lunch."

"Oh, okay." I grab my phone from where I left it on the floor. "Hey, what were those books for?"

Phoenix pinches his nose. "Yeah, those. I keep meaning to donate them. Dylan did a book drive and I helped. Never got around to actually doing anything with them."

I nod, following Phoenix to the front door. "That's sweet of you. Oh, hey, I saw this post about an art fair not too far from here. Can we go tomorrow if you don't have plans?"

He smiles at me as he holds the front door open for me to walk through. "Sure, I can figure it out."

◆ ◆ ◆

"Whatcha doing?" I wrap my arms around Phoenix's shoulders, hands running down his bare chest.

He chuckles, his own hands resting over mine. "I'm writing my article. I've been getting behind."

I kiss his cheek, giggling. "I wonder why."

He spins around his chair. "I couldn't guess." He nods to me. "Maybe it has something to do with the fact that you're showing up in my office, half-naked?"

"Oh, that," I smile mischievously. "Well, I was thinking–"

"Not a good thing."

I pull my hands from his and smack his arm. "Do you want me to finish telling you why you see so much skin?"

"Yes, proceed." He leans back in his chair, cocking his head to the side and giving me his attention.

I smile again. "Well, I was *thinking* that the rule is three dates, right?"

"What rule?"

"The *when-to-screw* rule. It says you have sex on the third date."

He nods slowly. "Okay…"

"Yes, well, it came to my attention that our first date was a week ago, right?"

"Yeah, sure."

"Since then, we've spent every night together, but we take breaks in between to sleep. Okay? So by my calculations, we're on our eighth date right now, which means you need to fuck me."

Phoenix nearly chokes on his own throat, seemingly much more intrigued. "I'm sorry, say that again?"

"I said you're overdue. We should have had sex already."

I watch as emotions run over his face: confusion, excitement, and then confusion again. "Are you saying you want to have sex?"

"I don't think I could make it more obvious." I shrug. "But yes."

"What happened to taking it slow?"

I point at him, nodding in agreement. "Yes, that. Well, I've decided that I could be using this time to see you naked, completely and up close, and not just sit and ogle you from a distance."

"You're *ogling* me?"

"Mmhmm, yep. Though I'd much rather ogle all of it, so c'mon and take your pants off." I motion at him to get going.

He chuckles. "I think... I think my brain needs a moment to catch up. It's a little confused."

"Well, as it would be, but I need less talking and more stripping."

"I just... are you sure? I don't want to..."

"For the love of God." I groan, grabbing the hem of my crop top, taking it off. I throw it in his lap before taking off my shorts and dropping that in his lap too. "Now, this is as clear as I can be without taking your dick out myself, *so* if you could kindly—"

Phoenix jumps out of his chair, pressing his lips to mine just about as fast as I wanted him to in the first place. The clothes I had put in his lap fall onto my feet and I kick them to the side. Not two seconds later, Phoenix chucks his own shirt into the mix, my hands already running themselves over the divots of his abs. If I wasn't in the middle of kissing Phoenix, I think I'd be doing a little happy dance, maybe a jig, but my hands are preoccupied running themselves over just about every inch of skin they can. And my legs, well, my legs don't seem like they'll be holding me up much longer because I'm pretty sure I might collapse to the ground. We're doing it. We're not just doing something, we're doing *it*.

My fingers run through his silky smooth hair, my other hand gripped to his bicep as it flexes under my palm. He tastes like cinnamon and sugar, like sweet cinnamon buns. My brain is definitely fighting over whether to be nervous or excited during this experience. Just as nerves are about to win out, Phoenix pulls back from the kiss to yank me towards him. I ungracefully tumble onto him, dropping both of us onto his office chair, and not very comfortably.

I laugh, hair falling into my face. "What the hell was that?"

Phoenix snorts, moving us onto the floor, so I'm straddling his legs. "Just... ignore that. Pretend that was smooth."

"Mm-hmm. Okay." I shake my head, quickly kissing him again, capturing his mouth with mine. He responds with an equal amount of enthusiasm, pulling me so tight against him that I think I can feel his heartbeat mixing with mine. Or maybe it's my heartbeat mixing with his. Whoever's it is, it's definitely racing. I can feel my blood pumping in my fingers so hard I'm a little worried they may explode.

He moans into my mouth, making my whole body scream. The lingering smell of honey he always has on him from his soap smothering me in sweetness. If this man doesn't stop being so damn hot, I may not be able to function after this. Honestly, I may not even be able to function right now because somehow, I manage to get myself stuck in his hair. I pull away from him, trying to see what exactly I did. It's my ring. My wedding ring. I get it out, sliding off of Phoenix and staring at it.

Phoenix takes a deep breath. "It's okay, Maz. We don't have to..."

"No, I... I'm sorry. I didn't mean to be weird."

Phoenix squeezes my leg. "You're not being weird, I get it. We can go slower."

I shut my eyes, quickly shaking my head. "I want to. I *have* wanted to. We are screwing, right now." I look down at the ring, taking a deep breath before pulling it off my finger. I wait a minute, maybe to see if Roxanne strikes me dead, or maybe to see if the world stops spinning, but nothing happens. Everything is fine. I reach over to the desk and rest the ring on top of it. When I turn back to Phoenix, he has his eyebrow raised higher than it should be able to go.

"Are you sure?"

"Would you stop asking me that?" I chuckle, brushing hair off of his forehead.

He shrugs. "I want to make sure you're sure."

"I am." I nod slowly. "I'm sure."

"Okay, then get over here."

I lean forward and kiss him again, yanking on his sweats. "Take 'em off," I mumble against his lips.

He laughs. "Yes, ma'am." He pulls them off, throwing them somewhere else, forgetting about them instantly.

My eyes drift down, taking their time to *ogle* as much of him as I wanted to before and definitely enjoying the view. Just like every other time I've been here with Phoenix, I find my stomach squirming and my heart racing. I never stop loving the way his body looks, eating it up with the same eager gaze I have every other time before. I look up, meeting his eyes, and just like the times before, I'm captured by his stare. But this time... this time when he's looking at me like he couldn't adore me more, I'm actually embracing it. The times we've been together before have all been different than this time. This time we're *both* here, ready to commit, equally. There's nothing stopping us. There aren't any obstacles in the way.

As I move towards him, grabbing his lips with mine, it

feels like this is all I need. If the whole world washed away, I could stay right here forever. Phoenix reaches between my legs, rubbing his fingers right where I want them. If it wasn't super-duper embarrassment, I'd be making the noise of a whole damn orchestra right now. I open my eyes, not realizing I had squeezed them closed in the first place, and see Phoenix smirking at me. Just as I'm about to shut them right back, his fingers retreat. I take a second to compose myself, but then he throws composure to the wind. He brings his fingers to his mouth, sucking on them before dragging them back out, eyes stuck on mine.

My mouth must fall open a good fifty feet as I feel fire sprint through my veins. "Holy Hell, why was that so hot?"

"I don't kno– oh–"

I practically tackle the poor guy, not able to throw my leg over him fast enough, frantically grabbing his dick and sliding onto it. I moan, any thoughts of embarrassing flying from my mind as I feel my breath hitch and I push my palms against Phoenix's chest.

"Why is *that* so hot?" He mumbles, pressing his fingers into my hips, guiding me up and down. He pushes his head back against the floor, making a noise in the back of his throat that makes my insides do a happy jump.

I feel my mind spinning, trying to process everything that's happening around me and *in* me. I can't take my eyes off his face, both pinched in concentration and full of relaxing happiness. The sharp edge of his jaw, the slenderness of his nose. His lips, slightly puffy and red, hiding that dazzling, panty-dropper smile. My gaze wanders to his hair, disheveled and flopped over his forehead, then to his eyes, that striking blue that sends shivers through my whole body like lightning every time he looks at me. Then my eyes follow his, looking at what he's watching so carefully. He's trained on where our bodies are meeting, watching the motion of use moving in and out with each other.

I've had sex with Phoenix before. Different ages, different places, and different ways. One thing that always manages to surprise me is how *good* this feels. It's like all of our pieces fit right into the right spots, forming a whole, complete puzzle. I like this puzzle. This is a great freaking puzzle, that's for sure. A puzzle that's getting really tiring. It forgot how much effort all this bouncing takes. I'm already out of breath. I try not to think of Phoenix making fun of my lack of endurance, since the man is a machine, and stop. "Switch."

"Switch?"

I nod. "Yes, switch. I'm out of breath."

"You're hopeless."

I roll my eyes as I climb off of him. "Not hopeless, just lacking in the cardio department."

He just smiles at me, leaning me, so I'm flat on my back before he starts to hover over me, grabbing my leg and pushing it up.

"Where do you think that's going?" I ask, a little concerned by this maneuver.

He looks at my leg then back at me. "Up there?"

"I don't know if I'm that flexible."

He pushes my leg farther up against my ear, leaning against it, trying to prove his point. "Yes, you are. See?"

"When I'm sore tomorrow, it's going to be your damn fault," I grumble, spreading my other leg open to give him room.

He kisses my leg. "I'll massage your leg and bring you breakfast in bed. Don't you worry."

"Oh, I'm... okay." I lose my words as he thrusts into me, not taking his eyes off mine for a second. "I'm going to be sore."

His lips stretch as he holds back a laugh. "I told you, I'll take care of you."

My mind trips a little hearing that. He didn't mean he'll take care of me forever, just tomorrow, but his care could make crappy days so much better. So what if that care comes after he bends me into shapes I definitely shouldn't be in? Just the thought of it makes my heart swoon. What happens when it actually comes true, and Phoenix brings me breakfast in bed, massaging my leg as I eat my French toast? Definite swooning. Then he's going to make a joke about *why* he has to even massage my thigh in the first place. Then I'll swoon some more and probably jump his bones like I did today.

I've been here less than two weeks, and in those two weeks, I've managed to not only suck his dick in a shower but then ride it days later. Either I'm just a sucker for his charm, or neither of us has much willpower. As far as I can tell, this is definitely not our third date, and if time spent together was the same thing as dates, then we'd be counting in years. So my logic was a little flawed, but I won't knock it, and I don't think Phoenix will either.

"*Mazey–*" He moans, pushing far into me and holding himself there as I feel my insides fill up. I look intently at him, both wanting to laugh at his face as he orgasms and feeling a strange, comforting blanket drape over me. After a moment, Phoenix drops his forehead to mine, kissing my nose. "Best fourth date ever."

I kiss him back on the lips. "I'll bet the fifth date will be even better."

"The fifth one?" He rolls off me, and I feel a whole bunch of liquid pools out of me. Phoenix grabs his shirt, wiping me off before looking at it and scrunching his nose. "I guess I could have thought that one through a little better."

I push the shirt aside, shrugging. "Thought through or not, you just got your own cum on your shirt."

"Yeah... I'll have to clean that more than once." He grins at me, and I grin back. "What?"

I purse my lips. "How about we have our fifth date right now and you do more of the fun finger stuff."

"Finger stuff? You sound like a grown-up."

"Oh, shove it. Preferably in there," I point in between my legs, making him laugh.

He lays me back again, pressing his lips onto my inner thigh, looking up at me from down my body. He looks up at me through his eyelashes, a sexy smile on his lips before he buries his tongue back where he was just moments before.

As the door falls shut behind him, Phoenix drops a plastic grocery bag onto the kitchen counter. I smile at him and point to the coffee table where the remainder of my Chinese dinner is sitting. Once the clock hit eight, I was too hungry to wait for him anymore. "I have leftovers for you."

He comes over, the contents of his plastic bag in his hands, leaning over the back of the couch and kissing me quickly before coming around to sit down. "Great minds think alike. I brought you some snacks." He hands me a pile of processed foods, keeping a couple protein bars and an apple in his own lap.

"Why'd you grab all this food?"

Phoenix shrugs. "I was at the store. I got you some of the snacks you like."

I look through the pile on my lap, seeing most of my favorite candies and snacks. "Thank you?"

"Yeah, sure." He flips the TV on and immediately turns

Netflix to the screen. "I saw this show on my recommendations the other day that I think you'll like. I watched the trailer, but we'll have to see if it's any good."

I open up my bag of mini Twix. "Well, let's see."

Phoenix turns it on, dropping the remote beside him, reaching for the bag of Cheetos.

I pull it away from him. "You're on a diet."

"Ugh, fine." He leans forward, grabbing the container of chicken.

When he leans back, I rest my head on his shoulder, taking a deep breath. This... this is what I want. I want to just chill, exist. Be able to lounge around with my favorite person, not have to worry about life or death. Be able to watch a TV show, curled up on the couch, snack on some food. I want to be able to spend a day not having to worry about anything else. Not think about anything else. Not even have bad memories surface. When I'm with Phoenix, I feel like I can take on the world, bear everything on my shoulders. Like the weight of what's happened is lighter.

When Phoenix smiles at me, laughs near me, talks to me, he makes my life better. He makes me forget all the bad and start remembering the good. Even something as small as bringing me these snacks makes me feel cared for and loved. He notices the small things and keeps them in his memory. He knows me so well I can just sit here and be. I didn't realize how much I missed this until now, sitting around completely comfortable. I twist my ring on my finger, smiling down at it. Someday I won't feel any more sadness when I look down at this ring, but for now, I'm glad that the pain hurts a little bit less.

"Mazey!" Phoenix yells from the other room like it's an incredibly urgent matter. The last dozen times he's done this, it ends up being something he could do himself. Like, get a drink. Or find a pen. Or whatever absurdness he's got this time. "Do you know where my phone is?"

I glance around the room until I see it sitting on the counter. "It's in the kitchen."

"Can you grab it for me?"

"You're right there, just come get it yourself." I turn my attention back to the papers in front of me, finding the numbers I was adding up before and trying to continue my math.

Phoenix comes into the room. "I just needed the date."

"Well, if you had asked for the date, instead of your phone, I would have told you that it's the twelfth." I look up at him, smiling at him with a bucket of sass.

He just shakes his head and runs back into his office. After a second, he runs back out, coming over to where I'm sitting on the couch, and throwing his arms around my shoulders from behind. "What are you working on now?"

I hold the paper up for him to see. "I'm trying to figure out how long it would take for me to start making any money while paying the baker, and the rent for space, and buying supplies... so far, all I've got is never. My math keeps coming up weird."

"Is that what the next step of a business plan is?" Phoenix walks around the couch, dropping down next to me, pressing his side against mine.

I shrug, putting the paper back onto the lap desk in front of me. "I have no clue. I don't know anything about business plans, and neither do you, Mr. Sports Medicine."

"I wasn't saying I do, Ms. *Biology*. So there's no need for sarcasm." He kisses my cheek before picking up my paper. "You know what I said; I can be your sugar daddy."

I fake gag. "Do not call yourself my sugar daddy." I turn towards him, resisting the urge to pout my lips and whine as I think about the negative numbers on my paper. "I'm worried that this may not be practical."

"Mazey, babe, don't worry about practical. I'll support you until you're on your feet."

I sigh. "No, I'm saying what if I never get on my feet? It's nice of you to offer, but I need to think about how much I could practically make. Don't they say you don't make money for the first six years?"

"I think it's five."

"Six years is a long time for you to be supporting both of us." I feel my brain halt, bringing a very important question to the front of my mind. What if we're not together for six years? What if I start down this path and halfway through Phoenix and I break up? Yes, we've been friends for years, but friends and partners are two different things, and we've been 'partners' for such a short time. Most people would wait months, or years, before relying so heavily on the person they're dating. I don't even know what this is yet. I have no clue if I'm his girlfriend or his fuck buddy.

Well, I'd guess not fuck buddy. He convinced me to leave my wife once upon a time. You don't do that unless you're serious, but what if he's not as serious a year from now?

"You're letting all the bullshit Roxanne shoved in your head take over. Don't let her keep telling you what to do. It was bad enough when she was alive, but from her grave—"

"Why do you keep saying that?" I put my lap desk on the ground, scooting away from Phoenix enough to be able to look at him. "You keep saying stuff about Roxanne. Why do you have to bring her up?"

Phoenix sighs. He gives me a condescending look, like

he's about to explain something complex to a child. "I'm bringing her up because she plays a huge role in this, Mazey. She's the whole reason you changed your major. Changed your dream–"

"My dream was Roxanne. It was to have kids, and to raise a family, and to be with Roxanne. That isn't her fault. That's what *I* chose."

Phoenix grabs my hand. "You didn't want any of that. Not until Roxanne told you that you did."

I jump off the couch. "Stop that. Stop trying to mess up the way I see Roxanne. I'm giving you a chance, okay? You don't have to dump on her to get me, 'cause I already said yes."

"I don't want to mess up the way you think about her. Mazey, nothing I'm saying is me trying to convince you to be with me, or–"

"Then what are you trying to do exactly?"

Phoenix stands, reaching out for my hand. I pull it away. "I'm trying to tell you that you can do whatever you want. You don't have to bend to someone else's wishes anymore. If you don't want to do the café, then that's fine. If you want to have a dozen cafés, that's fine too. I want you to do what you want. But *you* don't want to do what you want."

"That doesn't make any sense. Of course, I'm doing what I want."

"No. Kids, a wife, and a house were never your dreams. And no – *no*. Don't tell me they were, 'cause they weren't. When you first moved here, you came to my room once a week to have me help you with your bio homework. You said that you hated science and the worst thing about it was biology. That doesn't sound like someone whose dream was to study biology."

"I never said my dream was to study biology. I said my

dream was to be able to afford the things you need to have a family."

Phoenix looks like he wants to punch me in the face, but instead, he takes a deep breath before talking. "I remember when you were trying to figure all of this out years ago, Mazey. I was *there*. You talked to me about it again and again. She told you anything she could to get you to agree with her, that you'd be happier once you were making more money. When y'all started a family, you needed to be secure. When those things didn't work, she tried other things. That she didn't know if she could handle the stress of dating a small business owner, she wanted someone driven, and you just weren't seeming driven enough."

"I was there too. I remember."

Phoenix throws his hands into the air. "Then why can't you remember that you went from hating the idea to loving it. Not because of what you wanted, but because of her."

"I... I don't..." I find myself lowering onto the couch, trying to sort through all the memories and moments flying through my head. Roxanne and I used to fight. A lot. We always had, and I knew we always would. We *did* until the last second I saw her alive. Those fights always ended up one of two ways. Roxanne won, or Roxanne got too pissed to keep talking, in which case we'd do what she wanted anyway. So, in the end, she always won.

"I know you loved her. I did too. She was my sister, but you can't keep letting her make all your decisions and create all your dreams for you." He sinks into the couch next to me. We sit in silence for long enough that I'd usually start getting uncomfortable. As if Phoenix and I silently agreed we were ready to move on, he picks my lap desk off the floor and looks at the papers. "Now, tell me about how much you're selling your oatmeal chocolate chip cookies for. Those are my favorite."

I grab the page that shows my guesses for how much everything will be and point at the oatmeal chocolate chip. "For you, they're free, though." I kiss his cheek and rest my head against his shoulder. I open my mouth to say something, to acknowledge the overwhelming amount of emotion I feel in my chest right now. I can't find the right words for him, so instead, I say it in my head. *Thank you*.

I fall forward onto the bed, catching myself with my hands as my chest heaves, trying to catch my breath. A smile tugs my lips as I take a deep breath. "I liked that one more."

Phoenix flops onto the bed beside me, pecking my lips with a kiss before rolling his condom off and trying to throw it into the trash can by the door. "That's because you're lazy."

"Huh, excuse you, I am not lazy!"

"Yes, you are! Your top picks all involve me doing all the work."

I turn around, so I'm sitting on the bed, leaning forward to kiss his chest, "It's not because I'm lazy. It's because they feel the best."

Phoenix huffs. "Yeah, sure. Whatever you say."

I roll my eyes before stretching out onto the blanket with a yawn. "How long were we at it?"

"It's uh…" He reaches over and turns the clock so he can read it. "It's three in the morning."

I snort as I try to keep in a chuckle. "God, we're acting like sex-crazed fiends."

"Well, aren't we?"

"I hope not, geez." I grab a pillow from the top of the bed

and put it under my head. "I'm exhausted. I could just fall asleep right now."

Phoenix pokes my cheek. "Nope. You promised me we'd watch my movie."

I groan. "Ugh, yes, I did. Fine, but you promised me food, and I have yet to be fed."

"That's because we haven't gotten groceries in a week. The kitchen is empty."

"You better keep your end of the deal, or I'm not keeping mine."

Phoenix shakes his head, pushing himself off the bed. "Fine, I'll go grab some food. Tomorrow you'll get groceries. Do something other than sitting there and looking cute." He grabs sweats, pulling them on, then tossing a shirt on as well.

"You saying you don't like this?"

Phoenix slides one shoe on, "no," he slides the other one on. "I'm saying that if we don't buy food, we'll starve. I'd drag you out now, but it's too early in the morning. The grocery store will be closed." He comes over and kisses me before heading towards the bedroom door. "Stay awake while I'm gone."

"I have to take a shower anyway," I grumble as I manage to get off the bed with a small thud and not in a graceful manner, unfortunately. "Be quick, I'm starving."

"As you wish," he heads into the hall.

"Wait!" I call after him, trotting to the doorway to stop him. "Get more condoms. We ran out earlier."

Phoenix shakes his head, laughing. "Of course we did."

"Still be quick!"

Phoenix blows me a kiss. "Fast as lightning."

CHAPTER NINE

I look up from my list to ponder the massive pile that's over-flowing the sides of the grocery cart. I started all of this wanting to stay organized, but with Phoenix chaotically throwing things everywhere, it became disorganized very quickly. I only know for sure that we bought presents for *some* of the kids, and we missed Olivia, I'm sure of it. While I'm constantly trying to figure out what goes where, Phoenix is off running through the aisles of the store, acting free as a bird.

I try to work my way to the bottom of the cart so I can see what's down there, but I can barely get to the second layer of junk, let alone all the way down. I bend over, trying to look through the gaps in the side, sighing as I lose hope that I'll be able to see anything useful.

Phoenix drops another toy into the cart, grabbing the handle and starting towards the game aisle, a chaotic look in his eyes.

I catch up to him, grabbing his arm to slow him down. "Stop. I have no clue who we've even found so far. You keep throwing things in willy nilly. Like, for example, who on Earth is this for?" I hold up the Darth Vader figurine he just threw in the cart and look at my list. "No one asked for this."

"Yeah, it's for me."

"No!" I huff, turning him towards me, trying to stop him before something else on a shelf catches his eye. "No shopping for yourself. This is already going to be way more expensive than it needs to be, we don't need to be adding in anything extra."

Phoenix takes the toy from my hand, dropping it back in and offering me a reassuring smile. "Mazey, babe, you're freaking out. Calm down."

"Yeah, I'm stressed. Don't tell me to calm down. We have a cart full of shit and have no idea who any of the shit is for. You're just running off, finding something that's *not* on the list, and throwing it in!" I turn the paper towards him to show him. "See, we're missing Olivia. I think we're missing Dylan, but I don't really know. And I'm pretty sure Vincent hasn't gotten anything considering all he wanted was a bong or a grinder."

Phoenix looks at the list. "Is that what it's called?"

"Is that what what's called?"

"Grinder. Isn't that like a dating app or something?"

"It's used to grind weed, Phoenix." I have to take a deep breath to stop myself from snapping at him as he looks over to me with a teasing look in his eyes.

Phoenix snorts. "Smoking weed much, are you?"

I snatch my list back out of his hands. "No, didn't you smoke when you were younger?" I don't wait for him to answer; I'm not really in the mood to listen anyway. "Either way, that's just what he asked for."

"Well, on your list, it says he wants hair dye and licorice."

"He told me afterward. This list was sent to everyone, Suzan would have flipped if he had put bong on his Christmas list." I pull the cart over to the side of the store, away from all the shoppers. "Now help me take all of this out so we can go through it all."

Phoenix sighs. "Mazey, really, do we have to?"

"Yes," I start to empty the cart, tossing a stuffed animal onto the empty shelf beside me. "We're not forgetting someone because you're too disorganized to make sure we got them all presents."

"We still have two weeks until Christmas. We could just come back and get whatever we forgot." Phoenix takes the list as I push it into his hands.

I resist the urge to throttle him, taking a second to calm down. I'm getting too stressed, they're just presents. "The closer we get to Christmas, the busier the stores are going to get. I just want to get it done, okay? I don't want to risk something going out of stock."

After a second of thought, Phoenix stuffs the list in his pocket and looks at the cart. "Okay, fine. What do you want me to do?"

"We can start with the toys for the kids. Take them out one by one, and if it's something we want, then we figure out who it's for and I write it on the list. If it's something we don't want, then put it on the bottom and we'll return it to where we got it." We go through each item, making sure we mark it off and find who it was for. As the cart is emptied, it becomes clear that it would've only been half as full without all of Phoenix's gifts to himself. We spend most of the afternoon finding the rest of the presents and then going home and wrapping them until way after dinner.

By the time we're done, it's almost time to go to bed. I place the last present under our miniature tree in the living room, feeling accomplished as I look at the neatly wrapped gifts. Grabbing the list off the counter, I beam up at Phoenix, feeling the stress roll off my shoulders. "We did it!"

Phoenix high fives me before grabbing the list from my hand. After a second of looking at it, he grimaces.

"What?"

He shakes his head. "I don't know if I should tell you."

I grab it back, looking over the list, trying to see what he noticed. "What? What's wrong?"

"Well, we forgot to put Ashten on the list."

"God damn it." I scrunch the list in my hands, pinching my brow. I need a drink. I go over to the kitchen, slamming the wadded paper onto the counter and reaching for the cabinet I think Phoenix stores his liquor in. As I yank the cabinet open, Phoenix comes running over like his heels are on fire.

"Wait—"

As the cabinet swings open in front of me, I see a bunch of gifts wrapped up with cute little bows and cartoon penguins on them. I look back at him, over my shoulder, as he comes over and slams the door shut.

"I told you to wait."

"I'm sorry, Nix, I was already opening it. Why are they hiding in the liquor cabinet anyway?"

He presses his eyes closed for a moment like he's trying to process something, before going over and pulling a top cabinet open and getting a bottle of vodka. "It's not the liquor cabinet, first of all. It's where I keep my miscellaneous cooking supplies. I figured you wouldn't be going in there."

"Okay," I look down at the cabinet, then back up at Phoenix, deciding to close it before he freaks out any more. "Why are they hidden in the miscellaneous cooking supplies cabinet?"

He pours a shot of vodka and hands it to me. "Because I didn't want you to see them."

I take the shot, eyeing Phoenix as I set the shot glass on the counter. "And why not?"

He pours a second shot and takes it himself, still looking weirdly freaked out. "'Cause, uh, they're yours?"

"They're mine?" I look down at the now-closed cabinet, then back up at Phoenix. "I hate penguins. You know that."

He shrugs, downing another shot and then pouring me another one before he responds. "It was going to be a joke. I thought it was funny."

I eye him, trying to figure out what exactly is funny about how much I despise penguins. They're probably my least favorite animal aside from dolphins – hate those shits too. I take the shot. "I thought you said you weren't getting me anything?"

"Makes the surprise all that much better, huh?"

I bark out a laugh. "I guess. I haven't gotten you anything, though."

"It's all good, babe. I can return the gifts tomorrow if you don't want them." He takes a third shot then hands me one too.

I take it. "Don't do that. I don't want you to go to any extra trouble."

"It won't be." He comes over to me, pressing his lips to mine in a quick swoop, leaving the taste of vodka on my mouth. "Now," he kisses my nose, "how about we get you drunk and we pretend it's the night we met?"

I raise an eyebrow. "You want to get me drunk and take advantage of me?"

"Hey, there will be no taking advantage of anyone. I'm just saying, you're really freaky when you're drunk." He takes a swing straight from the bottle, walking towards me and backing me out of the kitchen.

I shake my head, a coy smile on my lips. "Fine, but you're taking care of me tomorrow when I'm hungover."

"Sounds like a deal to me." He shakes the bottle at me, waiting for me to drink some more before picking me up in his arms and carrying me off to the bedroom, my squeal following behind us.

"A man who brings the car to you." Olivia teases, poking me with her elbow. "Get me one of those."

Vincent rolls his eyes. "Remember when you said you were happy for her?"

"Yes, I do. And I am. I'm allowed to be happy for her and envious of her at the same time, dipshit."

"Dipshit?" Vincent holds his hands out in a 'what the fuck' gesture. "I say one thing and you jump straight to dipshit?"

Olivia rolls her eyes and turns towards me, her expression going from sassy to playfully pitiful. "I change my mind. I'll back you and Phoenix up at Christmas if you find me a man who picks me up so I don't have to walk like five minutes to the car."

I chuckle. "Liv, Christmas is in a week. I waited years for mine, so I don't know if six days is a reasonable time limit."

"Fine, whatever. I'll just be alone forever."

Vincent groans, his face seeming to toe the line between annoyed and bored. "God, you're so dramatic."

Olivia flips him the bird. "Shove it, *dipshit*. I have to pee, I'll be back." She pushes past Vincent, going back into the café we just finished having lunch in.

I turn to Vincent, grinning. "Okay, I've been waiting to ask you something."

"What?" He gives me a suspicious look, rubbing his hands together to ward off the slight bite of the air.

I try to calm the excitement on my face so I don't raise his expectations. "I knew I'd end up hurting Olivia's feelings by picking you, but..."

Vincent's brows furrow. "You're making me nervous, spit it out."

"I'm trying to open a little café. I want you to work for me."

He narrows his eyes at me. "Are you screwing with me?"

I shake my head. "No. Wouldn't it be fun?"

He thinks for a second, taking a moment to decide what he thinks. A smile tugs the corner of his lips as he answers. "Hell yeah," He holds his hand out like he's about to shake my hand but quickly pulls me into a hug instead. "This beats any regular job."

I bounce on my toes. "Yay, this is exciting! I'm excited."

On the street, a horn honks, and when I look over, Phoenix is waving at me. He's parked half in the road, interrupting traffic. "Geez, maybe don't get a man who brings the car to you." Vincent laughs.

"Yeah, I have to go before Phoenix makes someone crash their damn car." I open the car door, turning back to Vincent for a second and waving at him. "Tell Olivia bye for me?"

He waves back. "Sure. Love you."

I slide into the seat and yell back, "love you too," as I close the door.

Phoenix quickly merges back into traffic. "So? How'd it go?"

I bounce in my seat. "He said yes! It's going to be so fun... Vincent, the baker, and me. I feel re-inspired."

"*Re*-inspired? I thought you were always inspired. Have I not been inspiring enough?"

I go to smack his arm, but he catches my hand, lacing his fingers through mine, resting them on his leg. "I'm just saying that I'm glad he said yes, and I'm glad you showed up before Olivia got back."

"Yeah... doubt that would have gone over well." Phoenix chuckles, apparently amused at the idea of me having to face Olivia and her sass.

I shrug. "I know, and I wish I could think of enough work for both of them to do. She already has a job, and she wants to go to school out of state. Vincent is staying after he gradu- ates in May."

"I know." He rubs his thumb along the back of my hand. "I agreed with you, remember?"

I nod, snuggling into the seat, letting the seat warmer heat my body. "Mmm, I'm so excited. I want to go home and just... I don't even know!" I beam at Phoenix, already starting to make a mental list of what I want to work on when we get home. "I could keep doing all the math, but damn does that make my brain hurt. Oh! Salads. I haven't figured out all my salads. That's what I'll do. They'll be the best salads on the face of the freaking Earth."

Phoenix takes the red light we're stopped at as a chance to look over at me, eyes gleaming with as much excitement as I feel. "God, I love you so much. You're so cute when you're excited." He picks up my hand, kissing the back of it as he starts driving, laying our connected fingers in his lap.

I turn towards the front of the car, trying to get the wheels in my brain to start moving. *I love you*. He did not just say that. Twenty days – *twenty*. People don't say "I love you" after twenty days, right? But does it matter when we say it if it's been said before? He's told me a million times he loved me, both in a platonic way and a romantic one. It's never been so casual, though. When he's told me he was *in love* with me before, it was always a big deal, to both of us. Maybe that's the thing. Maybe he's just saying he loves me like he's loved me for ages – as a friend. Or does he mean he's actually in love with me? Why am I freaking out? It's not like I'm not in love with the man too.

Holy shit. I'm in love with Phoenix–

"Maz? You're spacing out. You building your café in your head?"

I spin in my seat to face him and stare at him wide-eyed. "You just said you love me."

He looks over at me for a moment, confused, before turning his attention back to the road. "Yeah? What–"

"Like you love me like you'd say you love a friend, or like... you're *in* love with me?"

Phoenix gives me a side-eye as he squeezes my hand in question. "What kind of question is that?"

"Answer it, Nix."

"Well, I'm in love with you, Mazey. When has that not been obvious to you?"

I stare at him, baffled by the blunt way he just declared his love for me. He's so confident in his feelings for me. Why can't I feel the same way? I think I love him... no, I *know* I love him. At the very least, I know I love him because I've loved him since I was sixteen. Over the years, I've been falling in love with him slowly but surely. And I've known that for a long time. Loving my wife's brother was always hanging over me and I didn't know how to stop it. When Roxanne and I were in Arizona or Seattle, Phoenix was in Florida. My problems were literally hundreds of miles away.

Now he's sitting right here, telling me he loves me. When I used to think about how much I loved Phoenix, I always felt that ache of guilt like I was cheating on Roxanne. I don't have to feel that anymore. Now, all those feelings mean is that I love him. So why can't I seem to open my mouth to say that? Why does it feel like my throat closes as I look into his eyes and see all the love he has for me? It should be as easy as just opening my mouth and talking...

Phoenix turns into a gas station parking lot, turning to me and grabbing my hands. "I don't mean to freak you out."

"I'm fine." I offer him a smile. "We're all good."

Phoenix's lip twitches like he's holding back a smile. "I understand if you don't want to say it yet if you're not ready. Or if you don't love me anymore," he drops his eyes, clearing his throat, "I get that too."

"It just feels fast." I spread out his hand, tracing my finger on his palm. "We've only been officially dating for a couple of weeks now..."

"I know, but I've been trying to get you to date me for years. I've loved you for a pretty long time. You knew that before. Why would you think that'd change?"

I shrug. "I didn't really think about it? So much has happened to me and with me in this last year. I guess I just didn't know if you still loved me. I'm a different person now."

"Just so you know, it will *always* be the case."

Yep. I love him. Just need to figure out how to say it.

"Another one?" Lincoln raises an eyebrow at me as I slurp up the last of my Mai Tai.

Phoenix places my cup at the end of the booth and waves at the waitress. "She's, uh..."

"I'm drinking 'cause I wanna." I pout as I slide down in the booth.

Phoenix gives Lincoln a *look*. "She's nervous about Christmas."

Lincoln reaches forward and pats the back of my hand. "It'll be okay."

I narrow my eyes at him. "Don't do that. You're making fun of me."

"Well, yes, but–"

I yank my hand off the table, sitting up straighter and leaning toward him. "Were you not right there when Suzan was screaming at me and embarrassing me in front of everyone?"

Lincoln flinches. "Well, yes. I was."

"Then shut up."

The waitress – *Cherry*, she said her name was – reaches our table, candy red lips smiling at Phoenix as she turns to him. "What can I help you with?"

"Can we get another one of these?" He pokes at the Mai Tai cup, smiling back at her with only half the enthusiasm as Cherry.

She nods, leaning down to pick up the glass, taking extra care to show off as much of her cleavage as possible. "Anything else?"

I lean on Phoenix, lacing my fingers through his and leering up at Cherry. "Stop flirting with my man, please," I feel my chest heave for a second, and I pause, trying not to puke. When I'm sure I won't be vomiting, I look back at the waitress. "Please and thank you."

"Mazey, babe," Phoenix sighs, giving the waitress a sympathetic look.

Cherry flicks her eyes up to me, grimacing as she backs away slightly. "Ha, uh, sorry. I didn't–"

"Lincoln?" Someone scoots in front of the waitress, who's now standing several feet away from the table, smiling down at Lincoln. As I see her incredibly kind looking eyes, I recognize her immediately. Lincoln's fiancé, Jenny, I think her name was, barely looks at Phoenix or I as she continues talking, just looking at Lincoln. "Sorry, she asked me a million questions when I was leaving."

Lincoln's eyes dart to me, then back to his fiancé, who's eyes jump to me as well. "Hey, Mazey. I uh–"

The waitress comes closer to the table again, standing on the side of the table Phoenix *isn't* on, with her pen in her hand.

"Oh, hi," Jenny looks up at Cherry, "I didn't see you there. Can I please have a diet Coke?"

The waitress smiles at Jenny, eyes skirting to me as she starts to back away. "Yes."

"I ordered you fries," Lincoln kisses her cheek.

I frown at the waitress, who's still standing there. "That's it."

Phoenix smacks my leg from under the table and gives me a look asking what I'm doing.

Lincoln gestures to his fiancé, clearing his throat. "Y'all haven't officially met. This is Jenny. And this is my sister, Mazey."

"Hi," I wave at her, "Lincoln talks about you a little *too* much."

Taking my comment in stride, she smiles up at Lincoln. "Yep, sounds like him. In the village where we met, he talked about me to everyone who would listen. I wouldn't be surprised if they ban him from Tanzania for talking too much. Luckily for them, we haven't been back, or he'd probably have given them all the updates on our relationship."

"That's cute," I mutter, looking over as the waitress walks up with our drinks, setting one down in from of me and one in front of Jenny, pulling her hand back quickly and leaving without a word.

"Thanks," Jenny calls after Cherry before reaching out and placing a hand softly on the table in front of me. "How are you doing?"

I bark out a laugh. "I'm doing just peachy, thank you so much for asking."

Lincoln rolls his eyes at me. "Ignore her being a bitch. She's drunk."

"Let me live my life, Linc." I scrunch my nose at him, sticking my tongue out at him before using it to grab the straw in my cup and slurping up the fruity goodness.

"Don't be a jerk." Phoenix elbows me, then turns to Jenny. "She's just nervous."

I remove my lips from the straw to frown at him. "She doesn't care about my dirty laundry, Phoenix."

She shakes her head, looking extremely sympathetic. "No, I totally get it. You're nervous about the whole Thanksgiving thing, right? Yeah, when Lincoln told me about that, I just felt so bad for you–"

"Great," I mumble under my breath, barely loud enough for Phoenix to hear, let alone Jenny.

"–haven't met your mom yet, so it's hard for me to judge her so quickly, but I just don't understand what compelled her to do that. I can see why going back so soon would be nerve-wracking." Jenny shakes her head in that way people do when they want to offer you good advice but don't actually have any.

We all look up as the waitress comes to the table, setting Jenny's fries down. "Enjoy."

Jenny smiles at her before grabbing a fries and biting off the end. "Anyone want some?"

Lincoln takes one. "Well, I have met my mom. Unfortunately, this isn't exactly far-fetched."

"Pfft, yeah." I take another sip from my drink, debating asking for something to make it a little stronger. "This was the *fourth*," I clear my throat, "the fourth time she's done this." I put my elbow up on the table, dropping my chin in my hand as I look at Jenny. "The first three times were right after everything happened, though. So that made more sense." I spot the waitress, and I'm about to wave her over to get more liquor but stop when I see Phoenix looking at me, a defeated and embarrassed expression on his face.

"She did this before?" Jenny shakes her head to shame. "I wonder what prompts these outbursts?"

I drop my arm back onto my lap and off of the table, laughing. I lift my arm back up, ignoring the heavy feeling of it, and point at Jenny. "I can tell you that."

Phoenix sighs. "Mazey, honestly, you're going to regret—"

"So the night my wife died," I pause, looking over at Phoenix. "Well, I guess she's not my wife anymore, is she, heh?" I roll my eyes when all he does is sink into the booth and continue on. "Anyway, the night she died, Phoenix called me up, and I went to his hotel, and we fucked." I widen my eyes and look at Jenny, "*a lot*. Like I didn't find my wife's body until the next morning *a lot*." I nudge Phoenix with my elbow. He just shakes his head. "During the investigation into her murder, I was a suspect at first. Turns out when your alibi is cheating on your wife with her brother people don't seem to like that too much, do they?" I poke Phoenix's arm, and he, in turn, pulls my drink away from me. "Hey!"

He knocks my hand away. "No. You're no fun when you're angry drunk. And *I* am going to have to hear all about how hungover you are tomorrow morning. No, thank you."

"Mmm, but I also get horny when I drink vodka, so I think it balances in your favor." I grab at the drink again, but this time Lincoln smacks my hand.

"Jesus, maybe you shouldn't come to Christmas if it's going to make you this crazy. Drinking like this probably isn't healthy. You're clearly stressed, Maz." He and Phoenix share another look for like the millionth time since I started drinking.

I poke Phoenix's cheek. "Why do you keep looking at each other like that? I used to be one of your best friends too. Share looks with me."

"Yeah, the looks are *about* you, Mazey. So, no. I'm ordering you food. Maybe it'll help soak up the insane amount of alcohol in your stomach right now." Phoenix flags down the waitress.

I drop my head on his shoulder. "Oo, food sounds really good right now."

"What do you want?"

Lincoln knocks on the table with his knuckles. "They have fried pickles, your favorite, right?"

"I–"

"Her favorite is the potato skins."

I nod. "I *love* potato skins."

The waitress comes up. "What can I do for you?"

"An order of potato skins, and can we get some of the classic wings as well?" He looks away from her quickly, no doubt making sure I have no reason to pounce.

She nods, writing the order down and scooting away.

Jenny munches on a fry as she points at me. "Do you like painting?"

"I dunno. Never really painted before." I loop my arm through Phoenix's, snuggling into his side.

She nods. "You seem like you'd be really good at painting. On my way home from the airport, I saw this little wine and paint shop. The two of us should go there sometime."

"What's a wine and paint shop?" Lincoln asks.

"It's like this little place where you bring your own bottle of wine, and they teach you how to paint something, like a tree, or a beach or something. They're super cute." Jenny looks at me, expectantly.

Phoenix tucks a piece of hair behind my ear. "That sounds like fun, babe."

I nod. "I like wine." I look up at Phoenix, "Colors are fun."

"Yeah, colors are fun." He looks up at Lincoln, a laugh

behind his eyes. He turns to Jenny, "When?"

"Can we go the day before Christmas eve?" She looks to me for confirmation.

"Uh-huh, sure." I poke Phoenix's cheek. "Remind me, 'cause I may not remember in the morning."

"Will do." He squeezes my hand.

I squeeze it back, turning to Lincoln and Jenny. "Now excuse me, 'cause I think I'm going to go puke."

I lay there on the bathroom floor, wondering why, how? Well, not *how* – I'm not stupid, I know how it happened. More, *why on earth is this happening to me like this*? I mean, we were being careless. There were a few times when the thought didn't even cross my mind and I don't think it was crossing his either. We should have been better about it. We should have stopped and thought about it every single time, because if we had, *this* would not be happening.

Okay, slow down. Technically nothing has happened yet. I could just be sick. Oh God, wouldn't that be the best thing in the universe? *Wanting* to be sick is a new feeling for me, and dear, Lord Jesus, do I want to be sick. I just have this stupid feeling in my chest, like I know I'm not sick, which is ridiculous because there's no way I could actually know. I may have missed my period, and I may be a puking fiend right now, but I couldn't know for sure if I'm pregnant or not.

I could find out. Right now, I could find out. I've been lying here on this floor for way longer than the time I needed to let the pregnancy test sit for, but as I stare at the ceiling, I keep thinking about the fact that if I look at the damn thing, my mind may explode. At least while I'm sitting here, unsure, my brain is just *close* to exploding. If I look at that test, then I'll *know*, and Phoenix won't know. God, I'm going to have to tell Phoenix. I don't want to tell Phoenix, I can't even think about that right now. Groaning, I push up onto my elbows and look at where the test is sitting on the toilet seat lid. It's like it's just sitting there mocking me. What a bitch.

"Mazey? Are you okay?" Phoenix knocks on the door.

I repress a groan, trying to think of what to say to him and coming up short. Thankfully, I was able to grab the pregnancy test while Jenny and I were out yesterday painting. We went to grab some wine and I managed to buy it without her noticing. When we finally got home, Phoenix was soundly sleeping, and I just couldn't bring myself to tell him before I knew for sure. We have to go to Suzan's house, and I'm sitting here worrying about if her son got me pregnant. I have no clue how I'm supposed to tell him.

"I, uh... I'm just..."

"Are you sick again? I thought you said you didn't drink that much last night."

I didn't drink at all last night. I've been drinking so much this last week that I thought all the puking was from too much alcohol. Maybe it wasn't... and maybe I've been drinking this poor fetus to death. God damn pregnancies. "Well, I didn't, I just... I'll be out in a second. I promise."

"Okay, we have to leave soon."

"I know." I stare at the ceiling until I hear him walk away. Then I take a deep breath, push myself onto my knees, and grab the test off the toilet, still not looking at the lines. "Please don't be positive..." I whisper, trying to squeeze all of my hopes into the pee stick. After I release my hands, I turn it over and look at the symbol.

I'm pregnant.

Again.

CHAPTER TEN

I spend the whole ride over to Suzan's house staring down at a book in my lap. I brought the book so I could have an excuse to not talk to Phoenix, but I don't read, ever. So it took me a good five minutes to even convince him that I actually wanted to read it. *Then* I couldn't take my mind off the very obvious elephant in the room, or rather car, so I just stared at the book instead of actually reading it. Phoenix pointed out about ten minutes into the drive that I hadn't turned the page. So I spent the next twenty counting in my head and turning the page every five minutes. But my mind got lost again, so I spent the last fifteen staring at the pages again.

And oh boy, did Phoenix notice. He didn't say anything, but he noticed. He just kept looking over at me with this confused and worried look that makes me squirm, even just seeing it out of the corner of my eye. He knows something's up, and if I don't stop acting weird, he's going to start asking questions. When we finally get to Suzan's, I realize I have yet another problem to worry about, one that I had managed to not think about the whole ride over; I'm going to see Suzan again. I do *not* want to see Suzan right now.

Last time she was pissed 'cause I was about to kiss Phoenix. I wonder how much she'd flip if she knew I was pregnant with his kid? I don't know if I can handle another 'episode' from Suzan with everything else going on right now. As soon as I enter the house, I'll be a wide-open target for her to take a shot at. I take a deep breath, opening the car door, and stepping onto the sidewalk.

I stare at the front door's screen while Phoenix grabs the box of presents and the dessert. He apparently settled on berry pie, the kind I told Suzan was my favorite so long ago. When he finally steps past me, he gives me that same confused and worried look before balancing the box and opening the screen door. As I debate turning around and leaving or walking in with my chin held high, I feel a bitterness run through me.

Here I am, on a particularly shitty day, about to spend Christmas *Eve* – not even actual Christmas *day* – with Suzan, who has apparently decided we won't be mending our relationship any time soon. Add the fact that Phoenix and I are officially a couple and I don't see that changing. Who celebrates family Christmas on Christmas Eve? Well, Suzan, for one. She spends the entire actual Christmas at church or praying to Jesus. This is apparently something she's passed down to Phoenix, who told me this morning before going to the store that he has plans tomorrow. Plans on *Christmas*. Now, I don't claim to be an avid Christmas fanatic, but it's *Christmas*. With all those presents he has hidden away – the ones that disappeared the next day – I assumed he'd want to spend the morning unwrapping gifts. I even bought him some presents when I saw the ones he got me so we could make a whole day of it. Apparently, I'll be spending Christmas alone, just like I've been spending most of my time since I got here.

I sigh, looking at someone who's setting something down in the kitchen window to my right. I need to go in eventually; Phoenix will wonder where I am. On top of that, I probably look like a freak standing out here on the sidewalk. I start to walk up to the porch, and as I get close to reaching the door, I almost turn around and run back to the car to hide, but Olivia spots me and comes over to the screen door, narrowing her eyes at me.

"You gave Vincent a job while I was off peeing and then didn't answer my calls for the next five days."

I sigh, not wanting to deal with Olivia being angry right now. "He wasn't supposed to tell you about that."

Her mouth flops open as she huffs. "Well, that doesn't make it any better."

"Look, Liv–"

"Is he your favorite or something?" She barely turns to let me inside, slamming the screen down behind me. When I try to continue past her, she grabs my arm and turns me to face her.

"Olivia, c'mon, we can talk about this later." I try to think of all the reasons I had when I picked Vincent, but right now, my brain can't pry away from the other things it's chewing on.

She rolls her eyes. "Do you like Vincent more than me? Is that it?"

"No, Liv, I–"

She steps in front of me, eyes challenging mine. "Why didn't you tell me?" Her arms fold over her chest as she waits for an answer.

I sigh. "I was planning on telling you. I asked him not to say anything."

"Well, I–"

"Liv," I snap, instantly feeling bad about it from the way her face drops. "I didn't do it to hurt your feelings. We can talk about it more later, I can't deal with this right now." I push past her, heading away from the people gathering in the front of the house.

"Wait, Mazey..."

I ignore Olivia calling after me and continue walking. I'm about to go up the stairs, but I hear a bunch of the kids up there. I go past the stairs, darting into the laundry room on my right to avoid the living room to my left. I try to close the door behind me, but I hit someone, and when I turn around, Phoenix is standing there, the same look on his face again.

He blocks the doorway like he knows my first thought was to run and stares me down. "What's going on?"

I fold in on myself, sinking to the floor. "It's...it's bad, Nix," I mumble into my arms.

He kneels, picking my head up and holding my cheek in his hand. His eyes are full of worry, which they should be. I've been acting like a basket case all morning. He strokes his thumb across my cheek, giving me his undivided attention. "Hey, it's okay, alright? You can tell me."

"I'm..." I stare at him a moment too long and chicken out, but my brain jumps to something else, and words start flowing out. "What did you think when Roxanne and I asked you to be our sperm donor?"

He looks a little confused by that. "I, uh... I mean, I understood why. That way, the baby's DNA would be the same—"

"No, I mean about a kid running around that's your kid, but it's *not* your kid?"

He drops down the rest of the way to the ground, feet piled with mine, hands on my arm. "I didn't think about it too much at first. I didn't really make that connection. Once you told me that it happened, that you were pregnant, it kind of blew my mind."

"Blew your mind good, or blew your mind bad?"

"I guess bad. Bad because I knew that it wasn't going to

be my kid that you were carrying. She was going to be Roxanne's. That made it really hard, especially when you started showing. It was like a punch to the gut every time I saw you. I always had this dream that we'd have kids together someday, and you ended up having my baby with Roxanne." He squeezes my arm slightly. "Why? What brought this on?"

I sigh, leaning back against the washer, my feet sprawling out on either side of Phoenix. "I'm pregnant." It's such a low whisper I wouldn't have even thought he heard it.

But by the look of shock on his face, I know he did. His eyes don't leave my face as his lips part in stunned silence. I see the wheels turning in his head as he tries to figure out what I mean by *pregnant*. Of course, he eventually gets to the decision that when I say I'm pregnant, what I mean is... I'm pregnant. His eyes dart down to my stomach, boring holes through my skin like he wants to see the little bundle of cells in my uterus.

I clear my throat, trying to get the junk out of it from the tears pushing their way up but all it does is make my eyes start to water up. I look away from Phoenix, wiping my cheeks with the sleeve of my shirt to dry them, but they're wet again almost instantly.

Phoenix suddenly becomes mobile, moving to wrap his arms around me. "Okay, hey, babe. It's okay. Come here." He leans forward, pulling me into his arms, my face burying into the crook of his elbow.

"It feels so strange to know that the last time I was pregnant, I kept feeling like everything was wrong. I mean, I was married, and we had enough money and a spare room for the kid, and yet every time I thought about bringing a baby into the world, I felt defeated. And this time... I *just* started getting my life back together. We've been dating for like a month, and I definitely do not have the money to care for a baby."

"This is why you looked so stressed the whole way over?"

I shrug. "I didn't know how you'd feel. After Roxanne died and the baby... I just didn't know how you'd react."

Phoenix kisses my forehead. "I'm here, I swear."

"What are we going to say to people?" I groan, rolling my head back against the washer.

Phoenix grabs my hand and kisses it, offering me a half-smile. "We'll get through this Maz, okay?"

I nod, trying to smile back. "I can't believe we let this happen."

Phoenix chuckles. "Well, sometimes you're just too damn fine to wait or to think about anything other than you." He teases and nudges me until I smile at him.

"Ha, yeah. Blame it on my hot bod."

"Oh, I plan to." Phoenix stands, offering me a hand. "Come on. We should go out there."

I snort. "And say what? 'Oh, where were you guys?' Just telling Phoenix that he impregnated me. No big deal."

"Mmm, so now it's not your hot bod, it's my Olympic swimmers?"

I take his hand, letting him pull me up. "Yes, I like that better." I turn out of the room, grabbing Phoenix's hand as I go, and almost walk right into Suzan, who's standing in the hallway. "Suzan? What are you doing?"

Her eyes go straight to where our hands are connected. For a moment, I feel like letting go. But I don't, and neither does Phoenix. She turns the fire in her gaze towards me. "You come back to my house and *this* is what you're going to do? Ruin another holiday?"

"Wha..."

"I heard what you said." She snaps her eyes between the two of us, her face full of disgust. "Pregnant? You're pregnant? I can't even begin to tell you– I just... " She shakes her head, honestly looking like she might puke.

"Suzan, please, we didn't come here to ruin Christmas, okay?"

She fumes. "You were hiding in my laundry room and talking about it."

Phoenix steps in front of me slightly. "She just told me, okay?"

"So you're lying to my son now, too?" Suzan looks at me with a fierce challenge in her eyes.

I feel my eyes roll so far back in my head that they may have popped out if they went a little harder. "I wasn't lying to him. I found out less than an hour ago. And it's not like I even *could* have kept the secret for very long. We've only been together for less than a month."

"Ha! For all I know, y'all were sneaking around behind Roxanne's back this whole last year." She throws her hands in the air. "You're just making me look like a fool. My old foster kid and my son hooking up?"

"You seem to forget Roxanne was your daughter too, so it's not all that different."

She barks out a laugh. "Ah, you're right. So you like to go for my biological kids? Maybe you'll try Ashten next."

Before I'm even fully aware of where my hand's going, it's smacked against her cheek, making a horrible sound. I look at the shock on Suzan's face, then feel Phoenix's hand squeeze mine. I just smacked Phoenix's mom. How do I even move forward after doing that? After all the horrible things she's said to me and all the ways I've felt she's been in the wrong, I had never laid a hand on Suzan before. I've never slapped anyone, let alone Suzan. Honestly, though, with everything she's saying to me, she deserves it. I want to keep going, call her a bitch, or maybe just stand a scream at her.

Not right now, though. "I'm sorry, Suzan. That wasn't what I should have done, but you have absolutely no right to talk to me like that. I didn't want to come today because I didn't want you to do something like this again. I'm already here, though, and I don't plan on being pushed out by you on yet another holiday. *So*, if we can please just stop with all the shaming of me and Phoenix, I think that would be just swell."

Suzan huffs, looking like she might just smack me in return. "You do *not* speak to me like that in my own home."

"You know, this used to be my home too." I stomp away, not able to look at her face anymore. This feeling I have right now is so different than before. The first time she decided to start this whole thing against me, I was in such a low place I didn't want to defend myself, let alone be *able* to defend myself. At Thanksgiving, I was just so shocked that she was willing to put all of my private things out there on display like that, I didn't know what to do. Besides, Phoenix got me over it pretty quickly.

But this time, I feel much more than shame or shock. I feel anger. Blood-curdling anger that makes me feel like I'm going to explode. So instead, I go into the living room, where the gigantic tree sits, covered in many of the same decorations it's been covered in since before I even came here. The kids are all gathered around the tree, picking up presents and shaking them, trying to guess what's inside. Dylan is searching intently for boxes with his name on them and making a pile to one side of the tree.

"Mazey?" Nikkie comes over and gives me a hug. "I'm glad you ended up coming. Vincent was telling me you didn't know if you would."

I try to smile back, but it falls short. "There's more to Christmas than just one person. Plus, I missed last year. I wouldn't want to miss anymore."

He nods thoughtfully. "I'm glad you're back." He points to the tree over his shoulder. "I brought you a present just in case."

"Thanks," I look around the room. "I brought gifts for

everyone too. I have no clue where Phoenix put them, though."

He shrugs, clapping me on the shoulder. "We'll open them soon anyway, right?"

"Yeah," I watch as he heads back over to Eric and his girlfriend from Thanksgiving and drops down next to her. I wander back into the hallway, trying to find the presents, and find Phoenix and Suzan standing by the stairs.

Phoenix is talking harshly to Suzan, towering over her with fire in his eyes. Suzan doesn't seem to be thinking about backing down and holds her stance, arms crossed over her chest. "There is *no* reason why you shouldn't be willing to support us. I know it took you a little while to be okay with her and Roxanne being together, but you did. You never screamed in her face about it. And you know what, Mom, it's been *nine* years since we first met. Honestly, from the day we met, I was over the moon about her. So why can't you just give her a damn break?"

"Because she wasn't there while my baby was being murdered and raped. She should have been, she should have stopped him. How can she not blame herself for that?"

Phoenix's jaw twitches like it does when he's about to go off the rails. "She *does*, Mom. Is it impossible for you to see that everything you think, she's already thought about herself? After you blamed her and pushed her away from *you* the first time, she couldn't look at me for months. She felt so bad about what happened, and she shouldn't have! She didn't kill Roxanne, Mom. Bryan Johnson did. So if you want to go shit on someone, it should be him."

"Phoenix Sawyer Hickerman–"

"Nix?" I step forward, grabbing his arm and giving him a reassuring squeeze.

As he looks down at me, his eyes soften. "Are you okay?"

I nod. "I don't want you fighting with your mom because of me."

"I just—"

"I appreciate it," I kiss his shoulder, "but the conversation we need to have doesn't involve her. I came here to have fun with my family, so let's just go set up our gifts and let Suzan finish the food."

He doesn't take his eyes off me, slowly nodding. He kisses me before turning to Suzan. "She's right, it's Christmas. If you really want to fight about this, we should at least wait until afterward."

Suzan looks over my shoulder. When I look behind me, I see several people standing there, watching us. Lincoln looks like he wants to come over and join in the conversation. "I have to get the ham out of the oven, or it'll burn."

Of course, she doesn't just want to agree. She can't be willing not to fight to spare our feelings, she has to have another excuse as to why she's throwing in the towel. I watch as she takes a slow, deep breath before going past Phoenix and into the kitchen. I feel my body slump, my forehead resting on Phoenix's arm. I remember a time when Suzan inviting me into her life was a dream come true. She was going to be my savior. But now...

"Why don't you go sit? I'll grab the presents and you can put them under the tree." Phoenix kisses the top of my head.

I nod. "Uh, yeah. I'll..." I feel someone's hand rub on my shoulder. I look behind me to see Lincoln.

"Come sit with me." Lincoln starts leading me into the living room.

I plop down on the couch and Lincoln sits next to me with a defeated sigh.

Lincoln looks at me with somber eyes. "You doing okay?"

"I just..." How do I even tell him about me being pregnant?

"It's okay, Maz. You don't have to tell me yet." Lincoln squeezes my shoulder.

I lay my head down on his shoulder, sighing. "When did life get so... strange?"

"Hmm, probably around the time you had sex with Phoenix in a bar?"

I don't even have the heart for a comeback. I just nod slightly.

Lincoln pats my leg. "Well, for what it's worth, Mom is wrong. You didn't have anything to do with Roxanne's murder. If you were there, then chances are both of you would be dead right now. None of us would want that. We all love you too much."

"Doesn't seem like everyone agrees. I think..." I feel my breath hitch as I open my mouth to continue. It hurts to think about it, let alone say it. "I think if Suzan had the chance, she'd trade my life for Roxanne's. I think she'd let me die if she got Roxanne back."

Lincoln stiffens, sitting quietly for a second, which isn't like him. He always has something to say, even if it's not the right thing. "I... I'm sorry, Mazey."

He can't even deny it because we both know it's true. If she could, she'd find a way to do it, looking into my eyes as she did. She has always been willing to put Roxanne before me. At first, I understood. I was a new foster kid, and Roxanne had been her child for seventeen years. Why wouldn't she choose her over me? But as time went on, and I felt more and more like I was a part of this family... I just thought it had stopped. That somewhere along the lines, she had started looking at me like I was part of her family, not just something to distract Roxanne. Her true colors showed when she found out I cheated on Roxanne. She didn't hold back and at the time, I didn't think she should have had to. Her daughter had just died.

But while her daughter had died, my *wife* had just died too. I never meant to hurt Roxanne, and I wish I could take back messing up my last night with her. If I could go back, I would have said and done everything differently. But I can't, and I've beaten myself up over it every day since it happened. I've finally been able to feel some joy without the guilt of Roxanne not being able to feel it too. Suzan seems set on taking it all away from me. If we can't fix this... if Suzan doesn't forgive me, will I have to give up my family too? Will I never be able to spend another Thanksgiving, Easter, or Christmas with my sisters and brothers? Will I have to avoid her at people's birthdays and weddings? Will I be able to meet the new foster kids, or will they become strangers to me in Suzan's house?

There was a time that I felt like I owed Suzan the world. She took me in, gave me hope, and made sure I had a home. But the moment she chose not to adopt me because Roxanne asked her not to, she picked Roxanne's small wants over my need to have a place to be my own. By the time I found out, when it was too late, all she had to say was that it's what *Roxanne* wanted. She never even asked me what I thought, what I wanted. Ever since then, it's like I'm just sitting on the outside, not really a part of Suzan's family. If Roxanne and I hadn't ended up staying together, Suzan may not have had me come back for the holidays. She may have looked me over when listing off the names of all her kids to her friends. Maybe she still does. Maybe I've just always been Roxanne's friend to her.

If that's all she sees me as, is there ever going to be a way for me to change it?

"Okay, here are all the gifts. Do you care where they go, or do you want me to just put them wherever?" Phoenix squats down in front of me, a box full of presents in his hands.

I look over at the tree, already packed with presents. "I

think the kids were making stacks for each person. You should put them in their piles."

Phoenix nods and goes over to the tree, where some of the kids are still messing with presents. He shows them the presents he got each of them, joking with them about what they may have gotten, only fueling their curiosity.

Lincoln nudges me, nodding to Phoenix, a deep and thoughtful air about him. "He's so great with all the younger kids, don't you think? I guess Mom bringing in new kids left and right when we were younger helped out a bit. Maybe it was something else..."

I open my mouth to ask what he means by 'something else' but decide I'm too tired for mind games. "I was terrible with kids until I got here. Olivia and Vincent wouldn't leave me alone."

"Well, there are two good things. You're better with kids, and you've got some lifelong friends." Lincoln pauses, seeming lost in thought for a moment or two. "I'm sorry she never adopted you."

I wasn't expecting him to say that. Not many of my siblings really ever say anything about it to me. I don't think most of them even think twice about it. To them, I'm their sister, even if there were no papers to call it official. "She claims she had her reasons."

"I understand why she did it. You had been with two of her kids. Both Roxanne *and* Phoenix. So declaring them your siblings legally seems a little..."

My nose scrunches up. "I try not to think about it. Besides, she didn't know about that until after she decided not to adopt me."

He stares at me intently for a moment, eyes darting all over my face. "Strange, though."

"What?" I resist the urge to cover my face.

He shakes his head, finally looking back at my eyes. "I just love you, Mazey. Okay?"

"Umm, yeah." I raise my brows. "Love you too?"

He rolls his eyes. "Don't be so weird, I'm not trying to make you uncomfortable. The opposite, actually." He squeezes my arm. "I want you to know that you're my sister no matter what, Maz. I know Mom is giving you a hard time and that everything probably turned out *way* different than you had imagined. I just want you to know that I'm here for you, no matter what."

I lay my head back on his shoulder, taking a deep breath as I mull that over. I wouldn't be surprised if Suzan started an argument. She did at Thanksgiving, and she was already well on her way to doing it now, and we've barely been at her house ten minutes. I have always had a weird combination of feelings for Suzan. On the one hand, she took me in and gave me a place to live when no one else would. She brought me into this amazing family that I wouldn't trade for anything in the world. Because of her, I met Roxanne, Phoenix, Lincoln, Olivia, Vincent, Nikkie, Eric... every single one of the most important people in my life. By walking into this house that fateful day my whole life changed.

But one thing that has always stung, and will always sit at the pit of my stomach, is that she went back on her promise to adopt me, to make me officially her's. She promised me that she'd adopt me. She promised, and when Roxanne told her that she wanted to date me, not be my sister, Suzan didn't bat an eye. She didn't ask, she didn't question. She just decided not to adopt me, and because of that, I wasn't officially anyone's. Ever. Not even my jackass biological parents are allowed to claim me. Not after leaving me to the wolves. Until I married Roxanne, I wasn't ever officially part of a family. That's on Suzan, just like it's on every other person who has promised to love and care about me and failed miserably.

I can't just blame Suzan, though. While she should have stood up for me and kept her promise, it wasn't all her fault. Roxanne was the one who started that train of thought in Suzan's head. She's the one who asked her not to adopt me because she had a crush. While I tried my best to move on and not let it bug me, it always was in the back of my mind, eating away at me. If I could go back, I wouldn't be adopted. If I had been, I would never have married Roxanne. That's not the point, though. The point was always that Roxanne chose that little crush over my life without a family to call my own.

My eyes wander to Phoenix, who's smiling wide at the kids as they put the last few presents into place. People start wandering into the room, finding their places around the living room. I look at the people around me, the people I've called my family for almost ten years, and I feel my heart squeeze with emotion. Happiness at seeing those I love, but also a twinge of sadness that Suzan is challenging this love. I feel my sad sack of a face start to smile. "Love you too, Linc."

He doesn't say anything back, just wraps his arm around me and squeezes, letting me know he agrees. I know he does. They all love me as much as they would have if I was adopted or biologically related to them. But for some reason, when I look across the room at all the happy, smiling faces, I feel like I'm in a completely different world than everyone else. They're all comforted by being here. They *want* to be here. After Roxanne died, I wanted to avoid this house at all costs. I knew it would hurt too much and burn too bad. At some point, the feeling changed into one where I wasn't avoiding Roxanne's memory anymore, but the house and what comes with it.

In the hall, I hear Vincent. He starts to walk into the

room as he finishes his conversation. "Yes, babe. Mmm-hmm. I promise. Yes, see you soon. Yep. Bye." He hangs up, looking behind him as he does, rolling his eyes. "She's so suffocating sometimes."

The person behind him chuckles. "You're head over heels about her, so shut your face." He walks into the doorway beside Phoenix. It's Jake, Vincent's friend who was about to smoke on the roof when I first arrived. He scans the room, eyes finally landing on me. He offers me a charming smile. "Mazey, right?"

I nod, picking myself up off of Lincoln. "Yeah, hi." I smile back, not failing to notice when his striking silver eyes land on my hand, where my ring sits.

He lifts his eyes so they meet mine. He lets them linger a little too long and Phoenix slides his arm around my waist. Jake doesn't even seem to notice as he moves his way over to sit by Heather, Vincent dropping on his other side. Vincent smacks his arm, nodding towards me slightly, saying something I can't hear. Jake shrugs and gives me a sideways glance.

This guy can't be more than eighteen, right? He's friends with Vincent, so I imagine he's going to school with him. So what exactly does he think he's doing?

Suzan clears her throat. "We'll be reading the Christmas story after we open presents, so you can all remember why we're gathered today. I'll assume presents are the reason you kids are bouncing off the walls, though? Go ahead, pass out the gifts."

The kids immediately jump into action, passing one present to each person around the circle. As Dylan comes over to me and hands me a present he points at it. "I got this for you with 'Livia. She promised that it'd be your favorite."

Holding the present carefully in my lap, I smile at him. "I'll bet it is. Thank you, Dylan."

He runs off to his seat with his own present tucked under his arm.

Suzan looks over at the present in my hand, sparks flashing across her eyes. What she's thinking, I can't tell. "Mazey, I didn't know if you'd be coming, so some people may not have gotten you anything..."

My brain jumps into a defense mode, fists up, ready to fight. I ignore my brain and just smile at her tightly. "That's fine."

Phoenix scoffs beside me, his hand tightening against my waist.

I look around the circle at everyone, feeling like I need to savor this moment. Like my whole world might come tumbling down with one wrong move, one wrong word. The laughter that fills the room makes my eyes prick with tears, a heavy pressure settling on my chest. I look at Olivia, whose dress is way too short and tight for Christmas, eyes wide and bright with joy. I see Dylan, who's ripping wrapping paper from the box in his hands and throwing it behind him. As I look at them... I just want to embed this memory into my mind.

My eyes drift to Suzan, who's sitting with her back straight, her ankles crossed, smiling with no teeth as someone else opens their present. Her strawberry blonde hair is so tightly pulled into her hair clip; I'm surprised she doesn't have a raging headache. Her icy eyes shift to me, the smile slipping slightly from her lips. She tilts her chin up, face full of determination. Some of that strong will power that she passed down to her kids.

I take a deep breath, my own eyebrow raising. If she wants to bully me, she's going to have to actually say something.

"Mazey?"

"Huh?" I look beside me to Phoenix.

He smiles lightly at me. "It's your turn." He nods down to the present, resting on my thighs while holding a hand-painted mug in his own hands.

I nod and turn my attention to my lap. I rip the wrapping paper off, slowly opening the box, making Dylan squirm where he's sitting. As I open the box, I see a frame lying in the box, turned over, so I only see the back. I pick it up, turning it over, and as I do, I feel my breath hitch in my throat. Sloppily glued together are pictures of Roxanne and me. The frame is colored, and on the top, it says 'love is forever' written by someone other than Dylan, but decorated afterward. I feel a burn move up my throat, then into the backs of my eyes, tears ready to flow.

Dylan crawls forward slightly, worry coloring his face. "Do you not like it? 'Livia promised you'd like it." He frowns at her, and she chuckles at him.

"I think those are good tears, bud." Olivia nods at me.

Phoenix leans over, looking at what's in my hands. He, like the others in the room, seems to be wondering what made my heart drop through my gut. When he sees what I'm holding, he makes a sound as if someone punched him in the throat.

Maybe someone punched me in the throat. I don't think I'm breathing. I take a shaky breath, letting air into my lungs, and try to move words in my head to form a sentence. I fail epically and feel my mouth flop open and closed as my eyes trail over every picture that was picked. In the center, the largest of all, is Roxanne and me at our wedding, a ring being slipped onto Roxanne's finger. I'm looking at her hand in mine, wearing the goofiest smile on my face, and Roxanne is staring at me, pure joy flowing off her features. Her gorgeous blue eyes, the ones that seem to run in the family, sparkle with love.

Beside that picture is one of Roxanne and I sitting on a

bench at Olivia's birthday party at the park. Roxanne's arms are thrown around my neck, her tongue stuck out, eye winking. I'm pursing my lips, hand up in a peace sign. Another picture of Roxanne and I standing in front of the Christmas tree our sophomore year of college, her arms around my waist, kissing my cheek, a Santa hat resting on my head. The picture below that is of mine and Roxanne's hands, an engagement ring on each, from the picture we sent everyone the night she proposed to me. A picture from my twenty-first birthday, and one of us in a pool, and one of us hiking, and one of us at the Grand Canyon, and one holding baby Georgie.

The one my eyes finally reach is of Roxanne on her knees, hands on either side of my belly, lips pressed against my five-month bump. She has her eyes pressed closed, but the crinkles around it tell me she's smiling on the inside. My eyes are fixed on something over the camera, looking at the person behind it – Phoenix. It was Phoenix who took that photo. He took this photo not long before Roxanne died, something uncommon with us. We hardly ever took pictures, especially during this time when we were always fighting. My fingers press against it, a croak falling out of my lips. The last picture of Roxanne and me.

Phoenix's hand squeezes mine, his voice thick as he speaks. "She... she looks so happy."

"Are those happy tears, 'Livia?" Dylan presses Olivia, glancing at her only briefly before crawling up to me and looking up at me with big eyes. "Are you happy?"

I feel a tear slip down my cheek, my nose already clogged. I clear my throat, tilting the frame so Dylan can see it. "Did you pick this picture?" I point at it.

He nods. "Yes?" He looks behind him at Olivia before turning his attention back to me.

"Do you know what's in this picture?"

He tilts his head as he looks at it. "That's Roxanne, and that's baby." He points to the picture, where my bare stomach is very obviously pregnant.

"Yes." I feel my heart shrivel up a little bit, a sharp pain in my chest taking its place. "This is, um... this is right before Roxanne died, bud. This is the last picture of us."

I hear several people start, seeming to be realizing what my reaction is, several pairs of sad eyes now trained on me. Dylan looks back at Olivia, frowning at her, an accusatory look on his face. "I thought you said she'd like it?" He turns back to me. "'Livia said you'd like that picture."

I nod. "I do, bud. I do. It just reminds me of something sad, is all." I hold the picture frame to my chest, sniffling as my nose starts to run. "Thank you, Dylan. I love it."

Suzan clears her throat. "When did you have time to make Mazey that gift, Dylan?"

"'Livia had us make 'em." He looks up at me, eyes huge, hope flowing through them. "You like it, right?"

I chuckle. "Yes, I do. Thank you."

Seeming satisfied with that answer, he goes back to where he was sitting.

Suzan turns to Olivia. "So you went behind my back?"

Olivia rolls her eyes. "It wasn't behind your back, I just knew you didn't have them buy Mazey anything."

I feel my heart drop at the thought that Suzan purposely left me out of the list. It's not like I hadn't already known, but hearing Olivia confirm it wasn't a great feeling.

"I didn't think she was coming–"

"Why not? Because you thought you scared her off last time? Do you know how hard it was to convince her to come back?"

Suzan huffs. "Well, I just thought–"

"She's your daughter too, *Mom*." Olivia narrows her eyes at

Suzan, looking like she's really ramping up, all her sass ready to overflow.

I sit forward, intervening before she says something she'll regret. "Liv, it's okay. I didn't even know if I was coming until we had lunch. It's fair to assume not to include me." It was so not fair, but I don't need Suzan blaming me, or worse, blaming Olivia if things go too far. "It's fine, really."

Suzan nods. "I honestly wasn't sure if she was going to continue to come over on holidays after Roxanne died."

"What?" The word slips out of my mouth before I can stop myself, and my mouth keeps going, too. "Why wouldn't I come anymore?"

Suzan purses her lips, eyes looking at me with an unfaltering gaze. "You were Roxanne's wife, and once she died, that was no longer the case."

"I–" My mouth snaps shut. What do I say to that? Of course, I'm Roxanne's wife. What does that have to do with me coming to the holidays anyway? "What do you mean?"

"Just that, honey, you don't really have a reason to keep coming back." She turns her eyes to Phoenix. "Though, I guess since you're shacking up with my son, you probably feel like you do."

I feel my mouth fall open slightly, trying to form words but not being able to navigate through all the confusion I'm feeling. I close my mouth, leaning forward and looking directly at Suzan. "Are you saying that if I'm not dating Roxanne or Phoenix, I don't have a reason to be here?"

She shakes her head slowly. "No, just that... just that you may not *feel* like you have a reason."

"I'm part of this family. That seems like reason enough." I watch as Suzan looks down at the ground, avoiding my eyes, some of the confidence wavering slightly. I feel the rush of emotions come back to my throat, tears pushing against the backs of my eyes again. "Suzan? Do you see me as part of the family?"

Suzan clears her throat. "Well, you obviously know that no papers were ever filed–"

"I'm saying you specifically. Do *you* see me as family?"

"It's hard to really say, because of your relationship with Roxanne, and this with Phoenix... it's not something you do with your brothers and sisters."

I feel Phoenix's grip on my leg tighten. "Yes, I know. I don't see Roxanne and Phoenix as my siblings. I do see everyone else as my siblings."

"You can't make that distinction, honey. It's either all of them or none of them."

"I did. I can tell you what I feel about every person in this room, and I've got to say it's all platonic, except Phoenix. You *know* that I was willing to let go of Roxanne to be adopted." I feel the urge to stand up, to scream at the top of my lungs, but with everyone's stares on Suzan and me, the feeling subsides. I don't need to be ruining everyone's Christmas over this. I open my mouth to tell Suzan so, but she beats me to it.

"The moment you kissed Roxanne while you were under my roof, you chose to not get adopted, and you knew that. You were only in my house for a year, Mazey. You were barely here before you rushed off with my daughter. I don't think you were ever ready to make the sacrifice to be a part of this family. You didn't, and still don't, have a clue what family means." She seems oddly calm for someone who just burst my whole world.

My stomach tightens so much I feel like I'm going to puke, and then it feels so insanely large that I might explode. My brain ticks, not seeming to begin to process it all. Like if I listen to logic, what I know is true, instead of overthinking, I might be able to understand what Suzan just said. But listening to that logic would be admitting so many truths I've been keeping buried. Now is as good a time as any to let everything out, though.

I feel my throat bubble up with laughter, but I try my best to push it down. "God, you're such a bitch." The laughter manages to punch through my mouth, coming out as a deranged, sad-sounding giggle. "I... I can't believe you just said that." The laughter seems to keep pushing up my throat, coming out in little chunks, sounding strangely like a cat dumped into a grinder. I feel myself push to my feet, not really meaning to, but feeling much better once I do. "That's so stupid. I mean, my parents dump me once, like sixteen years ago, and somehow that means I don't know what family is?"

"Mazey..."

I wave her off. "Look, don't worry about it. It's nice to know that I don't have to feel so conflicted about hating you anymore. I guess this means we won't be burying the hatchet after all the things you said to me after Roxanne died? At least if we're admitting neither of us has ever thought of you as my mom I can just hate you and not feel bad, right?" I feel my throat close up as tears start to pool in my eyes. "Thank God you managed to wait until Roxanne was dead to tell me," I clear my throat as the waterworks start and the tears start to flood down my cheeks. "She would have been absolutely devastated to hear this."

I stare at her for a moment longer, maybe waiting for her to agree, or maybe to apologize. I don't know. But as her face turns to steel, I know it won't happen. She doesn't feel bad that I never found a place to call home, or that I can feel my memories of this place slowly crumble away. She doesn't care because she thinks I ruined her daughter. "Why did you even let me come back?"

"What?" She seems surprised by the question, like me not screaming at her is the last thing she expected.

I wipe my nose with the back of my hand. "Why did you let me come back to Florida to live with you if you were just going to shit on me the moment I got here?" The silence that follows cuts into my chest, twisting and pushing in deep. I can feel my throat, thick with the emotions pouring out my eyes.

Suzan, radiating calmness, rests her hands on her thighs, letting out a little sigh. "You were a mess."

"You had something to do with that, you know."

She ignores me, continuing on as if I didn't speak. "Look, Phoenix asked me to let you have a place to stay. If I had known it would lead you to date him—"

"So you did it because of Phoenix, not me? You did it 'cause your child asked you to, just like you did when Roxanne asked you not to adopt me." I wrap my arms around my waist. I don't want to be here anymore. Why haven't I just left yet?

"Him asking me isn't a good enough reason?"

I choke up a laugh. "There are a million better reasons to have let me come back. Like after there was a shootout on my front lawn with the man who killed my wife? Or after I couldn't afford a place to live, so I slept in my storage unit? Or how about after I gave birth to your grandchild? Did that not seem like a good enough reason?" I pull myself back, taking a calm breath as my sadness creeps into anger. "You know what, after what you've said today it's not like I should be surprised that you didn't care. Actually, I take that back. I think you did care. You didn't talk to me for a year. A *year*. And when you do you let me back to your house you're screaming at me a week later for how I fucked up with Roxanne, and here we are again, arguing over someone who is dead."

Suzan flinches when I say that, and I think if someone said that to me I'd be flinching too. Finally, something that hurt her instead of me. Out of all the times I've caused Suzan pain, this is the first where it was my intention. What kind of person does that make me? Am I as bad as her if I'm happy to see the misery behind her eyes? Maybe, but right now, with how terribly she's making me feel about myself, it seems I have the right idea.

I forge on. "I think you let me come back here so you *could* argue with me about this. Because you blame me for Roxanne's death." I feel my lungs collapse, the weight of our conversation pushing onto me, getting harder to hold up. Suzan looks broken, defeated. My tears still run down my cheeks, and I'd have to guess I look like a hot mess right now, but I have hardly any time to think about that while I'm finally finding the truth. "That's why you haven't let it go, why you're so pissed about Phoenix and me. You blame *me* for Roxanne dying, don't you? Because if you had your pick, you'd have had me there that night, while Roxanne was off with another woman, wouldn't you? You'd trade my life for hers."

"Mazey... I didn't mean..."

"You don't have to!" I choke on my tears, feeling every muscle in my body contract as my knees start to grow weak. The tears piss me off too, and I once again curse my inability to be angry without crying. "You... you don't have to."

"Babe?" Phoenix grabs onto the hem of my dress, looking up at me with so much pain in his eyes I think he might also feel the weight on his chest that I feel right now.

My eyes drift across the room, looking at all the people who I've called my family all these years. While I don't think they agree with Suzan, I don't think I can stay here with this 'family' when the person who's holding it together makes me want to gouge her eyes out and curl up into an unmoving ball at the same time. I'll never be able to come to another

Thanksgiving, Christmas, or birthday again. I'll be seated in the back of the church at weddings. I won't get to watch Georgie, or Dylan, or any of the other kids grow up. I won't be invited to the welcome dinner for the new foster kids. I'll be shoved out. I won't be a part of their family anymore.

"You got your wish, Suzan. I'm not a Hickerman, and I won't ever be. And now... I guess I'm not even part of this family either." I start towards the hallway, wanting to run away and never come back, but Suzan stops me.

"Mazey... there's no need to be so dramatic."

I snort, an extremely snotty snort, and shake my head at her. "Shove it up your ass, Suzan. I'm done with your shit." Leaving her with that shocked look on her face, I rush out of the room.

"Mazey, wait!" I hear Phoenix call after me.

"What the hell, Mom?" Olivia pipes up.

I ignore them all as I push through the screen in the front door, not stopping until I'm by Phoenix's car down the road. I yank on the handle, and of course it's locked. So in the most dramatic way I possibly can, I drop onto the road, pushing my head back against the car door. The ugliest sob crawls out of my throat with a gurgly, disgusting sound following it.

I feel like an idiot. Of course Suzan never saw me the same, I knew that. I just didn't know the extent of her comparisons. I thought at *most* it was her choosing Roxanne over me, and then later, Phoenix. While I wish it wasn't the case, I understood her favoring her biological kids. She gave birth to them, they shared her DNA, I could maybe understand that. But to just say plain out that she didn't see me as a part of the family? That I was at most her daughter-*in-law*, and nothing more? That now that Roxanne was dead I no longer had the right to hold that title?

It's bullshit.

I shouldn't have to lose everyone in my life because Suzan changed her mind. I didn't have any friends in Seattle, and I certainly don't have any friends here. The only people I have are the ones sitting in that room. It feels strange, knowing that with one word from Suzan I'm cast out. Well, am I? I mean, how many of them would just throw me out because Suzan said so? I don't think any of them would, but if that's the case, then where are they? I'm usually not an attention seeker, and I usually tell people what it is I want, but right now I could really use a hug, or a shoulder to cry on. I thought *someone* would have followed me out. Maybe I need to stop being such a cry baby and go back in there so I can tell Phoenix I want to go home.

Just as I'm about to push myself to my feet, Jake plops down next to me, scaring the crap out of me, a look of concern covering his face. "You okay?"

I laugh. "Uh..."

Jake chuckles too, shaking his head at himself. "Yeah, stupid question."

I look behind him, expecting to see that someone else followed him out. "How'd you manage to get the short straw? I assumed," I stop myself, my eyes dropping my eyes to my shoes. Maybe no one else offered to come out.

"They're kind of having a catfight in there. With all the commotion I just kind of snuck out. Vincent was too busy defending your honor to notice." He shrugs. "Doesn't feel like the short straw anyway. I felt bad for you back there. Now I want to ask if you're okay again, but it's still a stupid question."

I shake my head. "Not a stupid question unless you don't actually want to hear the answer."

"Well, hit me. I have no connection to this, I have no feelings about this, and you don't have to ever see me again if you don't want to. So lay it on me." He holds his arms out like he's offering for me to actually grab my thoughts and emotions and lay them on his chest.

Turning to face the road again, I let out a deep breath, "Hmm, where to even start?" I cringe inwardly at how stuffy my voice sounds. My nose is probably all red, just like I'm sure my eyes and cheeks are. Real cute.

"Ha, yeah, I wouldn't know." He kicks a rock with his shoe, his shoes that are so stark white I'd have to guess he's never worn them before. For some reason, he seems more mature than a typical high schooler would be.

I shake my head, hair falling out of my ponytail and into my face. "I'm pregnant."

Jake stops mid-kick, turning to look at me. "Oh, shit." He spins his body so all of him is facing me, giving me his full attention.

"Suzan overheard me telling Phoenix. I just found out this morning." I let out a sad little laugh, "It's stupid that I'm this surprised. I mean, you have sex with no protection, what do you expect? But it's," I pause as I try to decide if 'laying it on him' is really the best choice. Right now I need an ear to listen, and he has two. "I don't know how much you saw back there. I was pregnant when my wife, Roxanne, died. It, uh... well, I don't have a baby now. The sperm donor was Phoenix. So it's just... I feel like the world is just laughing in my face."

Jake nods thoughtfully, eyes locked with mine, which is kind of overwhelming with the intensity of the silver in them. "Maybe it is."

"Maybe the world is laughing in my face?"

He shrugs. "Yeah, why not? Seems like a lot of shit keeps happening to you, right? I mean, I've seen you twice, this is the longest we've ever talked, and I know that your wife was raped and murdered, you were pregnant with her baby at the time, but also her brother's baby, who you now happen to be dating, and who impregnated you. Again. That's not even mentioning your mom."

"And she's not even my mom, not really." I crack a smile as I realize he's right. "My life's a mess, isn't it?"

He holds two of his fingers up, barely touching each other. "Just a little bit."

My smile widens, lifting the weight off my chest slightly. Maybe that was a sign to think about something else. "So why are you here, anyway? Why aren't you with your family?"

"My family lives in Canada, and we're Jewish. So, not much reason."

I look at him with confusion. "Your parents live in a different country? Why do you go to school here?"

"It's a pretty good college, and Florida winters are *much* nicer than where I'm from."

I wave my hand. "Wait, back up. You're in college?"

He nods, eyes sparkling with amusement. "Yeah? Did you think I was in high school?"

"Well, yeah. You're friends with Vincent," I trail off, realizing that sounds stupid. "I just assumed you were in high school too. Some seniors look pretty old."

He snorts. "I'm twenty-two. I hope I don't look like a senior in high school."

"Well, you don't, I just," I shrug, lips pressed together, "never mind. How are you two friends then anyway? The school is like forty minutes from here, how'd you even met?"

For a second it looks like he won't tell me, but then he looks back up at me. "A party. I think he was there to buy pot, and just kind of got wrapped up in everything. I found him sleeping on a bench and gave him a ride to my place. He said his mom wouldn't be too pleased about all the drinking he'd been doing."

"Yeah, no."

"On our way back the next morning we had the whole

fifty-minute drive to kill. We talked. I guess now we're just friends." He shrugs, leaning his head against the car door sideways, and looks up at the sky.

I do the same, a sense of calm washing over me as I watch the clouds floating in the air. "I can see how. You're very easy to talk to."

"Why, thank you."

I sigh, letting my eyes shut. "Thank you."

"For what?"

I shrug. "I dunno. Listening?"

"Like I said," he pokes my arm, "I like listening."

I let my head roll so I'm looking at him. "Hmm, maybe we should be friends too. Can Vincent share?"

He nods. "I'm sure he can." He stands up, looking down at me.

"Well, then friends it is."

He holds a hand down, and I take it. He yanks me up, smiling as he responds. "Sounds like a plan to me."

CHAPTER ELEVEN

My Christmas morning consists of eating Captain Crunch on the couch while watching Hallmark movies in my PJs. Feeling like a sorry lump of a person, nose sore from all the tissues it endured last night, and eyes puffy from tears, I'm not in a good mood. My mood doesn't look like it's improving either, since I can't stop thinking about what Phoenix is doing. It's Christmas morning. On fuckin' Christmas morning, he's run off somewhere, without a word, and I'm left wondering. I'm on scenario twenty when my phone pings, alerting me of a text. Assuming it's either Phoenix or one of my siblings, I pick it up to answer. I'm surprised when I see Jake's name on the screen.

When he asked for my number yesterday, I was hesitant to give it to him. He had been making eyes at me a little during the Christmas debacle yesterday. I'm so not in the mood to be stuck in another love triangle, even if I'm not actively participating. But after the cackle he let out when I mentioned it, I feel better about it. I could use another friend, and he said he wanted one too. Though, when he said he'd text me to make plans, I honestly didn't expect to be hearing from him the day afterward.

I reply to his message asking me what I'm doing. I tell him I'm doing just what I had expected, which is nothing. He replies instantly, asking if he can come over since he's in the area for lunch with a friend. I give him the address and suddenly realize I look like a walking disaster. While I'm not trying to impress the man, I also don't want to scare him off. I huff, pushing myself off the couch and going into the bedroom to change my clothes and brush my hair. As I'm rinsing my mouth after brushing my teeth, I hear the doorbell ring.

I quickly wipe my mouth off and run to the front of the apartment. I open the door, smiling at Jake, who's standing out front with a bag in his hand and a backpack over his shoulder. I eye the label on the bag, not failing to notice that it looks like some kind of Italian restaurant. "You brought food?"

He nods, coming into the apartment. "Yeah, I was already at the restaurant when my friend canceled. Figured I'd bring us something to eat." He drops the bag on the counter and looks around the room. "Nice place, though not exactly the vibe I was expecting."

"Thanks, and yes. Not my place, it's Phoenix's. I lived in Seattle until like a month ago. I guess I technically still do." I grab forks out of the drawer and head towards the couch.

Jake follows my lead, bringing the food over and plopping down next to me, dropping his backpack to the floor. "Is that where Roxanne died?"

I feel my heart skip a beat. I don't know why, but the calmness of his voice seems strange to me. Maybe it's because most people have hidden questions underneath the one they're asking, or that the way they ask makes it seem more like they want gossip than to know about my life. Either way, it's different in a good way. "Uh, yeah."

"Sorry, is that not something you want to talk about?" He unpacks the bag of food but keeps his eyes on me.

I shrug. "I mean, I just normally don't talk to people who don't already know everything that happened, even the things I didn't want them to know."

He nods thoughtfully. "Sometimes, it's nice to let a new pair of ears listen to something. Do you wanna, I dunno, talk about it? I don't mean to cross any lines, but I usually do anyway."

I chuckle. "It feels like all that trauma is constantly in my head... I guess until recently."

"Like once you moved back here?"

"Once I started dating Phoenix." I open a container of baked ziti while Jake grabs the one with chicken alfredo. "Like I said, almost everyone I've genuinely interacted with since Roxanne died has known everything about me. It's so strange to know you don't know any of it."

He shrugs. "Maybe you want to keep it that way? I mean, Vincent never seemed like he wanted to talk about it, even got mad one time when someone asked about you. I think he wanted to let your business be yours. All I really know is what you told me yesterday."

I nod thoughtfully as I take a bite. "Maybe I'll be able to have a third section in my life."

"What do you mean?" Jake asks before he stuffs his mouth with pasta.

I finish chewing. "I've always seen my life split into two different sections. The part before I came to live with Suzan and the part after that. Not a single person from those two parts overlap. Not one."

"What happened to your parents?"

Keeping true to his word, he doesn't seem like the kind of person afraid to ask the questions he really wants to. He also just feels like someone I want to be talking to. A pretty good combination. "Oh, uh, weird shit, I guess. I don't know where my dad is, but he's wanted by the police. My mom died about two weeks after they decided to give me up. They think my dad killed her."

"Wow, that's a lot."

I shake my head. "That's not even the half of it. My childhood was... a mess. I'm surprised they kept me as long as they did."

"When did they give you up?"

"When I was eight. Though I guess me saying 'give up' is a little too generous. More like abandoned." I look down at the bowl of pasta in my hand, my throat tightening at the memories of the day it all happened. Jake looks at me with a look in his eyes that makes my heart open up and lets more words pour through my lips. "They asked me to go to the store to buy myself some lunch, so I walked until I found the nearest convenience store. Stole some canned something or another. When I went back, they weren't there. I waited for a while because I had assumed they just went off to buy drugs or have sex. They ended up not showing up the next day or the day after. On the third day, my luck ran out at that convenience store, and they caught me stealing.

"The police started trying to find my parents, but I didn't even know my mom's real name because she went by a nickname – Bunny – so I wasn't exactly much help. I only had a picture of the two of them to give to the police. When they found her dead body, it matched the picture. They sent me into foster care. I ended up moving when they thought it might be my dad who killed my mom, to protect me in case he wanted to kill me too. That's how I ended up in Florida."

Jake *hmphs*, leaning back against the couch. "Well, that's lousy, huh?"

"Yeah, well, I've had some other fun *lousy* things happen after that too." I shove another forkful of pasta in my mouth, talking around it as I continue. "I'm sorry, I'm complaining a lot."

Jake snorts so forcefully it sounds like it hurt. "You've had way too much shit happen to you. I think you've earned the right to complain."

I shake my head. "That doesn't exactly work when the things happened years ago."

"Fine," Jake turns, so he's leaning back against the armrest and facing me. "If you don't want to complain, then don't. I'm down to listen to a little bit of bitching, but maybe you're not in the mood to bitch. So instead, tell me what Suzan's so pissed about."

I tilt my head. "I'm pretty sure we went over this yesterday."

"Well, yes. You told me about what's happening now... congrats, by the way," he says as he points at my stomach.

"Hmm, maybe not a congratulations?" I find my hand moving to press against my stomach. *Pregnant.*

Jake rolls his eyes. "What are you supposed to say to someone in your situation? Let me know once you've kicked your fetus to the curb?"

"Eww."

"Exactly." Jake turns his insanely silver eyes on me, holding my gaze captive. "What I'm saying is that, like you've pointed out, I'm not exactly up to date. What happened with you and Phoenix before all of these new '*Suzan*' developments?"

I huff. "Like all the way at the beginning?"

"Well, the beginning is usually pretty important, right?"

I nod, leaning my head back and looking up at the ceiling. At the start? "Well, I met Phoenix before I met everyone else."

"How?"

"The day I was supposed to come to Orlando, my flight was late, we landed at midnight. I ended up missing the time I was supposed to meet everyone, meaning Suzan and all her foster kids at the time, so they put me up in a hotel that night. At the time, I was, uh, not exactly a golden child, and so I snuck out, used a fake ID to get into a bar, and decided I wanted a drink. When I got there, I saw Phoenix at the bar."

Jake whistles. "Love at first sight?"

I cough out a laugh. "Hell no. I mean, I knew he was cute, but I was just hoping I could get him to buy me a drink. He did buy me one, well, a couple actually, and then we went into the back alley and..." I scrunch up my nose, "stuff."

"Stuff?" He chuckles. "That's all I get? Did y'all bang or not?"

I shake my head. "No, I, uh, blew him, but at that time I was actually a virgin. I didn't want to lose it in an alley."

He narrows his eyes at me. "I thought you two slept together?"

"Umm, we did. He got my number and offered to 'show me around,' which I think was total BS. Like a million hours later, at like five in the freaking morning, I get a phone call from him, asking if he could come to pick me up. I, being a dumbass, said yes. We didn't leave the parking lot."

Jake gives me a look that has a little bit of concern and amusement mixed together. "So you didn't want to lose it in an alley, but you'd lose it in the back seat of some guy's car?"

"I didn't lose it then either." I eat some more of my pasta. "He ended up coming back to my hotel room, and we, uh, did more things. He fell asleep. Later that day, when I went to meet everyone, Phoenix was still asleep in my hotel room, so he wasn't there. When he finally came to the house... God, neither of us knew what to do."

He chuckles. "I wish I could have seen the look on your faces."

"It wasn't fun. Then he kind of tried to get me to date him, and I said no because I didn't want to mess anything up with Suzan, I wanted to get adopted. Everyone ended up finding out Phoenix and I had sex when Roxanne found out. She yells at about the same volume that her mom does, and the whole house ended up finding out." I shake my head, looking down at my lap, "She ended up kissing someone else to try to get back at me. She thought what I had done was cheating. Jokes on her, I didn't cheat until *much* later."

Jake looks like he's not sure if he should laugh or not. "The night she died?"

"Yeah," I nod, "that's the first time I physically cheated on her. I mean, Roxanne and I broke up *a lot*, and I won't say nothing ever happened during those times, but I didn't cheat on her. Emotionally, hell, yes. But physically? Not until the night she died."

"Emotionally?"

I sigh, slumping into the couch, feeling the twinge of guilt as I tell the story. "I've been in love with Phoenix for a long time."

Jake nods, seeming lost in thought. After a moment, he reaches forward, putting his pasta down, then turns to me, squeezing my knee. The gesture feels oddly comforting being from someone I've just met. "I'm sorry life keeps throwing more shit at you. Do you know what you're going to do about the baby?"

I let out a dry laugh. "We haven't really talked about it, but I don't want a kid."

"Weren't you going to have a kid with Roxanne?"

I nod. I was, so how do you tell someone you've just met that you regretted getting pregnant even while you held your child in your arms for the first time? "Uh, yes, I was. She really wanted kids."

"But you didn't?"

"Not really," I finch as the words come out of my mouth. I've never told anyone that I regret that entire pregnancy, and the first person I admit it to is Jake. "The only reason I had a kid is because Roxanne asked me to."

Jake scoots closer, legs crossed in front of him as he faces me. His eyes are full of pure interest in my story. "What would you have done?"

"What do you mean?"

"If Roxanne hadn't died, and you had the baby with her, you'd be a mom right now."

I feel like a wave hits me as that thought rushes into my mind. I honestly haven't thought about that. Even when I was pregnant, and I knew the baby was coming, I hadn't fully processed it all. It was like I wouldn't believe it was real until I gave birth and the baby was in my arms. After Roxanne died, it was like I never had to process it. I didn't ever think about what life would be like with a child because I didn't even think I would have one. "Yeah, I would be."

He tilts his head. "What happened to the baby?"

I look away from him, turning so I'm facing the TV, setting my eyes on the screen. "I don't know." I clear my throat, grabbing the remote, and changing the channel. "Wanna watch this movie? It had just started when you messaged me."

Jake turns on the couch, too, side-eyeing me. "Uh, sure, yeah. But after that, we should play some Mario. I see it on the TV stand."

I smile tightly at him. "Deal."

As I'm grabbing the OJ out of the fridge, I hear the front door locks turning. The thought of Phoenix walking through the door makes my heart flutter. I also start to think of the million questions I have for him about where he's been all day. I don't have any time to ask them, though, because he comes into the apartment full of energy. Phoenix throws himself in front of me, where I'm standing by the kitchen counter, a drink in my hand. He holds out a wrapped box between us.

"What's that?"

"A Christmas present." He beams proudly, holding it out for me to take.

I do, reluctantly, narrowing my eyes at him. This present is wrapped in a red sparkly wrapping paper. "Weren't they wrapped in that penguin paper?"

"Uh, yes. After you said we weren't getting each other gifts, I took them all back."

I look at the gift in my hand then back at him. "Then what is this?"

He shrugs. "I decided to get this, anyway."

"Well, I did actually get you some things. I thought we'd open them this morning." I put the box down, turning to get my gifts for Phoenix.

He grabs my arm, turning my back around, a mischievous look in his eyes. "My gift kind of has some activities attached to it."

"What—"

"It's more for me than for you."

"So you got yourself a Christmas gift? Not me."

He shrugs. "Well, that gift will make me want to give you more gifts."

"I don't know what that means."

He waves me off. "Just open it."

I rip off the wrapping paper, dropping it in the trash can behind me, revealing a garment box. I give him a skeptical look, slowly taking the top of the box off. Lying on top of white tissue paper is something red, strappy, and definitely some kind of lingerie. I take the two pieces out, putting the box down onto the counter. In the one hand is a red thong. In the other is something much more complicated. "What..."

Phoenix takes it from my hands, straightening it out. Two straps go down to two hearts that I'm *assuming* are supposed to go over my nipples. Underneath where my exposed boobs would be is a piece of sheer fabric that covers the back and side but leaves the stomach exposed. "You see what I mean now?"

"About the wanting to give me other gifts? Sure." I shake my head and examine the fabric. "I have no clue how I'll be able to get that on."

Phoenix holds it out. "Like this. Just put this part over your head, and then this part would need to be in the back, and–"

"I don't know if I'm in the mood..."

Phoenix rests his palm against my cheek, dazzling me with his brilliant blue eyes. "Let's spend the last few hours of Christmas together, right? Just you and me. Tomorrow, when we go to pack the last of your clothes from Seattle, we won't exactly have any time for any fun, right?"

I sigh, looking down at the strappy number on the counter. What does it hurt to just have a little fun, right? "Okay, I'll tell you what. *You* get ready to give me the best 'gift' I've ever had, and *I'll* go put on this death trap. Deal?"

Phoenix beams down at me, eyes full of devious thoughts. "Hell yes, you have a deal." He hands me the top, and I go to the bathroom.

I put the underwear on first, simple enough. Then as I try to pull all the straps onto the right sides of my head, I realize it isn't actually as hard as I had thought. With a little adjusting, it works. As I look at myself in the mirror, I shake my head. It actually looks pretty damn sexy. *He* better think this is the sexiest damn thing he's seen in his entire life, or this will feel ridiculous.

Trying to feel as sensual as possible, I open the door, expecting to have to go find Phoenix in the bedroom. Instead, he's just standing right where I left him, eyes snapping instantly to me and sparkling more the longer they stay on me. I saunter towards him, a coy smile on my lips. "So? How do I look?"

"Like perfection."

I finally reach him, my eyelashes batting in a slightly comedic way. "And those gifts you promised me?"

Phoenix picks me up, lifting me onto the counter. "Don't worry. You'll be getting several more tonight. Merry fucking Christmas."

"Was that a pun?"

"Mmm-hmm." He grabs the strings on either side of my hips, starting to pull them down my legs, not wasting any time.

I huff. "You're taking it off already? What's the point? Your gift to yourself could have just been me naked. Less money involved."

"Oh, *this* is staying on," he snaps the strap on my shoulder. "This, however, is in my way." He pulls the thong the rest of the way off.

I chuckle, leaning back onto my hands. "Yeah? In the way of wha— oh!"

Wasting no time, he leans down to fit his face right between my legs. His fingers dig into my legs, gripping them about as tightly as I'm holding onto the counter under me. As he settles in, he drapes my leg over his shoulder, pushing the other one aside.

My eyes flutter shut, my heartbeat already speeding up. In the last month, I've seen time and time again what I missed out on all those years ago when I chose a family with Suzan over a relationship with Phoenix. As I can attest to right now, that was definitely a mistake. I look down at where Phoenix is burying himself between my legs. He looks up at me, the gorgeous sky blue of his eyes glimmering, with a mix of mischief and desire. The sight of his face between my legs and those eyes staring at me makes a rush flow through my body. I squeeze my eyes shut, falling backward onto my palms.

Phoenix chuckles against me, and I swear I feel my entire body spasm. This man is going to give me an orgasm in seconds if he continues like this. The world may be stopping, or ending, or *something*, because this feels way too good. Maybe I've died and gone to heaven? Maybe this is all a dream? An amazing, perfect dream that needs to happen again. Phoenix's nails dig into my skin, prickling with pain, letting me know that this is, in fact, not a dream.

"Holy shit," I gasp, falling back even more so I'm lying back on the counter, braced on my elbows. It's not a dream, so it's the stars aligning or karma giving me something really good after giving me a boatload of trauma. Or maybe Phoenix is just really good at this, and since I've felt this a million times in the last month, I'll say it's the latter. He's just really, really good at this.

Phoenix pauses, looking up at me, wiping his mouth with the back of his hand. "You doing good up there, babe?"

I shake my head, taking a deep breath. "No. Keep going."

He chuckles, settling his head back between my legs. Against my neck, Roxanne's ring slides, reminding me of the only other person I've been this close to. Each day with

Phoenix eases the ache of thinking about her more and more. Now when she passes through my mind in a moment like this, I don't feel that wash of guilt, like I shouldn't be letting someone else move his tongue like this on my skin. I just enjoy the moment. And I am definitely enjoying this moment. Definitely.

CHAPTER TWELVE

Turning the key in the lock, I push the door open, revealing the absolute disaster I was living in a month ago when I left for Florida. I flip on the light, and from where I stand, I can already tell this is going to be embarrassing. There's trash covering tables, lots of empty bottles of alcohol, clothes that I left lying around on the floor instead of putting in the hamper, and a ton of other things no one should have to see. The bedroom floor will be worse. Oh, God, it's going to be worse. Phoenix comes into the room behind me, closing the door to block out the cold. Well, some of the cold. I turned my heat off before I left, not wanting to be racking up any extra bills, so the place is still pretty chilly.

After waking up at four in the morning to catch our flight, then a six-hour plane ride, we're both already exhausted. Not to mention Phoenix kept me up most of the night. Not that I'm complaining about *that*, I'm just saying that I feel like I might fall over any second. After all that time awake last night, the wait at the airport, and then the plane ride, Phoenix still wouldn't tell me what he was doing yesterday. I pointed out to him that it's weird to run off on Christmas. He pointed out that he just doesn't want to talk about it.

After that, I felt like an ass for pushing him about it. Of course, he has things in his life that don't involve me. I don't want to be one of those people who demands to know everything about their significant other's life. I've never been like that, and I really don't want to start now. But another part of me remembers all the times I was being secretive with Roxanne. It was never for a good reason, it was always a devious one.

I pull off my gloves and snow jacket, dropping them onto the floor beside me. "Well, here it is."

"It's nice," Phoenix says, kissing my cheek, eyes darting around the room. His face disagrees with his words.

I scoff. "It's definitely not *nice* at all. But the rent is really cheap and it's not like I can afford anything else."

Phoenix puts his jacket and gloves on top of mine. I had told him he should buy a real jacket and gloves for the trip. He stuck with his hoodie and the fingerless gloves. He has to be freezing. Every time I asked if he was cold, he denied it. "Well, it doesn't matter now anyway, because you can come live with me."

I frown. "I still think we're skipping some of the essential steps of a relationship *before* living together."

"We've lived together *before*." He takes off his baseball cap – also something he ignored me on – and tosses it on the pile.

I raise my brows at him. "Yeah, with Suzan. That doesn't count."

"Look, Maz, we've gone over this. You can find your own place if you want. I just–"

"You just think I should move in with you. You're only saying that for the sex."

He wraps his arms around my waist, his ice-blue eyes glittering with mischief. "The sex is definitely a plus," he kisses me with a teasing smile still on his lips, "but you know the real reasons. There's–"

"The money, and the commutes, and that you 'just like looking at my face.'" I mock him, a playful smile pulling at my lips.

He narrows his eyes at me. "Will I ever be able to finish a–"

"Sentence? Nope." I pull my beanie off my head, letting it fall onto the couch beside my leg. "But your points don't matter, dumb or not. I couldn't afford anything near you anyway. I'll just have to mooch off you until I'm raking in cash with my new café."

He nods. "Mooch away, babe. When your café becomes the biggest success in Florida, I'll mooch off you. So we'll be square."

"Sounds like a plan to me." I go into the kitchen, switching on the light. The bulb buzzes on above me, filling the room with a gross yellow tone, making the whole room look murky. I notice a pile of dishes – clean, thankfully – sitting on the counter, never put away. The trash is half full and smells absolutely atrocious. I don't even want to look in my fridge because God only knows what I left in there. The extent of my preparation for leaving for Florida was pre-paying for December's rent and packing my suitcase. That was it. It didn't help matters that I spent most of that time drinking or sleeping, so I wasn't exactly in the clearest state of mind when I was walking out the door.

Phoenix comes in behind me, scrunching his nose as the smell hits him. "God, Maz. What died in here?"

"Just my trash from a month ago." I decide to take the leap and open the fridge, and it's about as gross as I imagined. "*Ech*, why didn't I just do this before?"

"'Cause, you're a dumbass. Lucky for you, I'm here."

Phoenix reaches over my head, grabbing some of the bottles, avoiding things that look like they could infest his hand just by getting near them. He reaches over my head again, and I poke him in the armpit.

"You could reach around me."

He scoffs. "I'm almost a foot-and-a-half taller than you. Over is much easier."

I roll my eyes but don't say anything else, grabbing a dish-towel from the counter beside the fridge. Using the towel, I scoop the more disgusting things into the trash, making sure not to touch them. When we're done dumping out my entire fridge, spoiled or not, I tie the trash bag, trying to yank it out of the can and failing miserably.

Phoenix wears a smug smile as he comes over, pulling it out in one swift motion and carrying the bag out the front door. When he comes back in a second later, he holds his hands up in surrender. "I take it back. Maybe you couldn't have cleaned this place out before you left. Seems like you're not quite strong enough."

I gape at him. "Am too! I could have gotten that if I tried harder."

"Sure, whatever you say." He rubs his hands together, looking at the thermostat by the door. "Jesus, it's freezing in here." He taps the buttons, eventually turning to look at the rest of the apartment. "I have no clue where to start first."

I follow him out, looking at the cluttered space around us, already feeling unmotivated to do anything. "Maybe we clean first?"

"Maybe we pack first."

"If we pack first, we may not end up cleaning."

"Good. Fuck cleaning."

I roll my eyes. "Don't be a jackass. I want my security deposit back."

"Like you're getting it back anyway. This place looks *really* shady. They're going to keep your money wither way." He looks over at me, holding his stare for only a moment longer before sighing. "Yes, fine. We clean first. But when we get to your clothes, you're trying on your underwear for me."

I make a face. "Weird trade-off, but okay."

As he passes by me to grab the trash bags out of the kitchen, he drops a kiss on the top of my head. He brings the whole box back in, handing me one and then surveying the room. "How much were you drinking?"

"I, uh..." I look up at him and cringe at the concerned look he's wearing on his face. "A lot. But I'm fine. So, let's get a-cleanin'!"

Phoenix groans but quickly gets to work picking up bottles.

As I grab an empty vodka bottle, my phone pings. I pull it out of my pocket.

"Who's that?"

"Jake. I told him we landed a bit ago. He's asking me to bring him back a souvenir."

Phoenix shakes his head in wonder. "You two are bizarre. You just met and now he's texting you about every single thing he's doing."

"No, not everything. Besides, I like talking to him. It just feels so easy, even with random mindless stuff, like what our favorite snacks are. Plus, I've sent him like five texts since he left yesterday."

Phoenix pouts, a little bit of the green-eyed monster poking through. "You haven't texted me five times since he left."

I tilt my head, walk over to him, and drop my hand on his chest. "Is someone jealous?" He opens his mouth to respond then quickly closes it when he realizes he doesn't have a good rebuttal. "You are jealous, how cute." I reach up, pecking his lips.

He grabs my head, kissing me more intensely with his strong arms trapping me to his chest, his mouth laying claim to mine. With a sigh, he pulls back, kissing my nose. "I'm not jealous. I just think it's weird."

"If it's the texting thing, then stop being weird about it. I was with you the whole time after he left. We had no reason to text." I give him a look telling him I think he's being ridiculous and move towards the other side of the room to start gathering trash.

Phoenix starts dropping bottles in his bag, making them clang together. "We didn't text that much when we didn't see each other."

"That's because *you* suck at texting." I put my bag on the ground and pull my phone out of my pocket again.

"See? He's texting you again. Why can't we—" His phone pings, and he pulls it out of his pocket, reading a text off the screen. "Would you prefer we talk like this?" He looks up at me, eyes narrowed. "Haha, very funny."

I send him another text.

"Thank you, I thought so..." He rolls his eyes. "Okay, nice, point made. Now stop it."

I smirk at him. "So you'd rather us talk, then?"

Phoenix scrunches his nose at me. "Yes, now shut up and clean."

After throwing away all the trash in the apartment, I lay on the bed, definitely about to drift off, waiting for Phoenix to grab us food. Despite us getting extremely distracted, we managed to clean the entire place, not a single bit of trash

203

left. Which only leaves us with packing all of my clothes and shipping them before our flight tomorrow night. Every time I suggested Phoenix and I make a trip of this, stay here for a while to get away, he acted like it was the craziest idea he'd ever heard. I pointed out that it would take the stress off. We wouldn't have to worry about a time limit as much. He insisted on taking care of everything in two days.

So I'm selling all my furniture here and just... starting over. Starting over, again. I was hoping that wouldn't happen anymore, I guess now it is, and it's a good thing. I couldn't have just sat here in this apartment wallowing away in self-pity forever. I had to pick myself up and start getting my life back on track. And I am. I haven't just been soaking in my thoughts. I've been hanging out with people, I've been laughing... I've been happy. I'll be able to be a person again.

The front door opens and shuts. "Maz?" Phoenix calls out. The amount of bag shuffling I hear tells me that he bought a little more than food.

I groan, sliding off the bed and blinking my eyes open, trying to will away the sleepiness. "Coming." Cleaning all day is hard work – work I'm apparently not cut out for. I go into the living room, or rather the small room that's everything other than the bedroom and bathroom. Phoenix is setting up food on the coffee table as I come out. I point to the kitchen counter. "Look what I found while you were out." I hold up the bottle of vodka.

"Is that what this raspberry lemonade was for?" He looks from the bottle to me, wearing a concerned look on his face. "Are you wanting to drink that?"

I bring the bottle over to him and put it down on the end table. "Yeah. You know how fun I get when I'm drunk. Figured you'd be excited." I wink at him, grabbing a container of food out of the paper bag and setting it out.

He looks down, eyes locking on my abdomen. "I just..."

I look down too, my brain taking a moment to remember what it is he's looking at. "Phoenix, I thought we were on the same page about not wanting to have a baby?"

"Yes, it just feels weird to be ignoring it and drinking."

"The reason people *don't* drink while they're pregnant is to make sure the baby is born healthy. That's not a problem here." I grab his hands, looking into his eyes to try to find what's bothering him. "Are you wanting to keep the baby?"

He takes a second longer than I'd him to like before he finally shakes his head, "No, it just feels weird... or wrong, maybe?"

"The drinking or the abortion?"

He drops his eyes to the floor before answering. "Both?"

I press my hand to his cheek, moving so I'm in his line of sight. He looks so conflicted. "Tell me what you're thinking, Nix. I didn't realize you'd want to have a baby. If you do, then we need to talk about it. I mean, it's not like we had a long conversation about it. Do you want to?"

"I want to talk about it. I'm just not sure how to talk about it, or what I could even say." He pulls out of my hands and drops down onto the couch with a sigh. "What a strange thing to talk about, huh?" He chuckles, head shaking slowly. "Two years ago, you were talking to Roxanne about having a baby. Now you're talking to me."

I sit on the coffee table, squeezing his knee, hoping to reassure him. "The conversations would be extremely different, Phoenix. Roxanne... she never wanted to actually talk about it. She wanted to have a baby, and she wanted me to carry that baby. I went from college graduate to potential mom without much of the decision falling on me." My hand drifts to my stomach, pressing against it. "My life is so different now than it was the last time I got pregnant. My wife is dead, I want to start a business, we just started dating..."

"I know," Phoenix grabs the hand on his knee and holds it. "I don't think now is the perfect time for us to have a kid. I've wanted this for so long, being able to hold you, and love you without having to feel guilt or nerves with it. So now that it's here, and you have my kid in you without it being Roxanne's too... I just don't want to throw that away. Not so soon."

"The last time I gave birth, I was at one of the lowest points in my life. I don't look back at the day the baby was born with fond memories, Phoenix. When I remember being pregnant and having that baby, all I think about is the pain I felt, not physically, but emotionally. I think about how much I resented a newborn. An infant. How much I hated looking at her and knowing that she wasn't my dream. She was Roxanne's, and when Roxanne wasn't there to see her dream come to life, it wasn't worth it. It wasn't what I wanted."

Phoenix nods, leaning forward and resting his forehead on mine. "I know, Maz. But..." Phoenix trails off, taking a deep breath. I see his brain working a mile a minute, mulling over something that he's not saying. After a second, he leans back, seeming to decide against saying what he wanted to say, his shoulder relaxing slightly. "I know."

I try to figure out what he's really feeling, what he's really wanting. I can't decide. "I might want to have kids, Phoenix. But if I do, I want them *one day*. I want to be more mentally healthy, and I want to be able to have forgiven myself for my first baby."

"*Our* first baby. You didn't make that choice on your own. You did the right thing."

I move off the coffee table and onto the couch, next to Phoenix, resting my head onto his shoulder. "The hardest choice I've had to make was giving her up. I can't have another baby so soon, especially knowing I gave up on her just a year ago. I can't, Phoenix."

"I know, babe. I know." He wraps his arms around me and rests his head on mine. "What if we hadn't given her up?"

"What do you mean?"

"If we hadn't given her up, would you want to have this baby?"

I look up at him, trying to figure out what that would even mean. I mean, I wouldn't have wanted to keep her. If I had... I just can't picture my life with a little girl running around. "No. I didn't want to raise her. I'm not, so having this baby wouldn't change that."

Phoenix draws in a long breath, slowly nodding. "Then I think you should get the abortion. When you're ready... then we can figure it all out."

I squeeze my eyes shut, taking a deep breath. "Are you sure? You're not just saying that?"

"I didn't raise concerns because I want *this* baby. I raised concerns because I want *a* baby. I want to have a family with you." He kisses my head. "If you're not ready, then I'm not either. We have a ton of other things to explore and do before we have kids. Like clearing out this apartment of yours, for one. So, let's get to work, huh?"

I groan as I sit up. "I think we've done enough for one day. I'm down to eat dinner, watch a movie, and screw. We can pack tomorrow."

Phoenix chuckles. "So ladylike."

"Me not being ladylike is one of the reasons you love me." I kiss him before reaching forward to grab the rice.

He smiles, taking the fork I hand him. "Very true. Now let's eat fast. I'm excited for dessert."

Phoenix holds up a thong in his hand and raises a brow at me. "Huh?"

I continue to fold the shirt in my hands as I respond. "Phoenix? Stop asking about each one and just assuming I'm taking all of my bras and underwear."

"Even the un-sexy ones?" He holds up a pair of granny panties.

I purse my lips, resisting the urge to throw something at him. "Yes. Even those. I use those for when I'm on my period."

"What, you can't be sexy when you're on your period?"

"I mean, sure, but I don't want to bleed all over my nice, expensive underwear." I stare at him until he drops the clothing out of his hand and into the box. After another second of staring, Phoenix sighs and reaches into the drawer, grabbing all of my underwear at once. "Thank you."

He does the same to my bra drawer, closing the box when it's full and taping it. "So, what now? All the fun things are put away."

"Ha, hilarious. You can fold my pants." I nod towards the pile I made on the bed. "That sounds really fun, right?"

"No, what sounds fun is me watching you try on all the sexy clothes I just packed away in that box." He huffs as he makes his way over to me, grabbing a pair of jeans off the top of the pile and starting to fold them.

I kiss his shoulder, dropping another shirt into the shirt box. "If you stop complaining, you can pick what we eat tonight."

A smirk pulls at his lips. "Can I pick you?"

"You want me to eat myself?" I tilt my head. "Doesn't make much sense."

He groans and drops the jeans onto the bed, making them

unfold again. "That's not what I meant and you know it. You're no fun."

"I'm plenty of fun. Just not when I'm trying to finish packing. Plus, we have a flight to catch, there's no time for more sex." I put the last shirt into the box and close it.

Phoenix smirks at me. "There's always time for more sex."

I grab the tape gun off the dresser where Phoenix put it, taping the box closed. I write *shirts* on the top, so we know what it is, and drop the box onto the ground. "We should've started earlier this morning."

Phoenix puts a pair of pants into the box before wrapping his arms around my waist. "You mean you didn't like how we spent the morning?" He kisses my neck, which he has full access to since my hair has been up in a sloppy bun since I got out of bed. "I thought it was the perfect way to wake up."

I swat at his arms, turning around in his grip and clasping my hands behind his neck. "It was perfect." I stretch up on my tip-toes and peck his lips. "*But* I want to finish this last bit of packing before our flight, Nix."

Phoenix squeezes me, resting his chin on top of my head. He lets out a deep breath, not saying any words, but conveying to me exactly what he's thinking. This whole pregnancy thing is wearing on him. I'll be happy when he doesn't have to worry about it anymore. Every time I bring it up, it's like his mind starts racing a million miles a minute.

I slump into him, nudging my cheek into his chest, the smell of my lavender shampoo washing over me. The smell makes me smile as I remember the shower we took together this morning. My shampoo is a good look on him. "I love you," I mumble against his chest, eyes locked onto the wall as I say those words.

Phoenix stiffens slightly, and I can practically hear his brain working. He wants to figure out how to react to that: to make it a huge deal or take it in stride. He kisses the top of my head. "Love you too, Maz." He squeezes my butt before letting go of me and turning back to his box.

I roll my eyes at him, getting back to work. He chose right. One of the many reasons why I, Mazey Sutton, love Phoenix Hickerman.

CHAPTER THIRTEEN

After spending the last four days without a second of relaxation, I feel like shit. Since Christmas Eve, I've had a screaming match with Suzan, wallowed in self-pity, spilled all my life secrets to Jake, flew across the country, and packed my entire apartment up. Now today, back at home, I'm feeling exhausted for a different reason. Phoenix has barely spoken to me the entire morning. I know we didn't get sleep, and I know that today is going to be hard, but *I'm* tired too. It's going to be hard on *me* too. I can tell there's something wrong with him. I just wish he would tell me what it is instead of pulling away like this.

As we're riding to the abortion clinic, with Phoenix's hand gripping mine in his lap, I just keep trying to remember that this is what's best. I do love Phoenix, and we deserve to try for some kind of happiness. We deserve to figure out how we want our life to go and strive for it. Having a baby right now just wouldn't make sense. Not for my mental health, financial health, our relationship's health, or a million other things.

As we pull into a parking spot, Phoenix pulls my hand up to his lips, kissing it. He squeezes it. "Are you ready?"

I just nod and pull myself out of the car. Phoenix runs around the car quickly with the car keys gripped in his hand as he locks the doors. He doesn't waste a second before sliding his hand back in mine. As we're walking towards the door, Phoenix pauses, jerking me to a stop, my arm totally getting yanked behind me. I look back at him. "What's wrong, Nix?" I rub my thumb along the back of his hand.

He looks down at me, his eyes soaked in worry. Worry and something else. "I, just–"

I pull our hands to my chest, pressing them to my heart. "Babe, you have to tell me now. Because I can't undo an abortion once it happens. So I need you to tell me what's on your mind." I look back at where Phoenix is staring. I don't see anything. I move into his line of sight. "Nix? What's wrong? Talk to me."

He yanks his hand out of mine, taking a deep breath, locking his eyes straight onto mine, and pursing his lips. I might regret asking him to talk, but I don't have time to stop him. Instead, I watch as he opens his mouth and utters words I never thought I'd hear. "I still have custody of Roxy."

My heart drops into the pit of my stomach, then all the way to the floor. Okay, no. He has to be saying some ridiculously dumb shit right now. Some kind of stupid prank. It'd be a terrible prank, but he *cannot* be serious. Can he? I feel my stomach where it's resting at my feet, wither away as I try to make my brain say something. Anything. "I'm sorry, come again?"

He looks confused, wetting his lips and opening his mouth to speak again. "I'm still our daughter's legal guardian. I've had Roxy for the last fourteen months. "

A laugh pushes out of my throat, coming out as some deranged choking noise, which about perfectly describes what my brain feels like right now. Here I am trying to deal with one pregnancy, and he's bringing up one that was supposed to be done with a year ago. "So where the hell is she, then, Phoenix? You have to be fucking with me!"

"I... I'm not." He flinches back slightly but keeps his calm surprisingly well for someone who has been keeping my child a secret for a year.

I clench my fingers against my palms, probably drawing blood, but drawing blood is better than smacking Phoenix right in his face, and that is what my hand is telling me to do right now. And oh boy, is that a tempting thought. But slapping people – Phoenix especially – won't help anyone. Neither is this, whatever *this* is. I have an appointment. And I tell Phoenix exactly that. "I have an appointment to get to, Phoenix. You have incredibly shitty timing."

"Well... I, uh–"

"Look, I'm going to go get this baby sucked out of my uterus. You're going to go with me and hold my hand, 'cause you put the baby there in the first place, and when I've finished my problems with *this* baby, I'll handle the problems with *that* baby. Well, *your* baby, apparently." I whip around, starting back towards the clinic's doors.

Phoenix rushes after me, his hand gripping my arm. "Mazey, please let me at least try to explain what happened. I know it's a weird time to drop this kind of bomb, but–"

I spin around towards Phoenix again. "Is this why you were being so weird?"

"Weird?"

"Every time kids or the fertilized egg in my uterus was brought up, you were *really* set on figuring out if I wanted kids. Every time I said *maybe*, you acted like I was insane. Like I should be able to welcome a kid into my life with open arms right now." I shake my head, pulling my arm out of his grip. "You were trying to test me. See if you should tell me about the baby." I feel another one of those deranged laughs works its way towards my throat, but I shove it down, centering my pissed off eyes on Phoenix. "Well, did I pass? Do I get to know the status of my own child now, Phoenix? Or are you just going to lie to me again and say she was adopted? 'Cause if I remember, and I do, that's exactly what you told me right after *you* convinced me to give her up, right? That was you, wasn't it? Or do you also have an identical twin I should know about?"

He drops his mouth open like he's trying to figure out how to answer the slew of questions I just threw at him.

I take a deep breath, still trying to talk my palm out of the idea of connecting with Phoenix's disgustingly pretty face. Instead, I muster up as much sarcasm as I can and answer my own question. "No? Great."

"Shit, Maz–" I cut him off as I walk through the clinic door. Not exactly the place to have a huge fight, which is exactly what I'm counting on. I think if I hear him say one more word, I might just lose it. And I really, really, don't want to be a crying, blubbering mess right now. If I go into that room sobbing, who knows if they'll do the operation. I need them to do this, now more than ever. A minute ago, I felt good about my decision to make sure I didn't have any kids. If the decision is now two kids or one kid, one kid is enough for me. More than enough.

The receptionist hands me some forms to sign. I go over to the waiting area, plopping down in a seat at the end of the aisle. Phoenix walks over next to me. I shoot death rays his way, and he, being the smart fellow he is, moves down a few seats. My eyes drift down to the forms in my hands, only half reading the mumbo jumbo written on the paper. I sign them all without really paying much attention to whatever it was they said. It doesn't help that I feel Phoenix's pathetic stare on me. I can practically taste the desperation radiating off of him. It's just making the anger bubbling in my gut all the more present. I lay my head back, staring at the ceiling,

Phoenix staring at me, trying to take deep, calming breaths. It doesn't help. I still want to mash his face into a wall. Or maybe just send him straight to a personal hell. Only for a little while. I'm not that cruel. Plus, he *apparently* has a child to care for.

"Mazey Sutton?" A nurse stands in the doorway. I feel my stomach drop. This is it. Time to go. I stand up, taking a moment to realize the forms I had sat next to me are gone. I spin around, looking for them.

Phoenix hovers behind me. "I brought them up."

I huff, nodding. Time to throw pride out the window for a second. I look up at him. "Hold my hand?"

"Always." He grabs my hand, squeezing it, showing me he's there.

The only way this could go better is if he hadn't just thrown me one of the biggest curveballs in my life.

After arriving home and having Phoenix personally watch me drink a full glass of water, I tell him to leave me alone for a little while. Every once in a while I hear Phoenix outside the room. Never close enough for me to see him, but close enough that I can almost hear him breathing. The entire day is spent with me ignoring him as he brings me medicine and water. Luckily, I spend most of the day sleeping. It isn't until close to six in the morning the next day that I hear him outside of the room again, banging pots in the kitchen. The one thing that keeps swirling around my mind, not leaving me alone, is how unbelievably confused I am. And pissed, I'm really pissed.

I take a deep breath, squeezing the ring around my neck. This feeling of wanting to throttle the person I'm supposed to be so in love with is all too familiar. Roxanne screwed up so much it became part of our normal routine. I hated feeling that way. Knowing that every time she trod a little too lightly around me, I was going to find out something else. With Phoenix, it's always felt different. Like no matter what happened, we'd make it past it. I felt that way when we were friends as teenagers, and now that we're dating. I just feel so comfortable around him. That no matter what happens, he'll hug me and tell me it's going to be okay.

The smell of bacon fills the room as Phoenix starts making breakfast. I can't even think about eating, I feel sick to my stomach. I'm not sure who he's planning on making food for, but if he comes in here with that stupid smile on his face, acting like nothing wrong, I'm going to lose it. When I needed him to help me get out of the bed to go to the bathroom, I almost just didn't get up. I don't even want to look at him.

I'm struggling between wanting to scream at him and going in there to ask all the questions circling around my head. Where is she? Who's looking after her? Does she know I'm her mom? How is she doing? If I never went to Florida, was Phoenix ever going to tell me? Why did Phoenix keep her? Do I want to keep her? Would I even be a good mom?

I know Phoenix would be an amazing dad, but I feel the same way I felt when Roxanne told me she wanted to have kids. She would be the mom, and I would just be there, living someone else's dream. I didn't want kids when Roxanne and I talked about it or when I got pregnant. And now? I want kids even less than I did before. When he had me sign the papers to give Roxy up, it felt like this perfect decision the two of us made together. She'd have a better life with someone else. But that's not how it went at all. She's still out there, apparently legally Phoenix's daughter.

Actually, come to think of it, is she still legally my daughter? When they took her away, did Phoenix just never tell anyone what we had decided? Did he shred the papers and hide her away?

"Holy shit," I mumble, groaning as I pull myself out of the bed and head out of the room. I pin Phoenix down with my stare the second I see him. "Is she still legally my child?"

"What?" He turns around, a nervous look on his face.

I huff, stepping further into the room. "You heard me, Phoenix. Did you submit my papers to give her up, or is she still legally in my custody?"

He furrows his brows, eyes sparking with some kind of intense emotions. "Yes, I submitted them. When I chose to keep Roxy, I did it knowing you may never want to be her mom. I didn't try to manipulate you into keeping her, Maz. Your parental rights are gone. You can get them back, but right now, they're gone."

I feel a little of the pressure ease out of my chest. At least there's that. At least he didn't lie to me about that. He has lied to me about other things, though. There's a whole human being that he's been hiding from me. How did he even keep that kind of secret? How did he not slip up and tell someone? When a person has that kind of thing buried inside them, it feels like every word out of their mouth might give it away. That every time they breathe the wrong way, their whole world might crumble around them.

That's how Phoenix has been living these last few weeks. Talking to me every day, about *everything*, and this just never came up? "Why?" I sigh, my shoulders slumping with the weight I've felt on them since he told me. "Why did you do it?"

Phoenix looks like he's trying not to shatter a particularly fragile piece of glass as he steps towards me. "Because... because when they asked me if I wanted to hold her, and they put her in my arms, I just – I couldn't see myself not loving her more than anything in the world. I couldn't give her up. Not after that."

"I held her too, but I still managed to stick to what we agreed on."

"When you held her, the only thing you were thinking about was Roxanne. Hell, you even named the kid after her. When I held her, it felt like a future. It felt like there was a chance that maybe, someday, we'd love her together and we'd all be a family."

"We weren't even dating when I had her!"

"I wanted to be dating and you know that."

"That doesn't mean you hide something like this! Is this why you were so distant after I had her? You were caring for an infant?"

Phoenix shakes his head, looking like he wants to walk closer. He doesn't. "I didn't mean to leave you alone, Mazey."

"Yeah, well, you did. That whole time I thought you were too heartbroken to look at me. That you were feeling the same sadness and guilt I was feeling over giving her up, but you weren't. You were calm and happy, and not even thinking about what I was going through!" I feel my throat close up as tears prick at the back of my eyes. Now is not the time.

"I thought about you every day."

"Not enough to call. Or to stop by. Or, come to think of it, to tell me you kept my baby."

"Our baby."

"She was never meant to be *your* baby, Phoenix. You were going to be signing the papers months before she was born. You were going to be giving her to Roxanne and me before she was even alive."

"But I didn't, and just because I was going to give her up *legally* doesn't mean I was ready to give her up *emotionally*."

"Emotionally? What emotions did you have for her, she was an infant!"

"I'm her father. I always was, and I always will be. I understand that you're upset. I'm sorry, Mazey. I am *so* sorry that I kept this a secret, but our decisions on Roxy were separate. You couldn't have taken care of her before, but I could. And you can now if you want to." Phoenix steps forward, reaching forward for my hand. He stops at the last second, sighing. "I want what I've always wanted. For us to be together. I love you, but I love Roxy too. When you came back to Florida, I was so shocked I didn't even know where to begin. I shouldn't have started anything with you without telling you everything. I just got swept away, but I've told you now. So it's up to you. A life with me and Roxy, or a life without."

"Excuse me?" I fume, at a complete loss of words. This shit hole of a man gets Lincoln to convince me to come back, then starts making moves on me immediately, pulling at my heart. He made me fall in love with him again. He made me go through an emotional rollercoaster trying to get over Roxanne to be with him, and now it's suddenly my choice? Like he didn't start all of this in the first place. But I can't get any of this out. "Where is she, Phoenix? I mean, I've been living with you for a month. Where is she? Is that where you've been going every day?"

He puts his palms out, face down like he's trying to calm an angry animal. "She's, uh, she's at Lincoln's house right now."

"Lincoln!" Of-freaking-course he knew about this. He invited me home when he knew Phoenix was keeping this shit from me. "She's been living at Lincoln's house?" My mind suddenly jumps somewhere else. "That's what that third room is for. Holy fuck. Oh my God, it's been right there the whole time. I've been so tempted to go in there, and I haven't. I could have stopped this shit weeks ago." A deranged laugh escapes my mouth. "My goodness, you have a lot of faith in me to not go in there."

"I just—"

"What would you have done if I found something of hers? I mean, is all of her crap at Lincoln's house, or is it at your apartment? How easily could I have found out?"

Phoenix looks at his feet. "You, uh... you did find some of her stuff. The books and the presents. They were her's."

"God, I'm an idiot. Jesus." I shake my head, turning around and pacing in the hall. "So, your daughter has been living at someone else's house without you, so you could shack up with me?"

"Yes."

"That—" I spin around to face him, my hands shaking at him. I just can't even fathom someone doing that. "That's so fucked up, Phoenix. Yes, I decided to give her up. For her own good. And I never lied to anyone about it or hid it from anyone. I just... hiding your daughter away? What does she think is happening? Are Jenny and Lincoln watching her right now? Your brother has been watching *your* daughter almost every night for the last month? I mean, I know he's good with kids, but Jesus, that's ridiculous."

Phoenix's face is dropping so much I'm surprised it can drop anymore. "I didn't want you to leave."

"That's—" I press my lips together, trying to find the right way to tell him what I feel, and what I feel is that this is fucked up. "That's fucking pathetic, Phoenix. You manipulated me, just like Roxanne. All my life, people have been telling me what to do, what to think, what to feel. I'm so done with it. I thought you were different. But you're not, you're just like your whole freaking family. Your mother, your sister, you... you're all so self-centered. You feel like you can make people do whatever you want. You made me fall in love with you again. You told me you thought Roxanne was shitty for forcing me to have a child. You're doing it too!"

"I'm not forcing you to do anything."

"You brought me back to Florida and started flirting with me, saying you wanted to start dating. You told me you loved me, you slept with me. You— you guaranteed that I'd end up heartbroken when you did that. And now I don't even know what to do. I feel like I can't even look at you." I push past him, grabbing my purse.

He turns toward me and takes one step forward. "Mazey..."

That's all he can do. Just stand there like a lump on a log. "Does anyone else know?"

"No. Lincoln is the only one."

"So not only have you been lying to me, you've been lying to them? You're raising this girl without a family. The only person she has is you. Why do that to her when she could have a huge, loving family? Give her a good life. If you're going to do all of this, at least make it worth it for her."

"I love her enough for everyone." He tilts his chin up like he's trying to prove to me it's true.

I grab the doorknob. "Go get your daughter. She hasn't seen you in a while. I'll figure out what I'm doing on my own."

I sit down on the cold, hard dirt in front of the tombstone, my nose frozen from the wind just like the grass and weeds sitting around me. The jacket I'm wearing does very little to help against the bite of the breeze. I clutch the flowers I bought to my chest and bury my face in the petals for a moment. After a long, deep breath, I set them down, resting against the stone sitting in front of me. I reach forward and run my finger against the engravings. April 12th, 1993 - June 15th, 2018. Reading those numbers, looking at those dates, they seem like they're so far apart. Like someone could live a lifetime in that span of time. And for Roxanne, it was her whole life, born and killed during that time. But she didn't *live*. Twenty-six years was all she got.

If these twenty-six years were all I got, what would that say for me?

I reach my hand up to the ring around my neck, stroking the gem with my thumb. I feel tears prickle in my eyes as I sink into the ground. "Hi, Rox."

It's times like these that I wish I believed in an afterlife. I can almost feel Roxanne sitting next to me, wanting to wipe away my tears, and trying to give me unasked-for advice. But I know she's not, and it makes the cold surrounding me that much more obvious.

"I know it's been a while since I've been here... I hit kind of a rough patch there for a little while. After I got that job, I just felt like I should pretend nothing had happened. It was nice to forget for a while. I've been forgetting a lot recently. Does that make me a bad person?" I shake my head, sighing. "I don't want to forget *you*, I just want to forget the pain that comes with it. It hurts so much, babe. It just feels like everything I had figured out about myself and my life got thrown out the window. I'm still trying to figure it out, and it's been a year and a half."

I pick one of the petals off a rose from the bouquet I brought and twirl it between my fingers. The tears rolling down my cheeks leave a stinging trail as the wind whips the wetness they leave behind. "I'm going to start a bakery. Ha, I know. Me, baking? I haven't done that in a long time. I used to. I used to bake you things all the time when we first met. I loved it. It's what I want to do. Phoenix is really helping me go for it."

Phoenix.

"I know this is probably the absolute worst thing to talk to you about, I mean, your brother did nothing but try to steal me from you while you were alive, and now he has stolen me... but I don't know what to do. He screwed up. Big time. I just have to figure out what it is that *I* want. When I was younger or when we got married, and people would ask how many kids I wanted, I'd always give some dumb answer. *Ah, I don't know. A few. Not now, in the future.* But, Rox, I never wanted kids. I still don't know if I do. Not when I was a kid myself, not when we were married, and not now that I have a kid out there needing me as a mom. I just have never seen myself doing that. Being a mom. It was you who was going to be the mom. I was just going to be on the sidelines."

I press my hand against my abdomen. "I had an abortion this morning, you know. I got pregnant. Yeah, dumb, I know. When I had that pregnancy test in my hand, and I saw that it was positive, the only thing I could think to myself is that I didn't want a baby. I wasn't happy. I was scared, sad. I wanted to curl up in a corner and cry. When I had the chance to get that abortion, I took it. So, what's that got to say about this other kid. *Our* kid, Roxanne. She was supposed to be our kid, and now she's going to be mine and Phoenix's? It doesn't seem right. We already messed up so much when it came to you when you were alive. Shouldn't we be honoring you now that you're gone?

"I don't want a kid. I gave her up. I gave her to someone else. I signed the papers. Crossed my *T*'s and dotted my *I*'s or whatever. I made that decision over a year ago. Phoenix changed that decision for me. Without asking, or talking to me, he completely changed my daughter's life. How do you make that kind of decision? How do you look at a newborn, who has one mom murdered and another depressed and spiraling out of control, and decide that the best thing for her is to keep her? She should be with a happy, loving family. A family that's excited and ready for a kid. Not with a dad who's been keeping her hidden and a mom who didn't know about her.

"God, Roxanne, I just wish you were here. I wish you could just hold me and tell me what to do. Better yet, if you were here, we'd be a happy family, curled up in our little condo we had, taking care of our kid together. She'd be named Sarah or something traditional like you wanted. You'd feed her, hold her, and love her more than anything. I don't think I can love her more than anything. I just don't think I can, and don't you need that? Don't you need that unconditional love to be a parent?"

I look down at the ring in my hand, my heart spinning out of control like my head is. I unclasp the necklace, holding it in front of me. "I was ready, Roxanne. I was ready to actually go somewhere with Phoenix. I had such a hard time trying to get over you and move on, but I was doing it. I was getting there. I was going to stick with him. Date, get engaged, get married. *Then*, maybe, have some kids. Now I have a bigger decision to make. How much do I need Phoenix in my life? If I leave him now, I'm not sure we could be friends. I think it's got to be together or be nothing. But do I love him enough to forgive him for this and then welcome our daughter back into my life? Do I love him enough to change the vision I had for myself?

"I loved you enough, but I had *years* to prepare for kids. You told me from the start you wanted kids. I always knew I'd have to change my dream for you. With Phoenix? When you were here, alive, it felt like *you* were what I'd have to give up to be with Phoenix. That if I was with him, I'd get the dream job and the dream life, but without you. Now he's changed that. I won't be having a dream life. How could I start a bakery when I have a one-year-old to care for? To support? He's changed our entire life without talking to me. What... what do I do?"

I rest my forehead against the cold stone, squeezing my eyes closed. Tears slip down my cheeks as my throat starts to close. I feel all the thoughts and emotions I've had sitting there, on the surface, finally overflow and tip out. An ugly, breath-catching sob starts racking its way through my body. I feel all the pain and anger pour out through my tears, my whole body aware of the emotions. I reach my hand up and press my palm against the cold stone, trying to feel Roxanne. Trying to hear her answer. All I want is for her to be here so I could see her again.

The one thought that becomes clear to me, circling through my mind, is that this sucks. I had finally started to see a new future. A future without Roxanne, but with Phoenix. I could see it building in my mind, right out of reach. I was set, ready to ride down this new path. Now I have to change everything I was set to go towards and figure out a new path.

I have to start from scratch. Again.

This feels like the time when I should beg for a sign, a way to see what path I should pick. As I see it, I have two options: option one, pick a life without Phoenix, open this bakery, start over with a new life, find new people to love. I could meet someone else, someone who's not related to my foster mom or deceased wife. I could move on from Roxanne and get over Phoenix. I could do something completely new. Option two, I pick a life with Phoenix and Roxy, Phoenix uses his work-from-home job to take care of Roxy, and I sit on the sidelines, watching. We get married, raise Roxy, and die together, old and wrinkly.

How the hell am I supposed to make a decision like that?

I turn over, resting my back against Roxanne's tombstone. The sobs subside until all I'm left with a snotty nose and water-soaked cheeks. "You know, if I got to pick, I would have cremated you and spread your ashes in all of your favorite places, but your mom wouldn't let me. She insisted on a grave she could come to. I guess now you'll be stuck in the ground."

In my coat pocket, I hear my phone ring. Pulling it out, I see a Florida area code. Trying my best to clear my throat and not sound like I just cried my eyes out, I answer the phone. "Hello?"

"Hi! Can I speak to Mazey Sutton, please?"

"Uh, yeah, that's me."

"Awesome! Well, I was just calling to confirm that you did get approved for that loan you applied for. I know that they were having a little trouble getting it through, so I just wanted to give you a call and let you know! Now I'm sure Josh gave you all the paperwork and information the last time you came in?"

"Yes, he did."

"Okay, well, if you can just come in some time so we can finalize it all, you'll be all set!"

I pick my head up off the tombstone, smiling at the sky. "Okay, awesome. Thank you."

"You're most certainly welcome. Have a wonderful day."

"Thanks, you too." I hang up the call, dropping my phone on the ground. I got the loan, so I can actually start putting all the pieces together. I'll actually be able to get this bakery started. As I'm about to start jumping with joy, a thought pops into my head. I was looking for a sign, something to tell me what to do, and this can't be a better sign. The loan for my dream job going through? Could the universe be telling me to pick my life? I sigh, sitting up. As I shift my eyes around the graveyard, my universe theory goes out the window. In the distance, standing against a tree, and watching me with hawk-like eyes, is Phoenix.

The man I've loved most in my life, watching over me, checking up on me. He knew exactly where I'd go to try to find answers. If that's not another great sign, then I just don't know what is. "Damn it," I huff, pushing myself up. While I'm done talking to Roxanne for the moment, I definitely *don't* want to talk to Phoenix. Not until I figure something out. So instead of heading back to the main entrance of the graveyard, I turn to hike it towards the back. Hopefully, I can find the bus from that end as well.

CHAPTER FOURTEEN

As I lay in the bed, the pitch-black room surrounding me, all I can hear is his breathing. It's like no matter how hard I try, I can't drown it out. I can't stop paying attention to the sound of his breath. The movement of his chest is becoming traced into my mind. All I know is that I'd rather be stuck here, not able to focus on anything other than listening to him breathe than have to be alone with my thoughts. Since I walked out of Phoenix's apartment that day, all I can do is think of him. And Roxy.

No amount of distractions, conversations, or soothing words can stop me from thinking. Or apparently from listening to *him* breathe. I roll over onto my back, letting out a sigh and staring at the ceiling. Not that long ago, I heard my phone vibrate, no doubt a text from Phoenix. I haven't checked it; I don't think I can handle any more of his messages. It's like he has a timer in his brain, so every hour, he has to remind me that he exists. Like my own brain isn't doing that enough as it is. If I could stop thinking about him altogether I would, and maybe then I could sleep. So the last thing I need is my phone adding to the things to think about.

Not that I can really say much. I keep my phone on. While I *really* don't want to be reminded of Phoenix, I'm thinking of him anyway. At least with his constant texts, it helps me remember why I'm so mad. It keeps the fire stoked, so I don't go running back to him. The bed feels cold without his arms around me, and the air seems stale without the sweet smell of honey he always has on him.

My phone vibrates again. I turn my head to look over at the brightness that illuminates the room. Next to me, I hear breath hitch. I lean on my elbow, grabbing the phone to look at the message. Usually, he doesn't send two in a row. As I look at the message, I feel my heart drop. He wants to meet up. Why does he want to meet up? I drop my phone on the nightstand much harder than I intend to. "Shit."

Jake's breathing goes from calm and steady to a groan. He looks over at me as he rubs his eyes. "What the hell are you doing?

I look down at the phone, then over at him. "Oh, nothing. Just can't sleep."

Jake looks at the clock sitting beside him, groaning again, tugging the covers up to his chin. "It's four in the morning."

"I know."

"What time did I fall asleep?"

I shrug. "Sometime during fast and furious... I think at midnight?"

Jake sits up in the bed, running his hands through his dark hair. "You've just been sitting there, doing nothing, for four hours?"

I sigh, fully aware that Jake seems to have decided we're going to start a conversation. Sitting up, I lean my head against his headboard. "Yes. What else am I supposed to do?"

"Something. Anything."

"Well, I can't do anything in here, or I'd wake you up—"

"You did that anyway," he chuckles.

I ignore him. "And I can't do anything out in the living room. Your roommate is already pissed I've been here so long."

Jake rolls his eyes. His roommate is *not* his favorite person. "It's been two weeks. Two freaking weeks. He needs to chill out."

I hold my hands up in surrender. "I'm not the one you should be complaining to. Though, you shouldn't be complaining to him either. It's his house too. Having some random chick here can't be that fun."

Jake just stares off, seeming like he's lost in thought a little. After a moment, he reaches over and turns on his lamp. We both flinch at the sudden burst of light. He turns to look at me again. "So, what's on your mind?"

I scoff as I look over at him. In the short period of time we've even known each other, it feels like we've found some kind of secret understanding. If something's wrong, he can sense it. It can be both very helpful and very annoying. I look down at my phone and resist the urge to throw it into a wall. Phoenix Hickerman and his stupid messages. "Phoenix sent me a text."

"Hasn't he *been* sending you texts?"

"Yes," I deflate, sinking into the headboard, blowing air out of my cheeks. "He said he wants to meet up."

Jake leans forward. "He wants to meet up? Are you ready?"

I shake my head. "I don't think so."

Jake nods slowly, thinking before replying to me. "So, you're going to go, anyway?"

"Probably. I hate hiding out here. I feel like my life is on pause. Plus, all of my stuff is at his apartment. I need to get it sometime, right?"

He slides back down the bed, laying his head on the pillow and looking up at me. "While I like having you here –

it's a treat – I'm pretty sure people are going to start thinking we're together if you keep sleeping in my bed."

I lay down too. "I haven't even told anyone where I am."

"Well, I'm sure Vincent told Olivia after he came over the other day. Based on what you've told me about her, she's probably already ready to tell everyone we're screwing."

I roll my eyes. "He wouldn't have to jump to conclusions if he'd have just let me freaking explain."

"Besides, my roommate probably thinks it anyway."

"You're the one who rolls out of bed every morning looking like you went for a romp in the sheets." I nod to his hair, which already looks like someone was running their hands through it over and over.

Jake chuckles, reaching over for the lamp, about to turn off the light, but pausing. "Fair enough. And, hey, if you need to stay here, we can tell him to fuck off anyway. I've wanted to for a long time."

I nod, smiling at him. "Alright, I can get behind that."

He looks at me for another moment, silver eyes searching mine for something. When he either finds it or gives up, he rolls over, turning off the light and mumbling under his breath. "Good night, Maz."

"Night, Jake." I turn onto my side, too, looking down at my phone. A third text comes through, and it consists of one word: *please*. How can two people go from being so happy to so broken?

I stand outside of Phoenix's door, trying to decide what to do. On the one hand, I have the key to the door dangling from my finger. On the other, I haven't been here in over two weeks. I don't want to just barge in on him. He told me that Roxy wouldn't be here, she's on a play date with a friend. Thank God, because otherwise, I could *not* be here. I was barely able to convince myself to come back to see Phoenix, let alone my abandoned daughter. I stare at the door handle, trying to convince myself to just put the damn key in the lock when the door swings open on its own. In front of me, Phoenix stands with a weary smile on his face.

"Hey," He opens the door wider, letting me walk in.

I do, dropping my purse onto the table next to the door. "How did you know I was out there?"

"I heard something by the door and looked through the peephole." He shoves his hands in his pockets, looking at me, studying me. "You came." There's a small, hopeful tone to his words.

"Yeah, I said I would." I stand awkwardly in the middle of the room, not really knowing what to do.

Phoenix nods. "I know. I just didn't know if you were ready to forgive me."

Ready to forgive him? "That's not really why I came..."

"So then, why did you?"

I shrug. "You said please?" I watch Phoenix as he moves to the kitchen island, leaning against it. "It's hard not to want to please the people you love."

Phoenix's eyes light up. "So, you still love me?"

"Yes, of course. There hasn't been a time I stopped loving you, even if I wasn't always *in* love with you. Plus, it's been two weeks. I couldn't get over you in two weeks if I tried."

He pulls his hands out of his pant pockets and shoves them in his jacket pockets instead. "So, you haven't been trying?"

"To get over you?" I shake my head. "No, I haven't. I've been trying to process everything."

"Process Roxy?"

I nod. "Roxy and you."

He steps closer to me, looking down at my hands. After a moment of debate, he reaches forward and grabs them. "And what have you processed?"

"I really don't want to lose you. I just got you back, and you're standing here in front of me, and all I want to do is lay in your arms." I look down at our connected hands and take a deep breath. The next part will be the hard part. The part where I tell them that while I don't want to lose him, I already have. Before I can say that, though, Phoenix squeezes my hand.

"I'm so glad you think that too." He smiles and shakes his head quickly. "Here, c'mere." He leads me over to the couch, sitting me down on it, while he kneels in front of me on the floor. "Mazey... I've already done this once. And when I did, I was so filled with love and hope. Even after everything else that happened that night, I still meant everything I said. And this time, when I ask, I mean it all the same."

Holy shit.

If I wasn't clenching my jaw with all the force in the world, I think my mouth would have fallen open in shock. He isn't doing what I think he's doing. Because if he is, then he's going to mess everything up. I stare down at my hands as Phoenix runs his thumb on the back, smiling up at me. He's smiling. He thinks I'm going to say yes. Holy crap. "Nix..."

"I do, Mazey. Do you remember what I said to you that night? I told you that when I was falling in love with you all those years ago that I knew you were the one. And you still are, Maz. You're my one and only." He chuckles, shaking his head. "That sounded cheesy, but you know what I mean."

I do. I feel the same way. He's my soul mate, the person I'm supposed to be with. But I've been crying over this huge mistake he's made for the last two weeks. I haven't been able to *look* at him, let alone think about actually getting married. What the hell is he thinking? Now is *not* the time for him to propose. "Phoenix—"

"I took your advice. I didn't propose in Frank's bar again. To me, it's the place my life began. I think you sometimes feel the same way, but now we can make new memories here. I've always known we'd find our way together again." He reaches into his pocket, and before I can stop him, or run and hide, he's snapped open a ring box in front of me, sparkling and glittery.

I almost want to cry. The ring he picked is perfect. It's a classic diamond, but at the base, I can see hints of colors, like the colors in Roxanne's ring. God, this man knows me so much. Well, apparently not enough to see that for the second time in our lives, I'll be turning down his proposal. My heart shrivels up in my chest, burning long and hard as I reach forward, closing the ring box and sighing. I see the light in his eyes start to dissolve as I take a deep breath. "I'm so sorry, Phoenix, but I can't."

I watch as he opens his mouth to speak but just stares at me instead, his smile slowly falling. He pulls the ring back into his body, practically cradling it in his chest. "I, uh, no?"

"I'm sorry, Phoenix. I just... ever since you've told me that you're raising Roxy, I've been trying to figure out how to even begin to understand what you did. I haven't even fully figured out how I feel about the fact that Roxy is here, in Florida. I definitely haven't had time to forgive you. Even if I had, I don't want to get married, Phoenix. I just... I've been trying to decide how to leave you. I didn't know how to tell you."

"It's been two weeks." He stands up, jamming his hand through his hair, his jaw twitching. "Obviously, you've been hurt, I haven't seen you this whole time, but when you agreed to meet, I thought that meant you were ready to get back together."

I shake my head. "I'm sorry, Nix. I didn't mean to trick you or anything. I just didn't know how to tell you, or what to say..." I get up, grabbing his hand. "I don't want to lose you, Phoenix."

He scoffs. "I know I should tell you that you could never lose me, but honestly, Mazey, this is the second time that I've been confident that we could spend the rest of our lives together, and you're saying no, again. I just thought I knew you better than this. Not that long ago, you had been professing your love for me and swearing you'd leave Roxanne for me. That we'd be together. You had a baby then too."

"That's completely different and you know that." I feel tears prick my eyes as the realization drops on me like a ton of bricks. I've been trying this whole time to make sure I don't lose Phoenix, but I lost him the moment I chose not to be in Roxy's life. I've just been kidding myself since then. Just like I've been off track since then, so has Phoenix. If he's been thinking that since I told him I'd leave Roxanne for him that we'd be together no matter what, then he's been wrong about that too. The night that Roxanne died, and I was with Phoenix, I meant what I said. I was going to leave her for him. We were finally going to be together. But when I went home afterward, and saw my wife dead on the floor, my entire world collapsed. To me, all promises made before that were erased. "When I told you I'd leave Roxanne for you, I didn't know she was being murdered right then. I wasn't thinking about what we'd do with the baby. We didn't have a deep conversation about what we'd do with our lives."

"Are you saying you wouldn't have kept her if we'd gotten together?" He watches me closely, really listening to my answer.

I huff, throwing my arms in the air. "I wasn't even thinking about it! You know that I never wanted a baby. I had a baby for Roxanne. Now, do I think I'd have been okay keeping her if Roxanne was still alive and we got together? Sure. At the time, I was prepared to have a kid. I pushed aside tons of my own thoughts and needs for that kid, but Roxanne and I had also been talking about having kids for over a year. I had a year to decide what I really wanted and then wrap my mind around what was happening. You dropping this bomb on me and then proposing to me a month later is *not* the same thing."

Phoenix nods slowly. "I love Roxy more than words can describe."

My breath hitches, even though it shouldn't have. He loves her more than words can describe, but not me. She's his daughter, of course, he does. His love for her should be that strong. There's no way I'm winning in this. He's not giving her up, not now. And I'm not staying for her, not now. To be honest, I wouldn't want Roxy's dad to leave her or be stuck with a mom who doesn't want her. "I know, Phoenix. I'm not saying you shouldn't. I'm just saying that I don't. I can't make myself do that. Not right now." I shake my head, wiping the tears from under my eyes. "When you chose to keep Roxy you chose her over me, and that's okay, Nix, but when I gave her up, I chose you over her."

"No, Maz, you're picking neither of us over both of us."

"Looks like we both aren't picking each other."

He snaps his eyes to mine, then shifts them to something behind me. "Again," Phoenix practically scowls as he says this.

I flinch back. "What does that mean?"

He bites his lip, looking down at his shoe. After a second, he takes a deep breath. "Since the day you met me, you've picked other things over me. Mom, Roxanne, Roxy... I've always been there, on the sidelines, hoping that one day it'd be my turn, but it never really was, was it? You're always going to have something that's going to come first."

"You're really going to throw that in my face? Seriously?

Making me feel bad that after not having a family for eight years, I would pick that over someone I'd just met? And I never picked Roxanne over you. Never. I was always picking you."

"When were you ever picking me? When you two went off to college together? When you got engaged? When you decided to start a family with her? Or when you *did* pick someone you'd just met over having a family? Because you did do that. Just not with me."

"I never meant to. You know that! I wasn't the one who told Suzan about us. You know that I was calling it off. After she knew, and there wasn't any chance for me to get adopted anyway—"

"You could have picked me."

"She was hurt, Phoenix. I had to be there for her."

"You know she did that on purpose, right?"

I stop, taken aback by what he's implying. "What?"

"Roxanne? She got into that accident on purpose. She knew she was losing you and she decided to do something about it. Oh, and when she told Mom about you two? She did that for the same reason. She heard us and knew she had to act fast to figure out a way to keep you. Same reason she took you to Arizona for college. If I was a million miles away, then I couldn't bother you. When she proposed to you? She knew I already had, that's why she did it that night. Oh, and remember when she suggested that we have sex to try to make the baby instead of going through the doctor? She was testing you. God, Mazey, Roxanne was a manipulative bitch, and you've never seen it. You've been picking her over and over, just the way she was playing you too."

None of that can be true. Getting into a car accident on purpose? She'd have to be insane to do that. I was there. I saw her in the hospital. Plus, GCU had always been her dream school, even before I came along. Besides, I can't believe that

Roxanne would have proposed to me just because Phoenix had. "Stop, Phoenix. Don't say shit you don't mean just because you're upset."

He scoffs. "No, I mean every word of this. I should have said it a lot sooner."

"No, what you should have said a lot sooner is that you still have my fucking child in your custody!"

"Ah, there she is. The girl who can actually say what she's thinking."

"Shove it, Phoenix. You should have told me the moment you decided."

"You mean after watching how awful the birth was for you? You were a sobbing, snotty mess. You were miserable at the thought of having to bring Roxy into this world. I knew you wouldn't have agreed with me."

"Well, I don't agree with you now, either. You should have let her go. She was *not* your child. You didn't get to decide what happened to her."

"She is my daughter. She's my flesh and blood, just like she's yours."

"No, she was the flesh and blood of *Roxanne* and me. Us picking you for the donor was never supposed to be anything more than that: a donation of your sperm. We only picked you so that our child would have both of our DNA."

"Roxanne died, Mazey. She's dead. So it's not like Roxy is her child anymore."

I clench my fist, resisting the urge to slap him. "Phoenix, I'd stop now, before you screw up even more."

He runs his tongue over his teeth, locking his eyes on mine. "I love you, Mazey, as much as someone can possibly love you. More than anyone else has *ever* loved you, including Roxanne. But I love Roxy too. I'm not giving her up. So if you're not going to be okay with that, then I think we're done here."

Finally. He said the words. He told me he's picking her over me. We both knew it was true, but he kept acting like I was the one who was choosing to leave even though he's picking it for me. We can be done with this. "Great." I feel my throat catch as tears rush to my eyes. "Yeah, that's great. I'll see myself out then." I spin around, stomping to the door.

"Mazey, where are you going?"

"Somewhere where I don't have to look at you. Not right now."

"Mazey!"

I slam the front door, going down the breezeway as far as I can go before dropping to the floor and hugging my knees to my chest. The waterworks pour down my cheeks, soaking my face and my knees as I rest my head against them. I pick up my phone, fingers tapping away with minds of their own. As I drop my phone, I don't even remember who I sent a text to. It doesn't matter anyway. I could sleep right here, in the breezeway, all night, and I probably wouldn't mind.

Almost two months ago, I was sitting in my apartment in Seattle, feeling like a wreck. I felt like I would never get better, like I'd lost my chance at happiness. Then Phoenix swoops in, sending Lincoln out to save me when they both knew full well that they were going to drop a bomb on my life. Do I wish I never knew Roxy was still here? No. I'd much rather know what I know now than be in the dark for the rest of my life. But how can I ever forgive Phoenix for doing this to me? How can I forgive him for dragging me in, saying he would stay with me forever, love me forever, only for it to all be a lie?

I was moving on, slowly getting better and finding out what to do with my life without the Hickerman family. Then Phoenix drags me back, gets me to fall back in love with him, and ruins everything. He even took Roxanne down with him, making sure that while I was nursing my broken heart, I had to question my dead wife too. If he thinks all the things he was saying, how could he want to propose to me? I mean, did he think that saying he wanted to marry me would make up my mind? Make us all a family?

I loved Roxanne. I love Phoenix. How is it that no matter who I'm with, or who I'm 'picking,' I always end up being the one getting hurt? I spent the last year and a half of my life miserable and grieving and guilty. Then with Phoenix... he made it so when I woke up in the morning, my first thought wasn't of Roxanne, my dead wife. It was of him, the man holding me while he sleeps, the man who loves me too much. When I dreamt, I wasn't just seeing Roxanne, dead on the floor, I was dreaming of a future with Phoenix. When I was sad and feeling alone, I wasn't wishing for Roxanne's arms around me, I actually *had* Phoenix's.

What am I going to dream of now?

"Mazey?"

I look up at the sound of Jake's voice as he comes up the stairs and comes towards me.

"I came as soon as I got your text, what's wrong?"

As he comes closer, I jump to my feet, throwing my arms around his neck. I dig my face into his chest, letting the sobs rack through my body and Jake just squeezes me tight, whispering soothing sounds. As my breathing starts to return to normal, I press my eyes closed, trying to picture Roxanne. I sniffle, whispering into Jake's chest. "I wish Roxanne was here to hold me."

"Aw, Maz, come on, let's get you home." He picks my phone up off the floor, drops an arm over my shoulder, and leads me away.

CHAPTER FIFTEEN

After wandering around the city for far too long, wanting to get out of Jake's house, but not having anything to actually do, I find myself sitting on a bench, under some oak trees, staring longingly at the lake in front of me. Down by the edge of the water, some ducks roam around. A good distance behind me is a couple lying on the grass in each other's arms. But other than that, there aren't any people around, just like the first time I came here. Years ago, when I first met Roxanne, the two of us would come to this park, sit on this bench, and talk about... everything.

This place is where I learned about Roxanne's fears and dreams, her past, her mind. This is where we kissed for the first time, said I love you for the first time. Out of any place in the universe, this is where I can feel Roxanne the strongest. It's like she's sitting here next to me, her arm thrown around my shoulder, and her lips pressed to my ear, talking about things she'd never tell anyone else. I lean my head back, closing my eyes, and take a deep breath. The water moves slightly in the breeze, just like the leaves rustle above my head, and before long, I feel like I can hear Roxanne's laugh beside me.

"I swear! I mean, just imagine. Okay? Imagine being embarrassed to death? That's definitely the worst way to die."

I can hear her sigh as she thinks about how stressed a test is making her feel, cry about a friend screwing her over, moan as my hands roam her body. Roxanne, sitting next to me, smiling, a mug of hot chocolate in her hands, and a fuzzy blanket thrown over her legs. Her nose pink from the breeze, but still wearing a tank top and sandals.

"This is not *cold. We live in Florida. You were born in Vermont. You can't tell me this is cold."*

I grab the necklace hanging against my chest and squeeze it. *Roxanne.* I love her so much. Even now that she's gone, I still love her with all of my heart. But I've been wearing my dead wife's ring around my neck for so long now, it feels normal. That's not normal. I unclasp the necklace, laying it in my palm. The ring shines as the leaves above my head move, taking the light with them. It's like I hold my entire life in my hands, a small little piece of my heart sitting outside of my body. I've attached so much of my well-being to this ring that wasn't even mine to being with.

I've always thought that I was following my heart when I picked Roxanne. Now I realize only part of that was true. I was following my heart, but my heart was never *with* Roxanne. It was following her, too, just like everyone always did. Roxanne was someone you followed, not someone who followed you. I was always so entranced by her, wanting to make sure she was happy, that she had everything she could ever need. I can still feel the way her smile made my heart flutter or the way that her lips pressed against mine made the entire world fade away.

I can almost hear her next to me, her lips on my shoulder,

her hand squeezing my arm. She'd give me advice if I asked for it. *"There's nothing that your heart can't forgive, Mazey. You're too kind to hold something over someone forever."* When she said that, she was talking about herself. But does it apply to this situation too?

I don't think life is as simple as it was when she said that. Life has added too many things into the mix. My heartache over Roxanne and my grief over not being there for her. Phoenix adopting my baby, his anger over me never picking him. We have more baggage now than we did all those years ago, when I was just some rebellious teenager in a bar, and he was some drunk frat boy playing the field. Now I'm sitting in a park, crying all alone, with my dead wife's ring in my hand, and the love of my life sitting at home heartbroken over me.

The love of my life

I fall back against the bench, a harsh laugh rushing out of my throat. I squeeze my eyes shut, feeling what's about to come. As I will myself not to completely lose it in public, the tears come pouring down my cheeks, and a strangled laugh pushes through my lips. Roxanne would brush the hair out of my face as it sticks to my cheeks. She'd shake her head at me and say something that'd piss me off. *"Tears aren't going to get you anywhere, babe. Don't cry about things, it's not worth it."* But it always feels worth it. The tears feel like a release, like they're a gateway to letting me understand everything I'm feeling.

As I sit here, trying to remember how to breathe, I realize the one thing I wish I didn't have to. After all the opportunities I've had to pick Phoenix and be with him, I *finally* chose him, and it's too late.

My laughter stops, and I feel all my energy fall out of my body, my shoulders slumping, hands falling into my lap. I curl my knees up to my chest, resting the necklace on top, running my finger over the ring. I miss her. I miss her more than I've missed anything. I've had people die around me or leave me more than anyone should. I've had so much loss in my life. My mom died and my dad left me. No foster parents kept me. Suzan never adopted me, Phoenix and I always passing each other by. But out of all the people who aren't in my life anymore, Roxanne's death hurts the most. The way she was yanked away from me, with no warning, punched a hole in my chest I won't ever be able to fill.

Now, I have to leave Phoenix. Yet another person out of my life, someone who I thought was going to be in it forever. That hole in my chest is only getting bigger, harder to fill. This time it's my choice. It's something I'm coming to terms with. It's the *right* thing. For some reason, I think that makes this easier. Knowing that I've already hit rock bottom, that from here my life will only go up, means that I can do this.

I've been so stuck on these things and these people that were put into my life when I was only sixteen. No one sticks around with their high school crushes, let alone two of them. And now that I'm not a part of their family anymore, do I have a reason to stay? Do I need to be involved anymore? Should I be pondering this huge life decision? What will be my place with my foster siblings? Can I forgive Lincoln for bringing me back here when he knew about Roxy? Will I hang out with Vincent, Olivia, Nikkie, and Eric? With the kids who are young forget who I am? Do I go to birthday parties, weddings, school plays?

I can remember Roxanne and I fighting about this, what family does – what family is. She rolled her eyes at me, *"We don't have to go to every birthday or every holiday. I spent eighteen years in that house."* Now neither of us will ever go to one again. But just because I let go of Phoenix doesn't mean I have to let go of everyone, right?. So, this isn't a choice of having my family versus not. This is a choice of having a family with *Phoenix* or not. And I can't do that. Not now, when looking at

Roxy will only remind me of Roxanne. Not when I'm so hurt by this huge life decision he made without me.

I slide my legs back down, feet on the ground, taking a deep breath as I look down at the ring in my hand. I have to let go. Of both of them. A clean slate doesn't start when I'm still tethered to the most painful thing in my life by the necklace tied around my neck. I think of her when it moves against my chest, or people point it out, or when I'm anxious and fidget with it. I love Roxanne with all my heart, but that doesn't mean I need to be sad every second of every day when I think about her.

I slip off of the bench, onto my knees on the grass. Placing the ring on the ground, I start to dig a little hole under the bench that's deep enough that someone won't find it and take it. As I finish it off, fingernails caked in dirt, my heart squeezes in my chest. Two months ago, I was a blubbering, sad, drunk mess, hiding away from the world in my living room. Now I'm putting my wife to rest.

I grab the necklace, squeezing it in my palm one last time, before dropping it in the hole. I push the dirt over it, covering the hole. My hands stay pressed against the ground, unable to move. A breeze brushes over my shoulders, whisking my hair around. I relax, shoulders not as tense. It's okay. I can do this. "I love you so much. I won't ever forget you. I promise. I couldn't, not ever." I pull my hands away, getting to my feet, looking down at the little grave I dug for my memory of Roxanne.

I take a long, shaky breath, willing myself to leave. I count to ten, close my eyes, and whisper into the wind. "Goodbye, Roxanne." Then, I leave.

Knocking on the door as I open it, I slide into Phoenix's apartment. It only takes a second for my eyes to go to where he's sitting in the corner of the living room, knees to his chest, forehead to his knees.

He looks up as I enter, eyes redder and more swollen than when I left two hours ago. He still offers me a half-smile as I get closer. "Hey."

I sit down in front of him and give him a half-smile back. "Hey."

"Are you okay?" He reaches forward and runs his thumb across my cheek. "You look like you've been crying."

I lean into his palm, a sigh escaping my lips. "I could say the same to you."

He chuckles, leaning his head against the wall behind him. "Uh, yeah. I haven't been very manly these last couple hours."

I scoot, so I'm leaning against the wall, our shoulders touching. "Neither have I."

"You're not supposed to be manly. You're a chick."

"You don't have to be manly either. Not when someone hurts you." I look over at him, thinking about all the times I've gotten lost in these brilliant blue eyes and knowing I won't get to again. "I'm sorry."

He looks down at the ground, sighing. "You don't have anything to apologize for, Maz. You didn't do anything wrong."

"Maybe not, but I still hurt you. I'm sorry about that. I don't want you to be sad, Phoenix. I want you to be happy. Live a happy life. I want you to tell your family that you kept Roxy. Bring her to live with you. Be in her life."

Phoenix's eyes snap back up to mine. "Where did all of this come from?"

"I had shitty parents growing up. When they left me, I

never found anyone else to parent me. Not well, not lovingly, and definitely not permanently. You chose to be a part of Roxy's life. I know she's too young to remember what's happening now, but it'll still make an impression on her. It'll still affect her life. You need to be there for her. You need to stand by your choice. You want to be a father? Be one. Be a good one."

He shakes his head. "I never intended on being a bad father. I just didn't think it was my place to tell anyone about Roxy. I wanted to tell you before I told anyone else. It would have been too hard to keep her a secret if I told my family."

"I know. But I do know now, and it *is* your secret to share. She's not my daughter anymore, Nix. She's yours. You should love her, be proud of her, show her off." I feel my hand reach for my necklace, but I stop halfway there, dropping my hand into my lap. "When I was deciding if I should keep Roxy or give her away, I made that decision based on who I thought would take care of her the best. I knew I couldn't have taken care of her. Not in a million years. But someone else could, and you are. I need you to be the best father you can be. Make sure that you give her everything Roxanne and I wanted for her and more."

Phoenix nods. "I will, Mazey. I will, I promise."

I turn myself so I'm facing Phoenix and grab his hands. "I love you *so* much, Phoenix. You're my best friend, my happy place, the love of my life. You've been my rock since I got here." I take a deep breath, trying to muster up the courage. "*But* we both know we can't keep doing this. I meant what I said about Roxy. I want her to be happy and loved and have good parents, and I can't do that for her. I just can't. You better not ever let her go. She's in your life now, for good. So we need to stop whatever this is. We need to figure out our own paths and do our own things."

"Mazey, I need you in my life."

"No, you don't." I smile at him. "I learned that the hard way. Just because you think you couldn't live without someone doesn't mean you *can't*. Knowing that you're out there, alive, happy, thriving, will make it all okay. It will make stepping away worth it. I can't ever see Roxanne again. She's gone, for good. But us... when we've gotten over each other, and we've moved forward with our lives, maybe we can be friends again."

Phoenix squeezes my hand. "But not now?"

I shake my head. "Not now. I think we have to learn to live without each other. Not *just* live, but live happily." I drop his hands, brushing a piece of hair off of his face. "I know that when you made the decision to keep Roxy that you never meant to hurt me. But it does hurt, Phoenix. Knowing that you went behind my back, kept this secret from me."

"I—"

"Wait, just let me finish." I wait until he nods to continue. "I know that you weren't trying to do anything wrong. You were trying to do what you thought was best. That doesn't change that it hurts. I love you, a lot. But I'm angry, and I'm hurt. I'll get over it. It'll be okay, eventually. Okay?"

Phoenix's eyes dart around mine like he's trying to make sure agreeing with me is the right thing to do. The thing that will make me happy. As I smile at him, and Phoenix's eyes finally rest on my neck where Roxanne's ring used to be, I see his shoulders slump, almost like a defeat. His fingers rest on my chest, where it would have laid, and he smiles slightly. As his eyes meet mine again, he nods. "Okay. I love you, Mazey. I trust that we'll find each other when the time is right." He stands up and offers me a hand.

From the way he looks at me, I can tell he thinks that. He thinks we'll get together eventually. I don't think I can. I want to start over, open a new chapter of my life. Find out where I belong without the Hickermans in my life. But I don't need to tell him that, not right now. He'll get over me someday. "Thank you." I grab his hand, letting him pull me up. We walk to the front door, our hands still locked together. I kiss his cheek, let go of his hand, and walk out the door. *Goodbye, Phoenix.*

CHAPTER SIXTEEN

I stand proudly, smiling at the display in front of me. After all those long days and grueling hours, I'm just glad that it's all done. As a bonus, it looks amazing. Despite Trinity telling me she didn't think I could do it so quickly, here it is. When I sent her my progress picture this morning, she still didn't believe it. Yet, here we are, with a finished bakery case, filled with adorable little pastries and cupcakes. I pull my phone out of my pocket and take a picture of it for her. Then I go over to the register, looking down at my checklist. I mark off the last step, shine glass, and smile at the paper.

I did it. My second bakery to open, this time on the perfect day. I run my fingers over the apron sitting next to me, where the store name sits – *Roxanne's*. People used to tell me they thought it was cheesy. No one here really knows what it's from anymore. I don't talk about her much, and when I do, it's only to explain the name. When people ask, I just say, *my ex-wife*. Most people don't have many questions after that. Only the people from my old life really know what today means.

Just as my eyes start to prick up again, my phone pings. I

look down at it, expecting Trinity to have sent a reply, but instead, I see Olivia's name on the screen. I swipe it open to see a picture of her and her husband. The message below reads, *thinking of you. Love you, Maz.* I feel a soft smile pull at my lips as I look down at Olivia's glowing face.

I reply and set my phone back down on the counter, but as soon as I do, it pings again, and this time it is from Trinity. She sends confetti emojis in celebration of me actually getting everything done. When I look at the time, I put my phone back in my pocket and take a deep breath. If I couldn't be with Roxanne today, at her grave or at our bench, opening this place in honor of her is the next best thing. Tonight, I promise myself. I'll drive there tonight, no matter how late it gets.

I rest my hand against my chest, closing my eyes. *I miss you. Six years is too long without you.* Before I can convince myself to open my eyes and start the day, my alarm goes off. Time to shine. I unlock the door, flip the sign to 'open,' and head back behind the counter. Throughout the morning, I have several passersby come in and check everything out. Some people have the coupon I put on my flyers. Some people saw my Facebook posts. Some people heard it from a friend. I had one person who had been to my original bakery and was stoked that there was one here now. I have a couple of each thing I pre-made left as it's nearing the end of the day, but I planned on that. I didn't want to run out of anything.

Close to when I'll be closing, early afternoon, I'm in the back, already baking some of them for tomorrow, when I hear my front doorbell chime, letting me know someone opened the door. I drop the bag of flour in my hand, pull the apron over my head, and start towards the front. "Hey, sorry about that, I'm the only one here. What can I—" I round the corner, coming to a halt as I see who's standing across the counter from me. My whole body goes stiff, mouth half-open, eyes unable to move. They rake in every single memory attached to those blue eyes, that kind face...

"Hey."

I feel my body move again, but only enough to stand up straight and close my mouth the rest of the way. "Hey... What are you doing here, Phoenix?"

He jabs a thumb at the door. "I saw the sign out front, and I noticed the name. I didn't really think it'd be you. What are you doing in Tampa?"

"I live here now." My fingers fidget with the end of my shirt like I'm a fifteen-year-old talking to her crush. I squeeze my fists instead. "I started opening this place about a month ago. I officially moved five days ago. But why are you here?"

The corner of Phoenix's lip jumps up. "I live here too. I moved about two months ago. I got an offer to oversee the Tampa blog branch."

"That's amazing—"

"I have to pee." A little voice comes from behind the counter, and my heart stops.

Phoenix looks down. "Yes, sorry. I forgot, baby." He looks around the bakery, presumably looking for a restroom sign.

"There's one around the corner," I point.

Phoenix points as well, and as he does, a little girl, around six years old, walks over to the bathroom. Her red hair is done in a Dutch braid, a bow tied around the end, and her teal eyes sparkle with the same icy tone as her dad's. He watches her walk into the bathroom and closes the door. As the lock clicks, he turns back to me. "I didn't mean to bombard you with seeing her... like I said, I didn't even really think it would be you here."

"She looks so much like you," I hear the breathiness of my voice, most likely because I feel like my lungs have forgotten how to function. I stare at the bathroom door, not able to take my eyes off where the little Roxy was a second ago. "I can't believe how much she looks like Roxanne too."

Phoenix sighs. "She looks like you as well. She looks like the best parts of you and Roxanne."

I look back at him. "I hadn't seen her. People offered to show me pictures, but I never wanted to see them."

"I understand that." He nods, stuffing his hands in his pockets. "I never told her who you were. I didn't think it was my place to—"

"Yeah, no. That makes sense." I nod and offer him a half-smile. "I am really glad you were able to make her happy."

Phoenix laughs. "Oh yeah, and spoiled. I'm definitely wrapped around her finger."

The bathroom door swings open again and Roxy comes out, wiping her hands on her pants. She goes back over to Phoenix. He wraps his arm around her and hugs her to his leg. She looks up at me, then to the cupcakes beside me, and then to me again. "Are those your cupcakes?"

"Uh, yeah." I clear my throat. "Yep, I made them."

Roxy looks up at her dad.

"If you want one, you gotta ask her."

She looks back at me. "Can I have a chocolate one, please?"

"Sure," I grab the cupcake, set it on a plate, and hand it to her.

Phoenix helps her steady the plate. "Sit down while you eat it, or else you're going to drop it."

She goes over to the table, jumping into a chair.

"What time do you close?"

I look at the clock. It's five to two. "About an hour."

"Maybe we should get out of your hair then—"

"No, sit. We have five years to catch up on." I go over to the front door, locking it, and flipping the sign.

Phoenix smiles a knowing smile. He pulls a chair out and gestures for me to sit.

I do, eyes trained on the man I spent a large chunk of my life loving. In the time since we've been apart, I've grown. A lot. I learned how to thrive on my own, without someone there to be a part of my every move. Without someone holding me back or holding me up. I've figured out more about who *I* am in these last few years than I had my entire life up to that point. I know so much more now than I did then. I have new friends, a new home, a new job... a new life.

And Phoenix has grown too. A father. Like a real-life, full-blown father. He's so put together. He's holding himself in a different way than he used to. The look in his eyes is different. He's happy now, and isn't that what I wanted? For us to find ourselves away from each other. To know who we are on our own. To make sure that we're happy by ourselves before we're happy with someone else.

He once told me that he was confident that we'd find each other again when the time is right.

"I can't believe we both moved to Tampa around the same time." He chuckles, sitting down in his seat.

I smile at him, nodding my head. "Must be fate."

His eyes twinkle at me with that look he has always had. The look that says, *I could stare at you forever.* The look that says, *I want to jump your bones.* The look that says, *I love you.* After all this time and he still has those same looks. His mouth pulls into a smirk as he looks me up and down like he knows just what I'm thinking. "Must be."

ACKNOWLEDGMENTS

I have a lot of people that I'd like to thank for being a part of creating this book!

First, to my parents, Jon and Terri, for having to listen to me ramble on about writing at almost every meal together. If I didn't have a way to word vomit about this book, I don't know what I would have done. The number of random problems you've helped me solve is crazy (and they weren't even my problems, they were my character's). You guys are absolutely incredible to be supporting me through trying to achieve my dream. Thank you so, so much!

To my sister, Alyssa, for saying she's not reading the book, even if it is my debut novel (she loves me, she's just not a reader). You're a pretty cool sister, as far as sisters go, and since we don't do sappy, that's all I'll say about that, love ya. My grandparents, for their help with figuring out this whole publishing thing. To all my friends and family for being there to support me through this: every single excited person and motivational comment helped me push through and get here!

On the professional side, I'd like to thank Noor Abbas, my cover artist, for making some absolutely beautiful cover art and helping me find my vision when I wasn't even sure what it was to begin with! I'd like to thank Aline Legnaioli for making those awesome character renderings. This book had developmental editing by Tiensha Mix.

I'd like to thank Shari Chase, Natalie Jones, Kim Brewster, Kate Bloom, Randi Johnson Reed, Marva Seaton, John Watkins, Samantha S., and more, who asked not to be named, for beta reading my book. I got amazing feedback, some of which really transformed my book, and it would not be where it is now without each and every one of you. You're all so incredibly kind to have done this for me, and it is really, really appreciated.

I want to thank everyone who agreed to review, rate, talk about, or share my book to help me with this journey. Everyone who interviewed me, wrote a blog post about my book, or let me post about my book with them aided me into making my debut novel release the amazing experience it was! If you're one of these amazing people just know that while I don't have the space to write everyone's names (it would be several pages long), I am incredibly thankful for everything you did, and I wish you the best in your own book publishing, blogging, reviewing, and interviewing endeavors!

Last, but definitely not least, I want to thank you, the person reading this acknowledgment and this book. I've dreamt of being an author my entire life, and I honestly didn't think I'd ever get to a point where I was actually publishing a book. My goal when I started this journey was to sell one book to someone I didn't personally know. If you're one of those people you're personally making my dreams come true! The fact that I even finished the book was a dream come true, let alone that someone like you is reading it. Thank you so much for making my day, week, month, or year by supporting me and my books (ha, get it?). I look forward to hearing your thoughts, opinions, and questions about the books. I love you all!

I hope you enjoyed reading *Life 2.0* as much as I enjoyed writing it, creating the characters, and discovering Mazey's story. Her story was the perfect one to be my first published and I love that she'll be close to my heart always.

ABOUT THE AUTHOR

Hi, I'm Ciara Fineman, the author of *Life 2.0*. Thank you for reading, and I really hope you enjoyed the book!

I've always loved writing, and have been dreaming of publishing a novel since I was a little girl. After years of it being the "unattainable dream," it's actually happening. I'm writing YA and NA romances, and I'm so excited to share my stories with the world! As I'm writing this, in September of 2020, I already have some other books in the works, so make sure you check me out on social media to stay up to date on what else I have coming out. You can scan the QR code on the back cover, or check out the social media shout outs below.

Thank you so much, and I hope I run into you again in one of my books!

WAYS TO CONNECT

If you'd like to connect with me, or anyone who helped with this book, the information is all right here. Thank you so much for your support. All my links will also be in the QR code on the back of the book, or at the end of the book.

My Socials:
> **Instagram** *(Author)*: @Ciara_Writes_
> **Twitter:** @Ciara_Writes
> **Website:** CiaraWrites.com
> **Facebook** *(Page)*: Ciara Writes
> **Facebook** *(Group)*: Ciara Fineman Readers Group
> **Goodreads:** Ciara Fineman
> **YouTube:** Ciara Writes

Cover Designer:
> **Instagram:** @swagcorre

Promotional Art:
> **Instagram:** @ali_illustrations_

Post Reading Interview by Lily Fuller:
On my YouTube channel!

www.ingramcontent.com/pod-product-compliance
Lightning Source LLC
Chambersburg PA
CBHW020551180626
46810CB00007B/2465